# A Good Day for Pie

## The Collected Stories of Ramsbolt

### Jennifer M. Lane

Cover design by Alia Hess – cultofsasha.com


Copyright © 2020

Published by Pen and Key Publishing

jennifermlanewrites.com

ISBN: 978-1-7334068-8-8

# ACKNOWLEDGEMENTS

Thank you to Shelly Campbell, Essa Hansen, and Cheryl Murphy.

Special thank you to Alia Hess.

CHAPTER ONE

"You stay here." Kyle bent to rub the puppy's ears. The yellow lab wasn't welcome in the farmhouse. "You get under Zeb's feet, and it makes him grumpy. Not that he needs the help. Trust me. I'd rather be out here with you."

Jacques's puppy tail thumped the workbench, his jaw dropped in a broad grin. His ears flopped as he yipped a demand for attention.

"I gotta go. Fix a tractor while I'm gone, would ya? Better yet, go upstairs and make me some coffee. Pay some bills and clean up that apartment while you're up there. I'll be back before this fog clears."

Kyle tugged the barn door shut. It skipped in its track and creaked to a close, sealing the puppy away with his work. Half of it, anyway.

Gravel crunched beneath his feet, and he kept his head down, careful not to twist an ankle. The soles of his boots were as thin as his wallet, and he couldn't afford to be flat on his back. Not with a barn full of broken tractors and a boss who wanted him to perform a miracle.

He cleared the two-acre gap between the barn and the farmhouse and arrived on the porch with damp hair and muddy boots. He left mud and mown grass on the scraper.

Inside, Dan and Bern fought over the paper, their voices thundering through the screen door, tightening the knot in Kyle's stomach. He didn't hate them; he just didn't fit in with them. They all came from the same town. But Kyle's college degree and the years he spent in a corner office in Boston drove a wedge between him and the people of Ramsbolt. If Zeb wasn't waiting for him, he'd have turned back to the barn.

"Damn mud." He kicked off his boots and left them by the door. The screen door slammed behind him.

"I wanna read this stupid story about the stores." Bern snatched at the page in Dan's hands, and Dan held them away like a defiant older brother pushing buttons that would set off fireworks. Bern punched his arm.

"Go ahead." Dan threw the pages at him. "Nobody's gonna open a store in Ramsbolt, of all dang places. Ain't nobody here to buy anything. What're you gonna do? Open up a soap store? Finally learn how to wash your grubby hands?"

Kyle ducked his head in the fridge. Zeb kept drinks in there for the field hands, and if he was lucky there'd be enough sweet tea left from the day before to sugarcoat whatever financial disaster he'd been summoned to fix. The shelf was empty, but for half a jug of apple cider that floated on a bed of sediment.

"Kyle? Is that you out there?" Zeb's voice boomed down the hall. "I need you to explain this mess to me."

Bern snickered behind the newspaper.

Dan scowled and wagged a finger. "Somebody's in trouble."

He rolled his eyes as he plodded down the hall, stepping over lumps in the carpet. The faux wood paneling held onto more smells than it had been exposed to, rancid and sour. The den at the end of the hall was dark. Yellowing wallpaper peeled at the edges. Zeb sat at his metal desk, beard trailing into his lap, still wearing his thin blue pajamas.

"What the Sam Hill is this?" Zeb jabbed his finger at the computer screen. The monitor was ancient and took up half the desk. The other half was coffee cups and ash trays, littered with the cinder tumbleweeds of cigarettes past.

Kyle slipped behind the desk and stood next to him.

"That would be your bank balance. That's the cash you have in the bank."

Zeb spun to face him, eyes on fire, and Kyle stumbled back, taking shallow breaths of the acid air. "That's not enough. Not enough! I thought you were better with money than with those tractors. That's what your dad said. What you said. You did finance. Finance!" He waved his arms in the air. "For big fancy companies."

"Investment portfolio management." Kyle ran a hand over his face and squinted at the screen. "I can't make money out of thin air. What are you saying is wrong with that number?"

He'd worked with plenty of clients who threw temper tantrums when they didn't like the numbers, but none of them had half of Zeb's unbridled ire, and their offices smelled nothing like this one.

Zeb's eyes went so wide Kyle could see the white around them. "You paid the whole gas bill."

"That's what you do with the bills. You pay them. We've talked about that. This one has the biggest penalty. You don't want to take on all that interest."

Zeb leaned forward, pounding his finger on the desk like a teacher spelling out a wrong. "I need to pay my employees. If I can't afford to pay them, you'll be the first one not getting a check." He opened a drawer, pulled out a pack of smokes, and muttered as he tried to light one with fingers thin as twigs. "Too damn good at money for your own good, I tell ya. I hired you to fix some tractors as a favor to your dad 'cause he was a friend. Never shoulda let some city finance guy stick his nose in my damn books. Shoulda known when you blew all your own cash."

The lighter snapped and fire licked at the end of his cigarette.

"I didn't blow it. I took care of my father. I was trying to help. Him and you."

"You said you were good at it, though. You should have stuck to the tractors."

Kyle's blood boiled. He knew better than to react. Zeb was just trying to get a rise out of him.

Zeb took a long draw. Smoke curled from his nostrils. "You might be half as good at tractors as you are at finances, by your own standards, but at least I know what I'm getting out of you as a mechanic." He stood from his chair and cursed his knees. "All I know is you gotta figure this mess out. All of it. Ain't nobody around here gonna be happy until you do."

Zeb took an ashtray from the desk and scraped down the hall, brushing the walls with his papery skin and his thin pajamas.

"Hard work does not pay off around here, does it?"

His boss was too far off, and too hard of hearing, to pick up on his grievance.

"How did I even get here? And how the hell am I going to get out?"

Kyle fell into the warm seat and spun to face the numbers.

## CHAPTER TWO

Smoke billowed from a pan on the stove. Breakfast was ruined.

"I wasn't in the mood for eggs, anyway."

The smoke alarm blared. A screaming siren pulsed, and Jacques went flying. The yellow lab's puppy feet were too big for his body, and he tumbled head over heels into the leg of a chair as he shot under the card table Kyle used for everything. A stack of mail dumped on the floor.

"I'm sorry, buddy. I'll make it stop."

Kyle threw the window open. The alarm was two feet too high to reach, so he waved a baking sheet at the siren, offering words of consolation that were lost in the commotion.

The alarm silenced, and Kyle fell to his knees in the tiny kitchen, the *beep, beep, beep* still ringing in his ears.

"It's okay." He reached out a hand and rubbed the soft spot behind Jacques's ear. The puppy trembled. "It was just a scary sound. I stopped it."

Jacques licked at his fingers.

"I can't remove the alarm. I'm sorry. I need it in case one of the tractors downstairs catches on fire or something."

Kyle gave Jacques one last pat on the head and pulled the mail into a pile. Sales papers and advertisements, bills from his dad's game of assisted-living hopscotch and letters from the state—remnants from their battle over his father's care while his bank account drained. He shuffled the deranged deck of cards that had only played out in his favor when he was too broke to fight anymore. They landed back on the table with a thud.

He used the morning newspaper to fan the last of the smoke out the window.

"You're not the first to be disappointed by my cooking. You should have met Tracey." Kyle wrinkled his nose. "I used to be really good at this, you know. Back in high school, I loved to cook. I even cooked in a restaurant, and I was on a magazine cover once. Okay, it was a newspaper insert, but I was good."

Jacques bounded from under the table and attacked the leather laces of Kyle's left moccasin slipper, shaking his head from side to side with a ferocious puppy snarl.

"I just don't enjoy it like I used to. It's a shame." It seemed like everything he touched burned or boiled over anymore. "I guess I'm just too distracted by the real world to get enjoyment out of this like I used to."

Kyle stepped out of his slipper and left it behind while he poured the last of a box of cereal into a bowl, a mountain of sandy dredges landing on top and wisping into the air.

"I always thought I'd learn what I needed to know in business school, work for a while, save up some money, then open my own chain of stores. I wanted to make one of those lifestyle brand stores with stuff for kitchens and dining rooms, but affordable, you know? You don't need an eight hundred dollar coffee maker to enjoy coffee. But what do I do? I repair tractors. I don't even know how to repair tractors."

He plopped at the table with the paper. An article below the fold announced next year's arts festival. A committee was forming to run it. Funds from the first festival were used to improve the park, and Adelle—whoever that was—was praised for her artful plantings of spring flowers. He flipped the paper open.

The headline caught his eye. *Want to start a new business? Cheap rents for vacant downtown properties.*

"Wouldn't that have been great six years ago? Maybe I wouldn't be stuck in this barn."

*Anyone wishing to start a new business has their pick of properties. More than 20 retail spaces downtown are available at discount rental prices. Many include utilities and no rent for up to a year with escalating rents thereafter. Rent-to-Own Agreements will be considered.*

A plan like that would be great for the town economy, and as investments went, it was one he'd urge a client to consider. But it had nothing to do with him. He would have considered it himself six years ago, back when he could afford to take a risk. Maybe found an old place with layers of charm, polished it up and filled it with simple dishes and classic cookware. But he was far too cash-strapped and energy-sapped now.

He dumped the newspaper into the recycling bin, and Jacques went after it. The puppy threw his paws against the can, knocking it into the wall. With the paper tight between his teeth, he shook it from side to side.

"Go ahead and tear it up, if it makes you happy."

Kyle stood, leaving the puppy to chew on yesterday's news. He poked at the ruined egg with his spatula. "Must be nice to live such a simple life. Know what would make me happy? Enough money to get out of this dump. Less stress. Maybe I'd enjoy cooking again."

He ditched the egg in the trash. "I used to love this pan. The only thing I do with it anymore is burn food."

He crossed his apartment in a dozen steps and sat on the edge of his sleek, modern bed to dig socks from the drawer of his nightstand. Shrugging into a T-shirt from a stack he kept in an old bookcase, he bumped his elbow on a shelf of scavenged wood and weather-worn bricks. Tingling pain mixed with numbness shot up his arm, and he cursed.

Jacques wagged at his feet.

He rubbed at the twinge that shot through his elbow, waiting for it to subside. Stupid loft. It was too small, too cramped, too dark. It felt like his childhood home, raw and crowded. Not that his place in Boston had been colossal, but at least it had rooms and sunlight. He missed being able to stretch out sometimes.

"It's a good thing we don't hang out here that much, huh? You coming downstairs to work with me today? We have a barn full of tractors, and they all need something. Better than being bored up here."

Kyle jammed his feet in his work boots. He raced down the stairs through the morning chill, Jacques at his heels, and turned the corner. A scrap of paper dangled from a thumbtack in the open door.

Bern's handwriting left a lot to be desired, but the message was unmistakable.

*Ur late. Tractor now. R else. B back soon 4 it.*

Kyle ripped the page from the door, crumbled it into a tight ball, and threw it across the barn floor. Jacques scampered after it.

"You may be back for it, but it won't be ready."

Tractors and parts were sprinkled across the barn floor resting in puddles of oil and daubed with grease. A gray tractor took up more than its fair share of space, a month into waiting for a new engine that always seemed a day away. An orange tractor puked fluids on the floor, every gasket eroded by time. Bern only cared about the yellow one. Its engine was seized. Kyle had seen a lot in six years of squinting at ancient manuals written in languages he couldn't understand, but a seized engine was a new one. His rear end ached from days of sitting on the cold concrete floor, and he wasn't any further along than he was when Bern towed it in. And Bern wasn't the understanding type.

But the sun dove through the open door and crept across the floor as morning turned to lunch. With the book on his knees and his dog asleep at his feet, his stomach growled, and old dreams rattled in their cage. Kyle flung his head back, resting against the old yellow tractor, rust be damned. He traced the floor joists overhead, seeing past the spider webs and old wasp nests, finding promise in the voids.

"Wouldn't this make an awesome store?"

Jacques lifted his head into a yawn, paws outstretched.

"No, a restaurant. And a store."

His stomach growled again. Hunger always came with a twinge of shame and sometimes guilt. The shame of being hungry in public. The guilt of taking food from his mother who went hungry on his behalf. He pictured the barn full of tables, draped with cloths and shivered at the memory of cramming down his dinner so fast he felt ill, because his parents fought about money every night at the kitchen table.

Jacques pawed at his leg.

"You don't want a store? I do. Or I did. I wanted to prove to the world that being in a kitchen and eating a meal could be an enjoyable affair. Can you imagine this place cleaned up?"

Jacques rolled onto his back, begging for a belly rub. Kyle obliged.

"This barn would make a hell of a restaurant. Handmade tables with mismatched chairs. A big central chimney with a fireplace. All the food would be local. We'd make our own bread and serve hearty meals with fresh vegetables. Thick stews in the winter. We could throw some great parties in here. And a store, of course. Right at the entrance with spice blends and colorful cast-iron pots and utensils made from real wood instead of that plastic garbage."

Jacques gnawed on the corner of the book. Kyle distracted him with a stray leaf and stood, brushing chaff and barn grime from his pants. "Nothing's gonna get done if I sit here daydreaming."

He tossed the manual on his workbench and flipped to the troubleshooting section, a last ditch effort before—he had no idea what. But it might as well have been written in ancient Greek. Everything he'd learned had been trial and error, mostly error, and none of it came from that book.

Kyle scratched behind one ear with a greasy nail, smearing grime in his hair. He slammed the book shut and spun to face the eager puppy.

"That's it. We should knock off for the day. What do you say? Go upstairs and try to cook something? I've got half a box of pasta and some stale Cheerios. A dash of salt, a splash of lemon. We could make it come alive. What do you say?"

It sounded terrible.

Footsteps crunched on the gravel outside. Kyle bristled at the intrusion. He grabbed a wrench and a spray can of lubricant.

"Okay. New plan. Every bolt on that thing is rusted to the frame.

We'll get the bolts loosened, then we can go up for lunch. Pasta, no Cheerios."

Kyle slipped beneath the tractor, spraying down rusted bolts with lubricant. He'd learned the hard way that Bern would use anything against him, especially anything that resembled being idle. It wasn't just Bern. Every encounter on that farm was either awkward or painful or dripping with blame for things he couldn't control, whether it was a tractor or the farm's finances.

A pair of boots crossed over the threshold and Bern's shadow stretched across the floor. Kyle braced himself for a terse demand.

Bern leaned against the door frame, one eyebrow cocked. "I gotta get a water tank halfway to Kansas, and every machine we got is stuck up in here so I hope you got good news 'bout any of 'em. Something tells me you ain't got any, though."

Kyle nudged a wrench with his foot, and it scraped across the dusty floor. Stray nuts and bolts skittered against the wall. He wiped his hands on his jeans as he stood. "Not every tractor is in here. And I need parts for that one." He nodded to the orange tractor with its leaky seals. "It'll be here tomorrow. Coming from Vermont." He didn't know what to do with the parts when they arrived, but they would arrive all the same.

"Can't you borrow a part off something else? Frankentractor that thing or something?"

Kyle shook his head and wiped grease off his tools with a tattered red rag. "Not compatible. And you can't reuse a gasket." He could tell Bern didn't believe him. He knew he wasn't believable even when he did know what he was talking about. And he was running out of ways to occupy his hands.

"You sure?" Bern asked.

Kyle threw the rag on the bench. "Positive. Why would I withhold valuable equipment?"

Bern pushed away from the doorframe and folded his arms across his puffed-up chest. "We got harvest soon. You know that?"

"Like I don't know that, Bern. Like I don't know we need that money to make payroll." Tractors were only part of their problem. Without tractors, no one would eat, but they might all go hungry anyway. "Look, the new engine will be here tomorrow. I'll get it in as fast as I can." *And then I'll conjure a million dollars from thin air.*

Bern slinked to the workbench and jiggled a tub of rusty parts in golden liquid. "Looks like bolts swimming in caramel." He poked a finger into the bowl. "What's in here?"

Kyle grabbed Bern's wrist and pulled his hand away. "It eats rust off stuff. Hope you've had a tetanus shot." He threw a greasy rag at him and nudged him toward the door. "Out, please."

Bern wrinkled his nose and curled his upper lip in a sarcastic sneer. "Geez. A guy can't be sociable?"

"You're in the way." The quicker he could get Bern out of the barn, the quicker Kyle could go back to daydreaming about creamy béarnaise sauces loaded with tarragon.

Bern gasped in mocked shock. "I'm holding up your progress? Well, I'll be. I should just scoot along so you can stare at those pages some more." He sauntered toward the door. "Loser. Guys like you only care about people with money."

"What was that?" Kyle folded his arms and planted his feet. He'd heard it before, in loud accusation and whispered address. It didn't matter that he'd grown up in Ramsbolt or that he'd returned. They only cared that he left. As if it was a sin to chase a dream unless they understood it. Kyle never pushed the point, no matter how insulted he was. His silence gave him the distance he liked. But this time, it flipped a switch in him. Judgment and criticism was one thing, but dreams were all he had to live on, and they'd been interrupted a time too many. He could hold his tongue for Zeb, but he didn't have to take it from Bern or anyone else.

Bern rolled his eyes. "You heard me. You never get along here. I don't know why you're so rude. You came here with your fancy car and your shiny shoes, and you think you're special, slumming it with normal folks. But we see you. Guys like you only care about people who got money. We ain't got retirement funds or fancy accounts for you to manage, so you ain't got time for us. You just sit in here looking down your nose at people."

Kyle shoved his hands in his pockets. "Nothing could be further from the truth. I wanted to be here."

He had. When he reached the end of his rope and quit his job, he expected his parents to be appalled. They never wanted to see him settle down in this town, but he wanted the comfort of his home. Plus, his father was already starting to slip, leaving stoves on all day and forgetting to open the flue in the fireplace. His mother had been coughing blood into tissues for months. The timing worked out to move back home. And with no other jobs around, his dad had called his old boss for a favor; that's how Kyle found himself working for Zeb. It had been a dream come true with free rent and easy work. Then Mom died and the funeral was expensive. Dad's Alzheimer's got worse and the state wouldn't pay for his care. Ramsbolt started to seem more cold, less inviting then. It wasn't a lie that he'd wanted to be there, but it was a half-truth to say he was happy about it. It was one of life's hard compromises.

"You wanted to be here? Did ya now? The story around here was that you were some fancy finance guy. You were supposed to know your shit. That's what they really brought you in here for. But it turns out you're not so good at any of it." Bern scanned the room, a look of contempt lining his face. "We knew you weren't a mechanic. Turns out you're good at nothing. You got this job 'cause you failed at everything, and your daddy called in a favor from his old boss."

Kyle cocked his head to the side and raised his eyebrows. There was no use correcting the record or appealing to Bern's compassionate side. Only fools argued with men whose minds were already made up. But the switch had been flipped, his hair on the back of his neck raised with his ire, so he tried anyway.

"I can't get blood from a stone. This place is poorer than you know, and it's not for lack of trying. I'm an investor. A money manager." Kyle glanced down at his cheap steel-toed boots with their fraying stitches. "At least I *was*. Doesn't mean I ever lived a rich life. It's a lot easier to be rich when you start out that way. Little do you know that if I did a worse job at fixing the finances of this place, we'd all have been out on our asses a long time ago." He turned his back to Bern and opened the manual to a random page, to a sectional view of a power shuttle transmission. He recognized it right away. Maybe he'd picked up more than he gave himself credit for.

Bern kicked a piece of gravel across the floor. It ricocheted off the wall and skittered to a stop. His voice dripped with sarcasm. "You just keep looking, buddy. You'll find something you're good at. Eventually. I don't mean to hold up all this progress you got going on."

Bern left the way he came, kicking gravel across the lot, his stomps growing more distant until they were gone. Jacques peeked out from behind the workbench.

"Were you hiding? From Bern? He's not bad, just grumpy sometimes."

The puppy sat at Kyle's feet, leaf clamped in his jaw. He shook his head and slobbery shards of dried leaf sprayed Kyle's shoes. He shook some more and lost his balance, falling over, legs sprawling as he tumbled onto his back.

Kyle scooped up the squirming puppy and kissed the top of his head.

"Whoever abandoned you was cruel and stupid. I'm glad, though."

He hadn't been looking for a puppy when a car pulled up on a snowy afternoon and left a box of them by the mailbox. He'd found homes for all but one…the littlest runt who couldn't sit still. He named him after Jacques Pepin, the cook he watched on television as a kid. Strange name for a puppy, but it turned out he needed escape and inspiration just as much as an adult as he had when he was a kid.

"At least I'm not the only daydreamer around here." Jacques licked the side of his face. He let the squirming puppy jump to the floor and grabbed a wrench. "Okay. Back to work. Loosen these bolts then lunch."

He slipped beneath the tractor, wrench in hand, loosening bolts as rust stained his knuckles. His chest clenched. It wasn't just the tight space beneath the tractor. The walls closed in around him, too small to hold his dream, too cold to warm his heart. He never wanted to be a mechanic. It was supposed to be a brief waypoint on a journey, a momentary blip in his life. He was supposed to be somewhere else, doing what he loved, but he got lost along the way, sucked into saving this farm because it was his bread and butter, bland as it was. Every sunny thought he had about moving on was shadowed by the cloud of having nowhere else to move to, nothing else to lean on. No one in Ramsbolt could hire him for work he was qualified for. It wasn't like anyone there needed a financial guru. His work for the farm was his only security, and that wasn't saying much.

Over the years, he leaned harder on his father's friend, harder on the farm, and the guilt burrowed deeper with him. But Zeb leaned on him, too, asking for money miracles where none were to be had. Someday the farmer would wise up, take his advice, sell some land, and hire a real mechanic. Someone who could do the job better, faster, with more intuition. Zeb would find someone whose whole heart would feel a sense of duty to the place. But for now, it was him and his dog and the barn, dark and drafty and cold as it was, dragging around a heavy heart that wanted to be somewhere else—in a past he never lived and a future he couldn't have.

The bolt wouldn't budge. He bent his knees for the leverage and pushed with all his might, but the wrench slipped and he slammed his hand against the frame. He clutched his fingers, pain searing up his arm. Jacques flopped at Kyle's side with a broad grin and let out a yip.

"Damn farm. Damn this place." He let the puppy lick his wounded hand. *If I were smart, I'd stop dreaming, wasting time on stupid shit. Time to buckle down and get this job done.*

## CHAPTER THREE

"Come on." Kyle slapped the dashboard of his ancient Saturn wagon. The car heaved itself down the road, throwing him back against the seat before dashing him into the steering wheel. It lurched with a loud backfire, and Kyle steered through the turning circle, through the shadow of the sailor statue, and onto sunny Main Street.

He pounded the dash. "You really make me miss that old BMW sometimes. *Get the Saturn*, Zeb said. *It's cheaper to maintain.* Never should have listened."

He pulled up to the curb across from the market and the engine stalled. Ignoring the stares of the old men gathered outside the newsstand, he dug his wallet from his pocket. Just a five and a few ones in there. Broke until payday. Spark plugs would have to wait.

The slam of his car door echoed off the brick walls, and he winced. He wanted to be invisible. Head down, hands in his pockets, he rushed across the street and into the market. Food shopping used to be fun. Inspiring. Now it was his least favorite chore.

He pushed through the door and wove around tables stacked high with baskets of produce. His wallet couldn't afford those luxuries.

Aiming straight for the staples, he kept his eyes focused on generic boxes of pasta, but he couldn't resist pausing to run his fingers over the bumpy skin of an overripe avocado. There was a time he could afford such a thing, but the farm didn't pay him in fresh-guacamole money, and living paycheck to paycheck took the fun out of shopping for even the cheapest bags of cereal. Losing his one joy in life was punishment for turning his back on his old job and his financial security. He couldn't even remember how to make guacamole anymore. Avocados. Tomatoes. Lime.

A nauseating mix of roses and cigarettes pulled him back. A hand reached past him and clutched a plastic tub of blueberries.

"I do love these," she said. The woman was ninety if she was a day. "They would make such a good pie. I can never get it right, though."

"Mmm." Baking had never been his strong suit.

"Was a family here a million years ago. Lived at the end of the street. Woman sold blueberry pies from her window."

Kyle picked up a plastic tub and turned it on its side. Thick, plump blueberries rolled around. "I thought that was just a story."

"Not a story. Eloise Nolan made the best pie." She dropped the berries in her basket.

"Eleanor. Not Eloise. It was Eleanor Nolan."

The woman slipped her arm through the basket handle and pursed her red-painted lips. "That was back before the government said you couldn't give out food from your kitchen without paying them fees and going through hassle. Long gone now. Can't get pie like that no more. Don't know what happened to that family."

"I wasn't just a story." Kyle squeezed the plastic tub, and the edge cut into his thumb. It was a story his father told often. The details would change, but the facts were always the same. Kyle's grandfather died or ran off or was kidnapped, leaving a wife and a child behind. His dad was raised by his mother in the little house at the end of Main Street, where she sold blueberry pies from her kitchen window. "Blueberry Window Pie."

"That's it. Where Diane's Tea House is now. The family just up and left."

"They didn't leave."

"They just seemed to disappear. Left like everyone else, I presume."

"Nope. Still here."

The woman's eyes narrowed. "There aren't any Nolan's in Ramsbolt."

"I'm a Nolan. Eleanor was my gran."

She craned her neck back, scrutinizing Kyle down the ridge of her nose. "You're Eleanor's grandson? What happened to her son?"

"He married my mom. We lived about a mile outside town."

"I never knew he was still here. Nice young man. Quiet. He dated Birdie, the Kirleys' daughter. How you can go without running into somebody in a town like this..." She shook her head.

It was work, being that isolated. His father hid their poverty in shame. His mother scoured hers by doing laundry for families that were better off. But they stayed to themselves in their house outside town.

"I grew up here. Not *here*, here. Ramsbolt, but not downtown. Birdie was my mom."

"Whatever became of your father?"

"He worked at the farms. Never went out much. He's in a nursing home in Colby now."

She shuffled the basket to her other arm. "Sorry to hear that. Your mother?"

"Lung cancer. Five years ago."

Her bun loosened as she shook her head, and wiry strands of silver hair sprang from their nest. "I had no idea they had a son."

"Yup. That's me. We were a quiet family, that's all. I worked at that old steakhouse outside town. I went to college, worked in Boston. Moved back six years ago. Helped my parents for a while. Had a hell of a fight with the state to get him into a home."

"I bet." Her face fell. "He's lucky to have someone to help him."

"Yeah. I guess." His thumb was wet. A drop of blood had formed where he cut it on the blueberry tub. He wiped it on his pants and dropped the berries in his basket. It was two dollars he should have spent on other things, but once you bleed on them, you have to buy them.

"All those years I begged her to teach me how to make that pie, and she wouldn't let slip one word of that recipe. Was a shame when she died. We have no restaurants in this town, and your own cooking gets stale after a while. Until Marissa's opened, we had no deserts at all in Ramsbolt. God knows someone should teach people to cook around here." The woman patted his arm. "At least there's a lucky lady out there somewhere. If you're still making your grandmother's pie."

*Great. The only thing I can afford in here today are minor injuries and kicks to the gut.*

A relationship. It was all supposed to fall into place by now. He should have climbed the rungs of life's ladder, had a great career, corner office with a view of some city, earned enough money to start his own chain of kitchenware stores, bought enough free time to cook for fun. Then he should have found a partner to enjoy those achievements with him. Instead his ladder to success had been chopped up for firewood. Sure, he'd tried things out of order, but he never had enough time for Tracey. Six years had passed, and the breakup still stung. She'd hated his cooking anyway.

Kyle rubbed the back of his neck. He didn't put any effort into the smile he gave her. "That's kind of you to say. It's just me, but that means I don't have to share."

The woman leaned closer. "Wise man. If you see your father, you tell him Mrs. Dean says hi."

She winked and moved on, shuffling down an aisle toward the peanut butter, jellies, and jams. He didn't have the heart to tell her that his father's mind was gone.

Kyle aimed for the generic pasta in its plain white box. It was just as good as the fancy kind, but it hurt to know what was out of reach. Forty-two years old and he couldn't afford name brand pasta. He added a jar of marinara and a bag of puppy food to his basket then dropped his items on the motionless belt at the register.

The guy in front of him waited for change and chatted about potholes and the broken town clock. Kyle knew better than to seem impatient, though he itched to rush out the door. Ramsbolt would not be rushed.

"Adelle said it's only a matter of time." Shawn, the bag boy, handed the man a full paper bag with a loaf of bread jutting out of the top. "As soon as she gets some tenants, she says she's gonna get the sewer fixed. Then the potholes."

"That's what Warren said." The man nodded his head at old news. Kyle forgot how fast word spread among the people who lived in town. "Hope she fixes it soon."

"Don't we all. Have a great day, Mr. Hahn."

"Ayup." The man shifted the bag on his hip and moved to the door. "You, too, now."

Shawn shook open a new paper bag and waited for Kyle's pasta and blueberries to roll down the conveyor. "You read the paper?"

Kyle couldn't make eye contact with the kid. He'd seen the bag boy at least once a week for five years, and always tried to hide the shame of buying less than he wanted, just scattered items that proved he wasn't half the cook he used to be. Shawn was barely born when Kyle cooked at the old steakhouse, and had no idea he was once the town's best cook. But even so, spreading his groceries out on display was a bit like inviting the world to peer into his soul and find it lacking. He told himself the world was preoccupied with its own insecurities, and that nobody judged him for what wasn't in his cart. The truth was, no one remembered him at all. But a little voice inside his head wouldn't stop screaming about his failures. Everyone in this town was poor, and they all nursed wounded pride, but Kyle never got used to it. Not after having the kind of freedom money could buy, then throwing it all away.

"Sir? The paper?" Shawn raised an eyebrow. "Did you read it?"

Eyes fixed on the conveyor belt, Kyle shrugged. "I might have seen it."

Shawn grabbed a paper and gave it a shake. "You want a copy? The Ramsbolt Reader's free this week."

Kyle shook his head and dug through his wallet. "Nah, I got one. Thanks."

"It sounds great, don't it? I would love to open a music store."

Kyle handed over a five as his eyes fell on the headline. Shawn's voice faded into the background, along with the beeping register. He snagged one from the stack.

"Wait. This is different from what I got this morning."

Shawn straightened his apron. "Yeah, it's a special supplement thing. It just came out. We're giving one to everybody. Adelle has this plan to rent out all the empty stores down here."

"Yeah, I saw. I just didn't realize there were twenty-eight empty stores. When I was kid, downtown was really busy." Kyle straightened the stack of papers.

"You can have that, if you want. Man, a music store would be great, wouldn't it? I'd sell vinyl and old tapes and CDs. And I'd have a room in the back for music lessons. You grew up around here, didn't ya? There wasn't anywhere to get music lessons, was there?"

"Um." Kyle tucked the paper in his bag. "No. No music lessons I can recall. There was a guy who taught piano out of his house, I think."

"What would you open? What kind of store?"

The old dream snapped into focus. Shelves of colorful cast iron, shiny stock pots, rich wood cutting boards, and a cozy corner for cooking classes that would have made that woman's head spin. But some things were better left as dreams. Besides, without a dream, he'd have nothing left.

"I'm not the business-owning type."

"Yeah, I hear ya. All that finance stuff is scary." Shawn winced.

"The finances are the easy part." Kyle folded down the top of his bag. "Good luck with the music store. You should give it a shot. Before you get too old and settled and risk averse."

He gave Shawn a weak smile and grabbed his bag. Behind him, a woman unloaded an armful of baby food jars on the belt.

"You hear about Zeb's farm?" she asked in the whispered tone of someone who was going to unleash gossip whether anyone wanted to hear it or not.

Kyle shuffled his bag and his wallet. Jars rattled down the belt.

"No. Anything good?" Shawn clenched a little jar of mushed peas.

"Going under's what I hear."

Face burning, head down, he walked from the store, shame searing its hole in the pit of his stomach. One more failure to add to the pile.

He climbed in the car, held his breath, and turned the key. The engine grinded and churned before coming to life, sputtering and stuttering. He let out the sigh and eased his foot on the gas, bracing himself for the violent lurch. The two dollars left in his wallet weren't enough to fix the car. Like everything else in his life, spark plugs would have to wait.

# CHAPTER FOUR

Kyle glanced out his office window at the Boston traffic on the street below. He straightened his tie in the mirror attached to the back of his office door and smoothed his short, dark hair, plucking an early grey highlighted by the fluorescent lighting. Coworkers were already heading to the conference room, but it was too early to go back there. He pulled a book from a shelf and pretended to look something up, flipping the pages with a pained expression that wasn't fake. His insides were jelly, and his knees wobbled. He didn't want to look too eager or uninterested as people passed by. It seemed best to look busy instead.

His assistant peeked his head around the corner. "You ready? They're about to announce who gets the new client and that VP chair you've always wanted."

Kyle looked up from the book. "In a minute. Just a few things to finish up."

"With a cookbook?"

Kyle slammed the book shut and pushed it into place on the shelf. "Dinner."

He hadn't been this anxious since he interviewed for the VP position three years ago, which he lost to some bigwig's daughter. But this time the job was his; he could feel it. Weeks of working double time, exhausted, running on empty, preparing a financial plan to take the company's income from hundreds of millions into the billions. He was by far the most qualified to get the new account. Why they had to announce the chosen one in front of the whole office, however, seemed pretentious. But that's the way things were with them. Anything that could be competitive was cutthroat, and anything cutthroat was life or death. That's just the way money was counted.

He slipped into the stream of identical white men, white shirts with starched collars, bad lighting glinting off cufflinks. Polished shoes padding on the plush hall carpet. Their voices ricocheted off the glass walls, talking about sports and kids' ball teams. There was a logjam at the door for the ritual of back slapping and *no, after you*. It was a power play to see who caved first. The weaker man always took the first step.

Kyle slowed, merged, shifted so he didn't have to play.

He leaned against the window. The city bustled on the street below, wrapped in scarves and drab winter coats. A yellow streetlight switched to red. Around him, the sea of shirts and skirts ebbed and flowed as people shuffled for seats and made room for colleagues, but Kyle stood alone, arms folded. He never went in for all the banter, the power plays, the casual sizing up and taking down. He was there for the work, and it was about to pay off. His hands tingled.

A new guy, some Harvard heavy hitter who came from money and grew up knowing how to use it, stomped into the room, clapping his hands, declaring the party started. Kyle kept his eye roll to himself.

"That guy." Becker rolled his eyes and leaned against the windowsill beside Kyle. "He has a lot of maturing to do."

Kyle shrugged. "He'll learn."

Power was best exerted in silence. The *look at me* bluster was all effect, an attempt to make up for something lacking somewhere else. VPs never acted like that. If they were intimidating, it was because they were quiet. Kyle counted his breaths, waiting for patience to settle his stomach, but it seemed so far away.

"Rumor has it you know who the client is." Becker gave him a wink. "Wanna spill the beans?"

Kyle returned a knowing smile. "And ruin the soup? No way."

The crowd parted as Carter strolled in, carrying his trademark leather padfolio. He started speaking before he reached his chair.

"I'm not going to keep you all for long. There's work to be done. I'm sure some of you couldn't keep your mouth shut, so everyone probably knows that we've secured the contract for Wardenclyffe." Carter dropped his padfolio on the table. Half the room jumped. He gripped the back of his chair with a satisfied smile. "One of you will be taking on the account and will be promoted to a vice president chair. I don't have time for the niceties. It's a household name, so you know they have aspirations to land a man on the moon in a commercial craft. Their work will be absolutely confidential. So this role must go to the right person."

Carter scanned the room. Kyle forced his breath to deepen, calming his racing heart. It had to be him. No one else had the candor or the discretion.

"We're giving the account to Huntington. Congrats. Be in my office at five thirty. Everybody, back to work."

The blood drained from Kyle's fingers, and his grip tightened on his jacket sleeves. It couldn't be. Huntington never worked a minute of overtime. He never showed up on Fridays. Kyle's hands tingled and broke out in a cold sweat. He squeezed his fists and shoved them in his pockets.

"Tough luck." Becker pushed away from the windowsill. "The only reason he got that job was because he donated a ton of his daddy's cash to that art museum."

"What art museum?" Kyle fell into step behind him as the room cleared out.

"Carter's wife is on the board of that visionary art museum downtown. The new one that opened in that old warehouse that burned down."

"And he donated to it. Of course." Wardenclyffe would be relieved when they found out their slacker finance guru got the job because he supported art made out of bicycle chains and hair dryers.

"I'd watch my back if I were you. Get busy, real fast on other projects. Fifty bucks says if you look too available, you'll get pulled in to do the heavy lifting."

"Without any of the credit. Good call." Kyle paused outside his office door. It took two years to get that name plate. They made you earn everything. Now they were handing out VP roles and lucrative clients to anyone who could foot the bill. He wanted to rip it off the wall, shove it in a cardboard box, and slide into the throngs of people outside, shuffling off to God knows where.

He knew Huntington well enough. At every chance, the guy leveraged his Brown degree and the fact that he shared his alumni status with Carter and Carter's sons. Being an alumni of Ramsbolt High School and his tiny Maine University business school was no help at all. As much as he wanted to strangle the guy for accepting a role he wasn't qualified for, he couldn't blame him. If being a Ramsbolt graduate could get him anywhere, he'd do the same thing. With a little less damage, though.

"Anyway, wanna go to lunch? A few of us are going down to that new place where you get your premade food from a refrigerator and pay twice as much."

Kyle wrinkled his nose. "Appealing as you make that sound, I'll pass. On to the next thing, right?"

"You're a warrior." Becker slapped him on the shoulder and skated into the pack, off to lunch and office gossip.

Kyle closed the door and ripped off his tie. He rubbed the spot on his neck that was near raw from wearing his ties too tight. Nonstop work and weeks of stress. No sleep. He'd eaten nothing but crap. All of it left his stomach in knots. A constant burning pit made him worry about an ulcer.

He threw his tie on his desk, and the skinny end landed in his cold cup of coffee. It grew dark as it wicked up his abandoned mojo. He blinked at it.

There wasn't any point anymore. The enjoyment was gone. Watching a client grow, seeing them stabilize and plateau, take risks. The adrenaline rush was lost. All that was left was bland office food and Hermès ties. Even his time away from work was unfulfilling. He never even cooked anymore.

He rested his forehead on his office window and peered down at the street. The glass was so thick it wasn't even cold. He used to be so passionate about his future, working nonstop to save for some inevitable joy of owning a kitchen supply store that he deferred by necessity, afraid to leap without a financial safety net. Maybe that was the point. His dream had been somewhere else, sitting on the sidelines, waiting for him. It waited for him for so long it died. Nothing was left but a constant yearning for more or better, and in hindsight, that old dream seemed stupid anyway. Who dreams of owning a kitchen supply store? If he'd been focused on the real goal, the important work of securing the financial future of businesses, he wouldn't feel like this at all. And he'd be a vice president by now.

* * *

Kyle's knife scraped his plate. He winced at the sound. The restaurant was far too quiet for that kind of negligence. From across the table, Tracey gave him the kind of side-eye she reserved for his most egregious offenses.

"You seem so distant tonight. What's going on with you?" She peered over her water glass. "When do you find out if you got that account?"

He pierced a radiantly green piece of asparagus with his fork and cut into it. Smiling through a deep breath, he said, "I didn't get it."

Tracey gaped, eyes wide. "No. You worked so hard." But there was a flash of something else, something unsaid in her eyes. She set her wine glass on the table and looked down at her hands.

A waiter whisked her empty glass away, and she declined a third drink. She never drank two glasses of wine with dinner. Two years of dating and he'd never seen her drink two glasses of wine on a weeknight.

"Enough about me." Kyle swallowed hard. "What's up with you?"

There was bad news to break. He could see it in the deep breath, the exhale, the stiff lower lip, and the way her eyes darted to the side. She wouldn't look at him. She'd been looking at her hands all night.

"What's this dinner about? It's not random. We come here on

weekends.”

She was breaking up with him. The realization washed over him in a wave of numbness, taking away his horrible day, the big letdown, the sense of worthlessness. Somehow it broke a dam in him, and all the emotion swept out to sea.

“You’re breaking up with me.”

“I wanted to find the right words, but I can’t.”

“Start with why.” He folded his napkin in his lap.

Her sigh was so deep she could have sucked in the table.

“Oh, God. Just forget it, Tracey. Don’t bother explaining. It’s someone else, or you lost the spark, or I work too much, or you want to dedicate your love to rescue dogs. Whatever. Just go. I’ll pay for dinner.”

She leaned back in her chair. “It’s not like that.”

“Isn’t it, though?” Was their relationship that miserable that she couldn’t string together the words: *I just don’t love you anymore.* Christ. After two years, she couldn’t find the words?

“Kyle, you’re just not as fun as you used to be. I know that sounds shallow—”

“You’re not wrong.” He picked at his chicken. Bland, blackened slab. It needed onion powder.

“*But* you’re always stressed out, ruminating, talking to yourself in the shower about fights you had weeks ago. Running over the same torn-up paths. You’re not trying to be happy.”

He let his fork fall to the plate with a satisfying clatter. “I work. Hard. I have a dream—”

“You’re not working for it. You don’t even seem to want it. It’s just this part of you, this story you tell about who you are. It’s part of your narrative, but all you do is work all the time. You don’t even enjoy it.”

"How can you say I don't really want it *and* say I'm working too hard to get there at the same time? How can you not see how important this is to me?"

She was right. Time and distance had faded it all to some hazy picture like a fleeting childhood memory, a mere snapshot with the hint of emotion. He didn't remember what he loved about cooking or why he wanted to open that store, but he clung to the hope of it like a relic from before some war, like a reminder of what life was supposed to be.

Tracey blinked at him. "All I'm saying is that whatever you have going on in your head is more important to you than I am. It's been two years. Either things with us are progressing or they're not, and if you're not invested in this, I can't be either. I have to think of myself and what I want."

He gulped his wine for the courage. Tracey was slipping away. His head told him to do something—anything—to salvage their relationship and make her reconsider, but his heart didn't crave it. Rather, the insult was a challenge.

"Not invested? I cook for you all the time."

"You don't have to. Didn't have to."

He nodded. "So you're saying I did nice things for you to show my affection, but they weren't your style."

She lifted her napkin from her lap and placed it by her plate. "No. I'm saying I don't like your cooking."

Rage flared within him, creeping up his neck and heating his cheeks. She never left an empty plate, and she said she loved it all the time. "You lied to me? Why?"

"Jesus. I don't know." Hands on the edges of her seat, she looked ready to run. "I'm angry, okay? I'm frustrated. I keep investing in this relationship, and it's like you're an emotionally dead fish. You don't even like to cook anymore. It's frantic and messy. It doesn't look fun or relaxing at all."

"But it is. It's exactly what I want it to be. You don't have to like it, I'd just appreciate it if you didn't lie."

She leaned across the table, fury in her eyes. "Are you kidding me? That's what you're going to stick with here? That I didn't like your food? You are the most uptight, aggressive cook I've ever seen. It's like you take out all your anger at your job on the kitchen. You hate the city, you hate your boss, you hate the universe. It's like you're trying to get as far down the wrong road as you can. The only forward momentum you make is in the wrong direction."

His nostrils flared. She didn't know him at all. "Screw you." He regretted it as soon as he said it.

"I hope you find what you want. I really do."

Silence fell, an anchor between them as they bobbed in the tide. He counted his breaths. In for four, hold for four, out for four. If either of them lost their cool, he'd never be able to show his face there again. Not that he liked dropping that much cash on food, but it was *the* place to be seen, and he had a reputation to protect. With the resentment pushed back into the shadows, there was room for the sadness. Without Tracey, he'd have no one. His neighbors were nameless, faceless. All he had were some coworkers he couldn't trust. Would he miss her or the companionship? It didn't really matter.

"I wish we could start over," he said.

"Maybe that's what you need to do, go back and start over. Figure things out. Get back to basics. But without me." She stood and reached for her purse. She pulled a few bills from her wallet and tucked cash under her plate. "I'm sorry."

She pushed in her chair and left.

Kyle let her go.

He'd read somewhere when he was a kid that the body's cells replenish every three months. In three months, the woman who walked away from him, the curve of her calves and the skin on her hips, would be a new person. He would be new. There was nothing left to do but wait to be new again.

He counted her cash and pulled out his wallet, adding enough of his own to cover a sizable tip. The waiter nodded from across the room, and Kyle slipped through the lobby and into the street.

It was a quiet night. Dark and cold. The parking garage reminded him of Christmas, driving in circles looking for a spot, hopping in and out of stores to find Tracey the perfect present. Two holidays. This one would be lonely.

Maybe she was right, and he was fighting for something he didn't really want. If the world of finance was draining him instead of getting him closer to his dream, then what was the point? What would get him closer? Money meant success. It would mean he'd dragged himself out of Ramsbolt and into the real world where he could survive on his own. Success was supposed to be the means and the end. Somehow his dream got lost in the middle.

He pressed the button on his key fob, and his BMW lit up a cement wall. He didn't even like that car. It was a perfectly good car, but he'd always wanted a Jeep.

He climbed into the driver's seat and shimmied into place, settling into the well-worn groove. Tracey was right. His dream didn't fit anymore.

What if he could start over? Go back to Ramsbolt, back to the quiet life, to the little restaurant where he was happy and creative? What if you could point to a spot on a calendar and say to some shady professional in a dark alley, "Hey, send me back there please."

He turned the key, but the car didn't start.

"Are you kidding me? Come on."

He tried again. The starter clicked, and the headlights died.

# CHAPTER FIVE

Kyle tightened the last spark plug and wiped his torque wrench with a tattered rag. His credit card was worse for the wear, and he scolded himself for paying interest on twenty-five dollars' worth of spark plugs, but desperate times called for desperate measures. He slammed the hood of his Saturn, and Jacques twitched awake, lifting his head and stretching into a yawn.

"I don't miss a lot about my old life, but sometimes I miss dropping my car off at the dealer and not worrying about what it would cost."

Jacques looked up at him with an open-mouthed grin that made Kyle feel like a god. The puppy ran for the knotted rope and dropped it at his feet, begging to play.

"You can go from zero to sixty in an instant, can't you?" Kyle grasped the end with his clean hand and let the puppy tug with all his might.

"Listen, I have some bad news, little buddy. You're gonna have to make those puppy crunchies last until Friday, because we're out of money for the week. Okay?"

Jacques braced himself with his front paws and pulled, flinging his head from side to side. Kyle lost his balance, crouched, and tightened his grip on the rope.

"You're getting strong." He dropped the rope, and Jacques flung it into the air. The puppy let out a satisfied yelp. "Thank God you're around. I'd die of boredom some days."

"How could you die of boredom with all this work to do?"

Kyle spun. A small wave of adrenaline pounded ashore, and his heart leapt into his throat. Zeb leaned in a window, one arm extended to the orange tractor that lay in pieces.

"Work. Everywhere."

Wiping sweat from his forehead with the back of a greasy hand, Kyle shrugged it off. "Engine will be here later today. Tracking says it should be here by eight, so who knows what time. I'll drop it in as soon as it gets here."

Zeb swatted at the air. "I ain't here for that. I need a miracle."

"Again?" He knew that look. Letting the man down easy wasn't as simple as it used to be. Being prodded for a miracle might be better than being yelled at, but it came with its own high cost. The farm inched closer to bankruptcy each month, and Kyle inched closer to losing his home, his job, and the safety of having a routine. The farm might not be much, and it barely paid him enough to survive on, but it was safety and security. It was his home.

"I can't print more money, Zeb. We've pulled interest off savings, drained and merged accounts. Two credit cards are maxed out, and we can't repay them and offload that debt until after the harvest. You're too far in the red to get another loan."

"We ain't got no choice. Two plots of corn got leaf blight."

Kyle ran a hand over his face, cool grease streaking his cheek. Was this what drove the woman in the store to declare the farm on the verge of defeat? "What's leaf blight? Do I want to know?"

"Probably not, but it wiped out two whole fields."

In another world, in another life, he would have pressed a button on his phone and asked an intern to bring coffee. He'd have asked what caused it. He'd tilt his head and nod at the sad parts and ask how it would affect their business, how it could be prevented in the future. He'd have drawn lines between clients, offered referrals, pulled in favors to help mitigate the damage. And he'd structure the financing to help get through the hard part and make a secure future. But those days were gone. That life was over, and there wasn't any help to be had in a world of endless struggle. But he had to try. His heart had to try.

"What causes leaf blight?"

"Moisture. Humidity. It's a fungus. It lives in the soil. We'll have to till that ground extra to make sure it goes away before next year. We shoulda noticed earlier, but we didn't."

There was a time he loved the intangible nature of money, how it could move through invisible walls and grow and shrink. The ability to manipulate it, to make lives better, was a powerful force. It was easy in the city. It was all an elaborate game when the money belonged in tall steel buildings, but out here, out in the fields, money was tangible and nature would always win.

"So what do you need to get through this, and what's it going to cost?"

Zeb rested his chin on his hand. "We gotta put more money into corn next year. We'll have to buy a stronger hybrid seed to help get past the fungus."

"How much more?"

"Twice as much, maybe? I dunno yet."

Kyle bit his tongue and held his breath to hold in the groan. There was no way he could double the seed budget for next year. "There isn't any wiggle room. A penny more is too much. We're maxed out. Loans are getting harder to come by, and we have less collateral to put up every year."

The tips of Zeb's ears turned pink. He rubbed at one. "I hate telling you things sometimes, 'cause you always got the wrong answers. I ain't selling my land."

"I'm not saying to sell all of it. Just enough to loosen the belt."

The men locked eyes. Kyle wouldn't wage a battle of the wills with the old farmer. The land was his to do with as he pleased. All he could do was offer professional opinions, and his last ditch advice was his worst. Digging into retirement savings was a last resort. Zeb worked his whole life, and he deserved to live a comfortable future, simple as it would be. Kyle's might never grow again, and it had taken economic blows just like everyone else's, but he would hold onto that retirement account with his dying breath. It hurt like hell to even think it.

"The last thing I can suggest is to take some from your retirement. It'll be a tax hit, but you can pay yourself back later. You absolutely have to pay yourself back, though. You have to get rid of all this accruing interest first. Things are going to get a lot worse unless you cut back on the amount you pay in interest."

Zeb slapped the windowsill and leaned back into the midday sun. "I'll think about that. That's not a bad idea."

Kyle shook his head. He never should have said it, not to a man who was desperate to live in the here and now. It might make Kyle's job a little more secure, and it was nice to know his paycheck was covered, but not at the expense of the farm's well-being. Or Zeb's. "No, it's a terrible idea. It's not a miracle. It's the absolute last thing you should be doing. It's there to help you when you… In the end."

Zeb wagged a finger at him, eyes narrowed. "We don't live in your high-rise city world. Out here, finance is different. Robbing Peter to pay Paul is how farms run. It's just the way it is."

High-rise city world? Apparently Zeb hadn't seen the loft apartment he'd lived in for the last six years.

"The way things are isn't always the way they ought to be." He had never been above begging a client to make a choice. Not if it were for the greater good. "Please consider selling some land. What will happen to all of it if you lose this farm, huh? What's the point in keeping it together if it's just going to fall apart anyway?" He wouldn't be doing his boss any favors by not pressing the issue. Emotion and money were like oil and vinegar. They taste great when you put them together, but they separated too easily.

Zeb shook his head in staunch defiance. "This farm stays intact, Kyle. Do everything you can to make it work. Get creative if you have to."

Kyle folded his arms. His fingers dug into his biceps. "I'm doing all I can."

"You'll have to dig a little deeper and figure out if all you can do is the best you can do." Zeb kicked at something on the ground. "You talked to your dad lately?"

"About as much as anyone can. He doesn't know who I am anymore. I still go up every weekend, but it's more for me than it is for him."

The old man's mouth twisted into a gnarled frown. "Getting old is the worst. You tell him I said hi. Even if he don't remember me. But I ain't selling my farm." Zeb pushed away from the window and stomped across the field.

Kyle couldn't blame the man for being bound to the land. He'd found his own comfort there. After throwing in the towel on his career, the little shops, tiny streets, and the fields he knew as a kid were the kind of salve that money couldn't buy. And that sense of place had been a blessing since his savings had dwindled down to near nothing.

No amount of creativity would help. He got into financing to do things with money, to nurture it and watch it grow, not to do whatever this was. Scraping by. Having no money to work with wasn't very inspiring.

He gathered old spark plugs from the floor and tossed them in the boxes. He could get five cents back from each one he returned, and he wasn't about to pass up that deal. It wouldn't put a roof over his head if he lost his place in the barn, but it would buy him a can of beans. That was a whole meal. He slammed the boxes on the workbench.

"Shitty, meaningless, useless job. Why am I even still here?" He kicked the leg of the cast-iron stove he had to feed in the winter to keep himself warm. The place was hot in the summer and humid. It smelled like death warmed over. Miserable place to work. Nobody liked him, and he didn't fit in. He wiggled his stinging toe inside his work boot.

It wasn't like he could just go somewhere else or get a part-time job in a town with no prospects. And he couldn't have left while he was paying for his dad's care. What kind of son signs the checks but never visits? He was back and forth from state agencies often in those early days, trying to get his dad into a decent permanent home, and prove to them that his dad was so poor the house caved in. And he wanted to help Zeb, who'd been good to his dad over the years and put a roof over his head in exchange for some work. He lost so most of his own money along the way that sticking around and bailing out water was the only way to keep from drowning.

He grabbed the edge of the barn door, ready to put all his weight behind it and slide it shut, put up a barrier between himself and the world, but he couldn't. He needed it open. He needed to hear the birds and see them hop across the threshold looking for seeds and dried grass. He needed to hear distant tractors and signs of life from the other half of his codependent relationship.

Zeb and the farm leaned on him, and he leaned back, ignoring the worst of the job, making excuses for the rest. For six long years he figured something else would come along, some miracle to lift him up out of his failures, but nothing ever came. So he stayed. And he'd stay until it all fell apart.

"Ky-le!" Bern's mocking singsong tone echoed across the drive. Kyle braced himself for footsteps, but they didn't come. He clutched the edge of the workbench.

"What now?" he yelled.

"You got that tractor fixed yet? I gotta move that water tank."

"Jesus Christ, Bern. When the damn motor gets here, I'll put it back together. I paid for the damn thing with my own credit card, you know. I'm sure as hell not gonna forget about it."

# CHAPTER SIX

Kyle squinted at the monitor, at the farm's tiny bank balance, much smaller than the bills. He popped the last of his blueberries into his mouth. They burst, tangy and sour, but lacked the flavor of the wild ones that grew on hedges all over town. It was such a tease. Good thing he hadn't saved them to make a pie. There was only so much disappointment he could take in one day. Much like filling out the federal grant form, those blueberries didn't offer much reward for the effort.

The farm had one shot at a hardship grant, but it required seven years of financial history, and nothing sent him into a tailspin of melancholy faster than looking at seven years of disaster. It was one thing when it was a client. It was something else when it was the source of his livelihood.

Outside the office window, fifteen percent of the crop was gone, and with it, fifteen percent of their income. More would be felled before Dan and Bern found the edges of the blight.

Kyle's cell phone buzzed, and he dug into his old briefcase to find it. It was crammed in a front pocket between an old grocery receipt and that newspaper supplement from the market. He threw it all on the desk and clutched the phone.

Cadwalladr.

It made him smile all the same to see Jon's name pop up on his phone. He hadn't heard from his old client in years. They'd been close once, the way you were with people you saw at social functions vaguely masked as work. Jon was a rotund man who would sit next to Kyle at association meetings and country club bars, prattling on about how he grew his business the organic way, back before kids these days, before social influencers and email spam trying to sell followers by the thousands.

He accepted the call, though he was sure it was a butt dial. "Kyle here."

"No one else is half as good, and I demand you take me back." Jon had one of those dripping New England accents that barely rounded out its British heritage. Tracey had called it snobbery, but Cadwalladr wasn't that way. Once you scraped away a layer of tweed and baritone, the man was a giant teddy bear. A greedy teddy bear, and a man who gave what he got, but a softy at his core. "You're the most conservative investor I know, and I need someone to take this project to the next level. You always guaranteed me returns, and you delivered. Take me back."

Kyle laughed. "I wish I could, but I'm not a part of that world anymore."

"I know. You quit your job and moved back to your delightful small town." Jon's fingers drummed on some distant desk, tapping through the phone.

"You were my hardest goodbye." Jon had been his first big client, and he'd valued the man's mentorship. He'd tried to stay in touch, sending investment tips by email. As the years passed at the farm, the emails were fewer and farther between. His mother's funeral. His father's care.

"You know how it is." Jon was more apologetic than dismissive.

"I do. No hard feelings. Things are busy here, too, and I don't do finance anymore." That was the nature of business. There were only so many hours in the day, and in a world where time and money were the same, there wasn't any to waste on unprofitable relationships.

"Nonsense. I'm setting up a new venture, and no one else will do. You're my go-to guy. If I have to bring you in-house, I will. What scotch do I bribe you with?"

Kyle tapped his pencil on the grant application. If only Jon could see him. He'd gone from managing piles of cash to mountains of misery. "You can send scotch whenever you'd like, but unfortunately, I'm out of commission. I can't even offer a referral, really. I've been out of the game too long. My FINRA license expired forever ago."

For a split second, he wished he still had it, both the license and the energy. Working for Jon, even on the side, could get him back on his feet. But that was a job for a different man. He wasn't that man anymore, and he didn't want to be.

"What terrible news. I don't believe it for an instant. What are you up to these days? Surely the whiz kid who whipped me into shape is managing some new start-up of epic proportions. Are you running some new tech giant? You got me out of more than my share of scrapes. With all that magic, I bet you have a story to tell."

Hardly. He closed a folder of six-year-old tax forms, putting aside the misery of the present to bask in the pride of his past. The office chair sank a little when he reached for his coffee. It was nice to hear his old mentor have such high hopes for him, not that he'd thought of Jon as a mentor at the time. It would be painful to dash his expectations.

"You could say I'm in technology, yeah." It was a half-truth, but not much of a stretch. Tractors were old, but they were technology. And he spent plenty of time keeping Zeb's old computer running.

Jon cleared his throat. "Where are you these days? Still in Boston?"

"Goodness no. I'm back in Maine." He tossed the plastic blueberry tub in the trash and leaned back. The seat creaked.

"That's where you were from, right? See? I remember important things."

Kyle smiled. Jon was one of the few clients who took an interest in reality outside the corner office. "Yup. Tiny town called Ramsbolt. It's farmland out here. Slower pace. More fulfilling than the world of finance. In some ways." *That* was a lie. Pride got the better of him, though, and he lost control of his words. "I've been thinking of starting something new."

But he hadn't. He couldn't start anything new because there was nothing worth starting and no money to start it with.

"Interesting! Care to elaborate?"

Searching his scattered thoughts for some detail, however vague, was like shoving his hand in a bag of thumbtacks, painful and useless. He grabbed the edge of the desk to spin the chair, and his hand landed on soft newsprint. The town manager had a plan to change everything, the headline screamed. Anyone with a dream could apply.

"Elaborate? Wish I could." He tried to give it an air of mystique, to hide any embarrassed inflection. The man was a millionaire. An economic immortal. He'd looked to Kyle for sound investment guidance. What was he supposed to say? That his dream was to open a kitchen supply store, but he was too poor to do it? The last thing he wanted to do was run through his list of failures with a man he admired.

"Did I ever tell you about my first job?" Jon's hearty laugh erupted from the phone. "I worked at an insurance company run by my father-in-law. Right out of college. I thought I was the shit. I had an office with this great view of Hartford. Not that views of Hartford are worth bragging about, but if you can look out at a river all day, it's a lot better than staring at the back of an elevator shaft."

"I've had offices like that."

"Most people had to work hard to get a window, but Frank just handed it to me. Being nice to his daughter, I guess. But it's hard to be passionate about insurance. It was over from the start, but I didn't know it. Not until I was sitting in an appointment with a really nice client. One of those guys you can take your tie off around, you know what I mean? You could laugh or tell an off-color joke, and he would just roll with it. But there I was in my fancy office with my view of the river, and he's telling me some story about how his business was growing, and he needed more liability insurance to cover his ass, and all I could think was…man, my life is boring. My life is over if I stay here."

Kyle's insides braided. He didn't want to hear it—a story like his with a happier ending. What was the point in wallowing in missed opportunities, pretending to be thrilled for someone else's success if it didn't put food on the table? He'd blown his U-turn, and he was stuck on this highway with no exit ramp and no destination.

He held the phone away from his face and let out a gratifying sigh. Clicking the speakerphone button, he dropped the phone on a manila folder stuffed with tax forms and folded his arms.

"I know that feeling, Jon."

He'd asked himself a million times if his job here was done, if he'd achieved everything he could to make the farm the best it could be. Farms were cyclical. They went into debt for a harvest payday, and there was never enough money in savings to handle contingencies. Every little thing was a disaster. He'd lent his talents as much as he could, paying down bills and building up savings, but he'd hit a wall that couldn't be climbed, and he didn't want to hear any more of Jon's successes. He needed to stay in the here and now, to hold on as tight as he could to what little joy he could find in his days. It was time to buckle down. Dreaming wouldn't get him anywhere.

"Listen, I don't mean to cut you off, but I gotta get to back to—"

"I have to say, Kyle, I'm proud of you for taking a leap of faith. I was young when I did it, but it's not so easy once you're established."

"Don't I know it." He wiggled the mouse and woke the computer from its slumber, resisting the urge to throw it against a wall.

"I'm so glad I did it. My life turned out for the better. It was terrible at the time, of course, but I look back now and think *ah, those were the good ol' days.* I do have a secret to tell you, though." Jon's voice dipped to little more than a whisper. "You'll be shocked, of course, but I had to take some serious risks to get out of there. Frank, the father-in-law who gave me my first job? He'd put a lot of money into a retirement account for me and my wife. I never told him, but I cashed it out to buy the inventory for my first furniture store. You'd never have suggested such a thing."

But he had. To Zeb. It went against everything he believed about life, about how life should be. Saving for the future was the only way to keep from ending up like his father, every fiber broken by the constant battle to ransack pennies from a world that thought you weren't good enough to have them.

He grabbed a pen and stabbed the newspaper, dragging deep lines in the margins, gouging frames around the list of Ramsbolt's empty addresses.

"Not a chance, Jon. I never would have let you do that." He couldn't let Zeb do it, either.

"Of course you wouldn't. You're much wiser than I was at that age. I *know* your new tech venture will be the same rewarding adventure mine has been."

Kyle nodded, glad Jon couldn't see his emptiness. "Oh, I didn't ask. What's your new gig?"

"I'm pretty excited about it. I'm selling off my brand. My daughter has no passion for this stuff. She wants to build sailboats, of all things, so I bought a ski resort in Colorado. It's time to cash in my laurels and follow a new passion."

"A ski resort. That's a change of pace. Good for you."

"Thank you. It's been very good catching up with you. If you think of a way I can convince you to join me, you know where to reach me. Until then, keep your skis together."

"You, too."

The line went dead with a subtle click, leaving Kyle staring down at his dark phone. Papers littered the desk. Old tax forms and schedules and declarations of debt left little room for anything else. Zeb's ashtray sat in the furthest corner, full of soot and embers. Everything from the carpet to the ceiling reeked of neglect.

There was so much waste in his world. Time and smoke and land fusing into a shapeless form that couldn't comfort or guide him. The priorities were out of order. And all the need—the need for money, peace, security, and more time to find solutions—it blaring like a siren in his head. He couldn't concentrate with all that noise. That grant was his last ditch effort to save the farm. They were out of options after that. Zeb would never sell his land. He'd never do the smart thing to make ends meet, and he'd wear that cloak of pride until it wore so thin there'd be nothing left to keep any of them warm. Not Dan or Bern or even himself.

He hit the print button. The machine grumbled and purged.

He grabbed the forms and stacked them in a pile. A quick signature from Zeb, and he'd take them downtown. Throw them in the mail. Wait for word.

It felt like goodbye for some reason, collecting papers from the desk. There was nothing bittersweet about turning his back on the ashtray, the ancient PC, the shuffling of money. With the flick of his thumb, he turned off the computer and pushed the papers back into their folders, the newspaper and its list of addresses on top, framed in blue pen that he'd scrawled in frustration.

He shoved it all back into his old briefcase in a ragged jumble.

Tomorrow was another day. Once that grant application was in the mail, he'd need a new plan.

## CHAPTER SEVEN

The state-run senior center in Colby smelled like antiseptic and urine, like everything Kyle saved money to avoid. He waited on the rubber mat for the second set of automatic doors to open and let him out of the vestibule, then stepped up to the registration desk.

A chain held a pen to the counter. It barely reached the clipboard where he left his name.

"Kyle. How have you been?" The young woman behind the counter wore white, like a nurse, but she wasn't one. He'd asked once, just to change the subject when she flirted with him and told him he looked like Mo Rocca.

"I've been good. You?" He inched to the hall.

"Great, thanks. Your dad is doing well. He talks about you every day, and says you're coming to read the paper."

"He doesn't really know who I am. At least not when I'm here."

She gave him the sad, knowing smile she probably gave everyone but with a sparkle in her eye he suspected was just for him. "It's nice that you read to him. Maybe it'll jumpstart some memories."

"You never know." He waved the paper and turned down the hall.

The chalky cream-colored walls were scuffed by passing wheelchairs and beds. Ahead, a woman in pink scrubs pushed a cart with a mop. One wheel squeaked as she turned into a room. A persistent phlegmy cough pulsed from behind a closed door, and from some distant bed a man yelled out a one-syllable cry. He paused outside his father's door, hand on the stainless steel lever, and took a breath of purgatory air. He was never sure who he would be: his father's son, his father's father. One time he was the mailman. A doctor once said that it was easier not to argue, especially if his father was agitated. For however long he stayed, he'd be whoever his father wanted.

"Hey, Pops." The door clicked closed behind him, and he squeezed the newspaper in his fist.

His father was sitting up in bed. He wore gray sweats and jabbed at buttons on a remote. The television sputtered through channels.

"This damn thing. You know how to work these buttons? I can't get *Wheel of Fortune* on this thing. I know it's on. These people hide it from me. And that man down the hall. Aah." His father waved a hand in the air and mocked the misery around him. "Bunch of whiners."

"I'm not sure. I can try." Kyle reached out a hand for the remote, but his father pulled away.

"No. You'll break it. All you firemen are the same. Rushing in with a big axe when all you need is a garden hose." He jabbed a button the TV turned off. "You checked on my house? Can I get back in yet?"

Kyle's neck wouldn't crack. He'd have to settle for the tension. His father hadn't asked about the house in a long time. Sometimes he thought there'd been a fire, other times a flood. Kyle didn't want to be the one to tell the man the roof caved in, that the walls collapsed, and there was no going back, even if he could be trusted to live alone.

"Not yet. Can't get back in yet. You'll have to stay here for now."

"I need to get in touch with my son. He lives in Boston. Someone needs to tell him."

Kyle nodded and lowered himself into the stiff chair at the bedside. It was cold and impersonal, like something out of an office waiting room. "I know. We've been in touch with him. He'll be here soon."

His father slumped a bit, settling into the bed. The plastic mattress cover crinkled beneath him. "I hope he hurries. There's a lot to do."

"Sure. Hey, have you read the paper today?" His father had been a remedial reader, even when his eyesight was in its prime.

"Not today. You can read it if you'd like. Not too loud, though. I might take a nap until *Wheel of Fortune* comes on."

Kyle smoothed the paper over his knee, the one he'd collected at the market. It didn't matter what he read, if he started in the middle of a sentence or never finished a story at all. His father, a man who once raised barns, couldn't concentrate on a commercial.

He cleared his throat, and his eyes found a heading. "The empty store located next to Warren's Newsstand is eleven-hundred square feet on two floors. Ramsbolt residents will remember it as Peppermint's Candy Shop, long before Marissa's came to be."

"Ramsbolt was a hell of a place when I was a kid."

Kyle lowered the paper. It wasn't often his father offered a window into the past, but a crystal clear view was rare. When they did come these days, they were usually through the warbled panes of Alzheimer's glass. "Do you remember Peppermint's?"

His father nodded, eyes soft and fixed on some distant mark. "I do. I grew up at the end of Main Street, in an old house that sits by the church."

"It's a tea shop, now."

"I know it. Never been there, but I know it. My mother made the best blueberry pies in the country, and she sold them from our living room window. Not on Sundays, but any other day you could get a pie if our window was open. Everybody knew her and that blueberry pie. Ramsbolt's legendary Blueberry Window Pie."

Pie had never made his mouth go so dry. His hands slicked with sweat, and he wiped them on his knees. "Do you remember the pie? What was it like?"

His father's head snapped to him, eyes narrowed, like he was angry he had to explain water to a fish. "It was pie. Had blueberries in it. Stupid questions. You done?"

His father had mentioned the pies before, mostly when recalling his mother, but he'd never said they were a town landmark. No one had, until the other day at the store. He itched to ask more, every ounce of butter, every gram of flour. Where did the berries come from? Did his father collect them? But the fire in his dad's eyes said it was better not to push. He let the pie go.

"Do you remember anything else about that house?"

His father wiggled his feet. "I grew up in a mansion. We had the biggest backyard in town. We had servants who did our shopping and cooking. It was like being shut up in a castle. I never met anyone."

It was a past that never existed, a clever tale his father wove to make comfort from the chaos and sense of the senselessness and cushion their life of poverty. It was true they never had many visitors, but not because they lived in a mansion.

"We had such parties. A thousand people would come and drink champagne. I wore a suit, but I never wore tails."

The stories his father told of a lavish past were so opposite to Kyle's reality that they almost sounded like dreams his father never chased.

The door swung open, and the beeps and clicks of medical machines grew louder. The woman in the pink scrubs dragged a cart in behind her, and the sounds faded as the door closed. "I didn't know you had company, Mr. Nolan. I'm just here to clean the bathroom."

"I was telling this fireman here about the mansion I grew up in."

"Uh huh." The woman wasn't deterred. She slipped into the bathroom with a scrub brush in her hand. "That sounds wonderful, Mr. Nolan."

"It was five stories high. We had an elevator."

She poked her head out of the bathroom and leveled an eye roll at Kyle. "They do this sometimes. Almost like they're filling in gaps with old movie scenes. Don't take offense."

"None taken."

"It can be jarring for people who aren't used to it."

"I can hear you, Edna. Just clean the toilet and keep your jealousy to yourself." His father's arm flew up so fast that Kyle barely had time to duck. The remote flew through the air and smashed against the wall, batteries rolling across the floor.

Edna, if that was even her real name, was unphased. "Do not throw your remote, Mr. Nolan."

Red faced and hands balled into fists, his father's tide had turned to outrage. "I will throw whatever I want."

Kyle folded the paper and rolled it back into its tube. "It was nice talking to you today. I'll be back next week, okay? I have some errands to run, and I have to take my dog out."

His father couldn't hear him. All his attention had turned inward.

Kyle slipped into the hall with Edna in his wake.

"I'm very sorry," she said.

Kyle dug his keys from his pocket and found the one to his Saturn. "Don't worry about it. He thought I was a fireman today, anyway. We all just do the best we can."

He didn't wait for a reply; he didn't need one, and Edna had enough on her plate.

That night, in bed, as an owl hooted in distant trees, and Jacques snored at his feet, he couldn't stop thinking about blueberry pie. Blueberry window pie.

If the pie was so famous, why didn't his father talk about it? Why did so many years go by before he learned his grandmother had been known and loved by the whole town and been so famous for her pie? Because they lived a detached existence as far from the town as they could get, and it was a sin for him to step foot over that line and expose the family to ridicule.

Kyle had always known why.

He knew his mother saw their poverty as a disgrace. He'd always figured it was just her way of dealing with the things she couldn't provide. But he never knew how far his father had fallen. What a shame that his parents tied their virtue to their wallet, embracing all that misery.

It all swirled as the room spun. Their push for him to go to college. Their demand he leave and never return. When his dad called in a favor from Zeb and got him that job, and he swore he'd take it back if Kyle stepped out of line and acted like some big city fool. He wasn't worried Kyle would embarrass him or bring shame to their family. He was worried Kyle would wander into town, do well for himself, and succeed. He was worried Kyle would find happiness where he couldn't, and prove once and for all that misery wasn't the only company the family could afford.

What a systemic disease, tying character flaws to financial deficits.

Heat swelled between the sheets, and he kicked out one foot in search of cooler air.

What did it taste like, that blueberry pie? Did she pass the recipe to anyone? God knows his mother never would have baked it.

His mother's baking prowess ended at runny spritz Christmas cookies that lost their definition and spread like snowballs. Her pumpkin pies could have been a soup course if Thanksgiving dinner had ever been formal enough. He didn't fault her. He hadn't inherited any baking instincts either. There was a time he could pick a slab of marbled meat, season and sear it and grill it to perfection. Drizzle silky sauces on seasoned vegetables to please even the pickiest eater. But baking had never been his thing. When he got that job at the old steakhouse, she'd been so proud. She'd written down every recipe she knew and put them in an old wooden box for him. It had been full of scraps of paper with old family dishes. But he'd been far too creative to dig through it in search of gold. Besides, he loved modern cooking and some of those scraps had been pretty old.

There were old recipes in there.

He threw the covers back and slid into his slippers, careful not to wake Jacques when he stood. Somewhere in the kitchen was that old recipe box, wooden with a broken brass clasp. He'd thrown away dozens of cookbooks when he left Boston, tossed out pans that didn't please him and pots that weren't the best. But he'd kept that box safe.

The kitchen didn't hide much. Under the sink was all cleaning supplies. Cabinets of canned food and shelves of staples.

He found the box on top of the fridge, right where he put it when he unpacked his things six years before. He blew dust from the lid and fingered the clasp.

Inside, paper and cardboard shards jutted at angles. One by one, he thumbed through food that was Ramsbolt to him. He didn't have memories of downtown, of candy shops and window pies like everyone else. His Ramsbolt was toast and cheese, chicken livers, corn on the cob. His mother's scribbled recipes for green bean casserole and potato stuffing, things that weren't worth remembering and were memorable all the same.

A yellowed slip of paper, once torn and mended with tape turned to crisp, unfolded to reveal the thick handwriting of a much older pen. The sharp uprights and the loopy scrawl must have been his grandmother's.

My Famous Blueberry Window Pie. Top Secret.

It was the only piece of evidence Kyle had ever seen to prove that his family ever belonged.

CHAPTER EIGHT

The sunrise had barely tinged the horizon when Kyle fed Jacques and left his apartment. His car huffed and pulsed steamy exhaust into the morning chill as he drove into town on sleepy streets. He parked on Main Street, the slam of his car door echoing off the brick buildings, and he cringed at the disturbance. A flock of birds startled from a tree behind Diane's Tea House, spraying the air with morning dew. And there was the window. It was a six-over-six, just twelve glass panes. White-painted wood trim set into a brick storefront. No front porch to speak of, just a few concrete steps that led to the front door. His grandmother's front door.

He leaned against the car, wringing the newspaper in hand, trying to picture the house in a sepia setting with the window flung open and a curtain fluttering in the breeze. A gauzy curtain stained with fruit pie. His father as a little boy flying out the door, down three concrete steps to the street with a toy in his hand, off to some great battle. Kyle had never heard his grandmother's voice; she'd died when he was young, but he could hear her scream after her son not to slam the door, to be back before sunset, don't ruin his clothes.

61

But that's not what he was here for.

*It was stupid to come down here and feed that monster. What did I used to say to my clients? Dreams are free? It's a hell of a diversion from the real world, but chasing them costs more than just money. I can't afford this chase. I can't even afford cheap spectator seats.*

Kyle folded the newspaper and shoved it in his back pocket. The town was quiet, and his footsteps made for irritating company. The stores were dark except for the bakery where Marissa prepared the day's treats. She moved through the pastel-colored store, stocking her display with muffins and bagels in the graceful choreographed dance of a long-running one-woman show. It plucked some long-dormant string in him, a tune of isolation he'd forgotten the words to long before. He'd wanted to be a part of that world, to walk down Main Street with the people of Ramsbolt. To wave at someone he knew. He also wanted a bagel, but there wasn't enough time or money for that. He had buildings to peer into.

It seemed silly to miss an hour of sleep to look at derelict buildings. All the more reason to rush back to the farm. But his mind wouldn't rest until he'd exhausted himself, so he went from store to store, leaning his hand against cold windows and peering in, comparing each space to the dream he once had. Not one of the stores lived up to the fantasy. Quite the opposite—everything on Main Street was terrifying. The sheer thought of shoveling out broken ceiling tiles and scraping decades of lead paint off water-stained walls made him sick to his stomach. Rounding the park and walking toward the antique store, he couldn't help but think that it wasn't much of a deal at all. It would take so much money to make any vacant store habitable that it was a losing proposition. If he were advising a client, he'd tell them to set up shop anywhere but there.

It was a relief in a way to see the stores laid out like this, one after one, a parade of blight. But it made him yearn for the small slices of Ramsbolt he did know as a kid, hopscotching the stores for the few things they needed, bored to tears while his mom stared at fabric or his dad bartered vegetables for boot repairs. Back then, town seemed colorful. Magical. But standing there staring at the bones of an old store across from Sparky's small engine repair shop, it felt cold and broken.

His breath fogged the glass.

*Geez, what a mess. And that's the easy part. A broom and some elbow grease are free.* All he could see were dollar signs, and not in an incoming way. Buying shelves, hanging drywall, and stocking the store was something else entirely. *Thank God I'm not still feeding a delusion I can run my own shop. Imagine how much more trouble I could get myself into.*

He crossed the street as the sun began to kiss the windows, lighting up the town. One last store to see, one last square on his blight bingo card.

He passed Penny's Loft where a little orange cat glared down at the street from his perch, scrutinizing the morning light. The last vacant shop sat next door.

Kyle pulled the newspaper from his pocket and checked the old general store off the list.

The doorway was recessed, like those grand store entrances with little hexagonal tiles in gleaming black and white, scuffed and blackened by shoes and dirt from the street. Leaves huddled in the corners with cigarette butts and a few candy wrappers.

*I don't even remember an old general store.*

The deep windows showed no displays, just wooden risers once painted white, as if vacancy were the only thing for sale. The paint was peeling, and shards were missing, bare wood peeking through.

It would look great as a store, the shelves painted pristine white, covered with copper pots and mixing bowls in vivid colors. Maybe a holiday tree draped with cookie cutters. He kicked himself for the reverie; it would only lead to a hunger he couldn't afford to feed.

*If dreaming gets me through another day, it's energy well spent.*

He stepped farther into the entry and peered through the door. An old ice cream freezer sat to one side, its red script writing visible in the morning sun. *A Taste of Heaven.*

*How many square feet is this place? It's huge.*

The newspaper said it was one of the better locations. It needed less work and had more square footage. It was cheaper, too, farther from Main Street. He stepped back on the sidewalk to take it all in. The second-floor windows looked cracked and drafty. Layers of glossy paint flaked from the trim. But it was across the street from a cheery florist, next to the antique store, and just down from a toy shop. Plenty of visibility for people passing through town.

Three hundred dollars a month for the first year, negotiable. Slight escalations after that. The lease rate didn't include utilities, but they were cheap. He could picture himself living upstairs, Jacques racing through the store. Shoveling snow from the sidewalk, cleaning the windows in the summer and waving at neighbors. His heart raced as the picture took shape, and the thought warmed his skin.

It wouldn't cost anything to ask a few questions.

Adelle's phone number was on the back page, a number to text to ask for a showing. It was next to a list of discounts available at Carol's Hardware Store for anyone renting a new space.

*That's a nice benefit. Takes a little off the cost of cleaning up and doing repairs. It's money that can go back into buying inventory for the store. Someone could make enough off this to feed himself and pay the bills if he worked hard enough.*

He'd be in better shape than he was now. He'd be working for himself, and not stuck at a farm that was constantly on the verge of collapse.

It was possible. That someone could be him.

He filled his lungs with the cool air of a crisp summer morning and pulled his phone from his pack pocket with a shaking hand. He sent a text to the number in the paper. *It's only a question*, he told himself. *You're not committing to anything.*

He missed twice before he tucked his phone back in his pocket.

*She probably won't even respond.*

Kyle picked up the pace, his breath forming clouds in the morning chill. He hurried back to his waiting car and held his breath while the engine struggled to start.

The farm was barely more than a mile away, but it felt like ages getting down Ramsbolt's streets, across the bridge, and past the tavern. That old feeling of committing a sin washed over him, as if he was breaking hard and fast rules about being in town and daydreaming. Even worse, he was doing both at the same time.

A jittery impatience added weight to his foot.

He had nothing to hide, really, no one ever looked for him at that early hour, and what he did with his morning wasn't anybody's business. But it was just his luck that as he pulled onto the gravel drive, Dan and Bern pulled the barn doors open and flipped on the lights, a ray streaming onto the drive through the thin fog.

Kyle's insides went into a knot, and his mind raced, looking for a story.

*Just tell them you ran out for dog food. No, that won't work. It's closed. Just say you had to mail a package. Or you went to Marissa's for breakfast.*

The dream was still his. He didn't want to tell lies about where he'd been, and the truth wasn't worth their ridicule. He cracked his neck. Nothing would come of it anyway. The whole thing had been foolish, really. He steered his car to its usual spot behind the barn and slipped in the back door.

*Just say it's none of their business.*

"We been waiting for you for ten minutes." Bern leaned against the workbench. It wobbled against the wall. Dan stood in the middle of the room, hands in his pockets.

Kyle pushed past Bern. "I had errands to run. What do you need?"

Bern rolled his eyes. "Did you get 'em done? You got no bags."

Dan aimed his thumb at the door, toward the fields. "We had to get an early start to make up lost time after this tractor sat broke for so long. Now that new engine you put in broke down out there."

Kyle let out a deep sigh and tossed his keys on the workbench. In his pocket, his phone buzzed with a text message.

## CHAPTER NINE

Kyle washed his hands at his tiny kitchen sink, chunks of grime swirling down the drain. The coffee in his stomach felt the same, churning and roiling, agitated by the clock. 10:22. He was late for a 10:30 appointment that he never should have made. He dried his hands and texted Adelle.

*Sorry to delay you. I might be five minutes late.*

It had taken forever to tow the tractor back to the barn with Bern's old Jeep, then it took an hour to find the problem and longer to replace the broken spark plug. The poor thing snapped in half on a rough start, and the irony of failing spark plugs wasn't lost on him. If only he could get himself started, if he hadn't lost that spark, he wouldn't be stranded in those fields either.

Adelle replied. *No problem. I'm here. I run the flower shop across the street. Got the basic proposal you emailed. It looks good.*

He hovered over the autofill responses. Thanks? Okay? Got it? Nothing seemed appropriate, and his proposal was anything but thorough. All she'd asked for by text was a line or two about the kind of business he wanted to run. He'd hardly call it a proposal.

Jacques sat at his feet, an expectant wide-eyed gaze fixed on the cabinet where his food was stored.

"I hate to leave you alone, especially after I was out in the field all day."

Jacques spun and took the end of his leash in his mouth. It fell from its peg by the door and landed on the floor with a thud.

"I know you wanna come, but it might be unprofessional."

Jacques spun again. His nails scraped the old linoleum, and his tail smacked into a jacket, knocking it from a hook. It cascaded over the puppy, who barked his disapproval. Teaching him to spin around had been an adorable mistake.

"Do you promise to make a good impression? You do raise a strong and valid argument. If dogs aren't welcome, it's good to know now. And anyone who doesn't fall in love with you, well, they just can't be good people, can they?"

Jacques shook out of the jacket and mouthed at the leash. Kyle chased Jacques's collar while the dog spun in circles.

The closer they got to town in his old sputtering Saturn, and the closer he got to inspecting the store, the sweatier his hands grew on the steering wheel. He pulled down the alley behind the shop, wiped his hands on his knees, and ran one through his wild hair, wishing he'd gotten it cut. He spun in the driver's seat and unfastened Jacques's safety belt.

"Do I look okay? You can tell me the truth." He smiled wide. "Any food in my teeth?"

Jacques wiggled himself free of his restraints, and when Kyle opened the door, he bounced from the car and tugged at the leash.

"One second, buddy." Kyle shot off a quick text message to let

Adelle know he had arrived.

*I'm here! Sorry I'm late. I parked around back.*

He received a fast reply.

*No problem! Meet you around front.*

It was scorching outside for late September. With its late blow, summer put up one hell of a fight, and heat sizzled off the sidewalk ahead. When he turned the corner, she was there. About his age, early forties. Long brown hair tied back in a messy knot, jeans, and white Keds with a green florist apron. She carried a manila folder.

He stuck out a hand. "You must be Adelle."

Adelle ignored his handshake. "Puppy!" She dropped to her knees and tousled the dog's ears. He yipped and slobbered her hand. "What's your dog's name?"

"This is Jacques. Like Jacques Pepin. I loved watching cooking shows as a kid," he said.

"Me, too." She stood, brushed the dirt from her knees, and tightened her apron.

Her apron was embroidered with a white five-leaf clover. Behind her, another was painted on the sign above her store. Everything about her was immaculate in a way no human could manufacture. Her world looked like something out of a magazine, with planters and buckets of cherry-colored flowers, not a wilted petal that he could see. Her life seemed like a small town aspiration wrapped up in rustic bow, and it was intimidating.

"Sorry I'm late." Kyle shuffled the dog leash and stuck out a hand again. "And sorry for the dog. I didn't want to leave him in the car. Is it okay if I bring him in?"

"Of course! Don't worry about it!" She shook his hand and forced the key into the lock of the empty storefront. "The door sticks. It's old. You have to jiggle it a bit, and it'll open right up."

She pushed the door, and a wall of pulpy air hit him, thick with dust. Inside, ribbons of light pierced the shadows, flecks of neglect glittering through. Jacques bumbled in, undeterred, nose to the floor as he searched for something to chase.

"The store is a blank slate, really." She leaned against the old ice cream freezer.

As he scanned the ceiling and the walls, the cobwebs melted away, and the future took shape. The old tin ceiling tiles had a beautiful copper patina peeking out from layers of white paint. The floor was well-worn. A large wood table with little wells, as if it could have held nails or bolts, sat to the side. It looked handmade with giant wooden pegs holding it together. It would be perfect for displaying tiny things like napkin rings and place setting markers. But for now it sat covered in white dirt like a gingerbread house dusted with powdered sugar.

Jacques yipped and jumped, leaving circles of footprints in the dust that covered the wide-plank hardwood floor.

"What do you think you want to do with the place? I know you said kitchen supplies," Adelle asked.

"I always liked to cook. There's something about soup that's so comforting. When I was a kid, we used to just throw things in a pot. Chicken, celery, a few herbs from the yard. I don't mean I want to throw weeds from the parking lot in the food! I mean…"

He turned away from her, so she wouldn't see the blush that burned his cheeks.

*Stop sputtering. You sound like an idiot.*

"Anyway, I want to open a kitchen supply shop. Colorful dutch ovens, toasters, cast-iron pans, nice dishes, utensils. That kind of thing. Specialty appliances like coffee bean grinders. Half my business will be cooking classes, though. I really want to teach people to cook and love their food."

His eyes wandered to the back of the store. It would be the perfect place to set up a classroom.

"That would be fun." The floor creaked as she crossed the room. Kyle turned to see her run her finger across the top of the giant table. As she did, dark wood the color of chocolate frosting showed through.

"What was this thing for?" he asked.

"Candy was in here. Penny candy."

He nodded and turned away, walking along the far wall. "This place was a general store?"

Adelle tilted her head to the side, and sunlight picked up gold highlights in her hair. He looked away. "It was. They sold candy and ice cream and just about anything you can imagine. Somehow they fit the whole world in here. It's been gone a few decades though."

No wonder he didn't remember it. His parents couldn't afford candy. If they shopped there, they never took him along. "Maybe I can use that old table for something."

Adelle went to the counter where the outline of an old register had dug itself into the wood countertop. "You know, thinking about cooking classes. If you get that off the ground, we could even collaborate sometime."

*She talks like it's a done deal.* "Yeah?" He raised an eyebrow while Jacques nipped at her shoelaces.

"Sure. If you do a cooking class with local veggies, I could hop in and teach them about growing kitchen herbs. Maybe sell some vegetable plants. Something like that. I dunno. Just a thought."

"It's a good one." Kyle opened a door to an old bathroom. A ceiling tile had smashed to the floor and dust covered the porcelain sink. At least the fixtures were intact. "This place could use some cleaning, but it's a nice space. And the price is great. I thought I'd never be able to chase this dream."

*You still can't chase this dream.*

His chest tightened with the last of his words. It was as close to an admission as he'd been since one tipsy night when he spilled his heart to Tracey. Here, breathing in air thick with decades-old dust, within actual walls where a real store could go, it was more than just brainstorming and wishing, imagining a space. He was standing in it with the person who could make it happen. His stomach lurched. He'd never been so terrified of walls and a floor before.

Adelle smiled at him. "It is a little rough around the edges. It's been empty for a long time, but it is a lot cheaper than anywhere else, that's for sure." She folded back the cover of the manila folder. "I've got an application and contract here for you to look over."

She held it out, and he took it with a shaking hand. "This is a super simple process. The rental fees are really cheap, and it doesn't kick in for six months. You do have to fix it up, though, and all the terms are in here. You can do the work yourself, but it has to pass inspection before it opens. You call Martin for that, and his number's in there. There's a list of vendors and phone numbers, too, to help you out."

The application was short. The contract was only four pages, but the type was small and intimidating. It reminded him of tax law. At least he didn't need to write out a full business plan yet. "I know Martin. He comes by the farm sometimes. I've run into him at Carol's."

"Good! She can help with paint and drywall at the hardware store, if you need it. She even has some discounted items to help people opening up new shops."

"I saw that in the paper. Nice of her. No rent for six months, huh? Even if I open before then? That's an even better deal than the newspaper said."

"Yeah, the town board hadn't finalized the plans when the paper came out. They put together a really nice deal for this space, but it was after Stuart's news deadline. They really want this store in particular to fill in fast. It's such a landmark. It would boost morale to see it leased. The six months help get you on your feet. After that, rent kicks in, and it's really cheap for the first two years. After that, it increases a bit every few years. There's a lease-to-own option. It's all laid out in here."

"Have you had any interest yet?"

Adelle ran a hand over her hair, tightening the knot that held it in place. "A few. A restaurant guy seemed interested in putting something in here. And a woman who sells clothes. I'm not so sure she was serious, but the restaurant guy kept talking about how many tables he could fit in here." She shrugged. "He was here yesterday."

Kyle swallowed hard to unstick his dry throat, but the attempt was a failure. "This is really cheap. I could never afford to open a shop if it weren't for this. I've been wanting to open a little store for years. It's been my dream not to have to work for someone else."

He flipped to the application, pulled a pen from his shirt pocket, and leaned on the old counter, where the register once sat. Name, address, phone number. They gave him half a dozen blank lines to write a description of his business.

*Retailer of fine kitchen and dining wares.*

*It should be longer than that. They gave me six lines. Maybe I shouldn't say "fine." Ramsbolt isn't fussy.*

He ran a hand through his hair and over his face.

"Don't overthink it." Adelle picked at a fingernail. "It's just a basic formality. So they have something on file that shows you don't plan on doing illegal stuff."

"Right. Okay." It was an out-of-body experience, watching his hand grasp the pen and form the familiar letters that made up his name. He'd signed a billion things—legal documents, restaurant tabs, forms at the DMV—but this was the first signature in a long time that was entirely self-serving. He didn't have to do this. A wave of regret and fear slammed into him nearly knocking him off his feet.

*Slow down. You can't commit to this.*

"You're the first town tenant. It'll be nice to have a new neighbor."

*It's just a piece of paper. It's an application, not a contract.* "I bet you're tired of looking out the window at all these empty buildings." He clicked his pen closed and dropped it back into his pocket. *What have I done?*

"Nah. It's nostalgia. Sometimes I wish I could bottle it all up and keep it safe forever, but it's time to move on. This was a dry goods store in my great-grandad's time. They sold hats and ribbon and plain paper until about fifty years ago. Then it became a general store. That cooler over there had popsicles in it. When I was a kid, I'd sneak a quarter from the register at my grandad's shop and buy a creamsicle, the frozen orange filled with cream. I would hide around the corner in the alley and eat it."

He glanced at the cooler as hot bile rose in his throat. The place had so much history. It was loved by so many people. What if he did put his store here, and they hated it? What if they stormed the place with pitchforks and torches and burned him at the stake in the town park for the vile act of defiling a landmark? A little voice inside his head said he wasn't a deserving steward. He might be a native son of Ramsbolt, but he wasn't connected to it. A spark of anger rose at his father, for the poverty and pride that kept them away. He swallowed it back, like he always did.

"We never came in here when I was little," he said. "Couldn't afford to. I could get this cooler up and running. That might be a nice touch."

Adelle shook her head and wrinkled her nose. "I doubt you'd want to. It's been sitting there empty since the nineties, I guess."

He shrugged and leaned against the counter. "I could get a new one. I'd probably need one anyway for frozen foods." Frozen foods. For take-out gourmet meals. *Oh, God. This seems like so much work. Why do I care? Am I talking myself into this?*

"You grew up here?" She studied him with a narrowed gaze. "I don't remember you. When did you go to school?"

Kyle smiled as he bent down and ruffled Jacques's head, pleased that she changed the subject before he grabbed the papers from the counter, tore them to shreds, and ran screaming to his car. The puppy gnawed at his hand. "We lived outside town and didn't come this way often. I left to go to college and came back a few years ago. I do maintenance and help manage the books for a farm out that way." He nodded toward the town park. "I wish we'd spent more time downtown when I was a kid. I don't have many memories of what it used to be like."

Adelle waved a hand and dust glittered in the air. "Ramsbolt's been changing a lot. For the better, in the grand scheme of things. Growing pains are extra hard on little towns like ours, but there's a strong sense of place here, and people really care about the future of it."

"I can tell. Everyone's really nice." He stood and grabbed the folder, revealing a clean swath of wood counter where his elbow had been.

"We do like newcomers. Gives us someone new to talk to." She accepted the signed application, and Jacques jumped at her ankles. She bent to pet him goodbye. "I'll leave you to it. You probably want to measure everything and start making lists of what you need. I'll get this to the committee for a vote, and I should have an answer for you next week, at the latest. It's entirely up to them, of course, but I'd say your chances are really good."

It would take a while to come to terms with what he'd done, to steady his hands so he could drive back to the farm. He'd have to come up with some excuse, a reason to back out, something that sounded plausible and not like immature crippling fear from a man who'd wasted Adelle's valuable time.

His heart squeezed at the thought of walking away from it. Would he look back on this as a dream deferred?

"Thanks. You don't mind if I take my time?"

Adelle paused at the door. "Not at all. I have a guy picking up an arrangement for his girlfriend soon, so I have to run. I'm excited to see what you do with the place. Let me know if you need anything."

She turned the knob and tugged at the door. It gave way with a crack as the old paint let go.

*Dreaming costs you nothing. Go ahead.* "Adelle! I meant to ask! What about colors? Are there rules about what colors I can paint the outside trim? I know it's historic."

"Any color you want. She's all yours now. Well, almost." She waved the folder. Sunlight reflected off her necklace. He hadn't noticed it before.

"This is gonna sound strange." He gestured to her necklace. "Is that a real five-leaf clover? I saw one on your apron and your shop sign, too, so I had to ask."

She raised a hand to the pendant. "It is. I found this when I was eighteen."

"That's funny." He smiled, and Adelle's cheeks burned red. She looked at her feet. She really was charming in an honest way. "They're really rare. I found one myself when I was a kid. I have it tucked in an old copy of *Treasure Island*. Kept all my clovers in there."

"I kept most of my clovers in *Anne of Green Gables*. Except for this one." She grasped the charm.

"They say each leaf stands for something different."

"Faith and hope." She shook her head. "I can't remember the rest."

He counted them on his fingers. "Love, luck, and wealth. That's the five."

Adelle let go of the charm and pushed the door open. A blast of early autumn pushed in. Jacques yipped a goodbye and wagged his body with his tail. "Well, four out of five's not bad."

"There's hope for us yet."

He couldn't tear his eyes away from hers, but he was grateful she slipped out the door. Watching her cross the street, back to her flower shop, his stomach tied itself into yet another knot.

Jacques pawed at his ankle.

"I hope she has a boyfriend or a husband or a girlfriend or something because if she doesn't, she could be distracting." Focus had never been his strong point, and he was losing it in the vastness of the space. It wasn't even all that big, but what it lacked in furniture it gained in echo.

He scuffed through the dust to the bottom of the stairs. "What do you think? Big dog bowl right here, full of biscuits? It's fun to dream, isn't it, buddy?"

He sighed, but it wasn't gratifying. His nose was plugging up. At least there wasn't carpeting to deal with, not on the stairs anyway. Upstairs would have to wait for another day. It wasn't a done deal yet, anyhow. He spun and faced the empty space, taking it all in.

"Kind of a blank canvas, isn't it?" It really wasn't all that bad, other than the dust and grime. "It doesn't cost a penny to dream. Okay!" He clapped his hands, and Jacques jumped, his butt in the air, poised to play.

"Let's do it. Let's dream. If I put a store in here, I'd put a big farm table right at the window here, set up like a Thanksgiving feast. Shelves along this wall. Cabinets full of cookware. We'd make this place look like a big farmhouse kitchen and fill it up with things that no one in Ramsbolt would ever want to buy. That back area would be a bank of ovens set into island workstations, each with a small fridge. And then no one would come, and we could go bankrupt, and we'd move into the Saturn at the top of a hill and forage for berries for dinner."

The thick dusty air was suffocating.

"I can't afford to fill this place. I would never tell a client to do this. This goes against everything I believe in. This is not a leap of faith. This is an airplane jump without a parachute."

His stomach lurched, and his mouth filled with a sour taste.

He scooped up a squirming Jacques and carried him to the door. He crossed the street with the dog in his arms and grabbed the handle of the flower shop door. He had to tell her no, he made a mistake, rescind, take the papers back and shred them, burn the little strips of paper until nothing was left of this frivolous dream. But there she was, at the counter, head down while she tucked roses into an arrangement. She looked like someone he wanted to know. She had her life together. She was the kind of person he wanted to be.

Before she could see him he ducked out of view, his back to the warm bricks. He clutched the neck of his T-shirt. He couldn't go in there and make a fool of himself.

If he didn't take this leap, he would never feel that rush. And he'd never know if it was possible.

CHAPTER TEN

Kyle ran through the corn field. Twisted, distorted leaves and stalks lashed his face. He couldn't catch his breath. His chest heaved and sharp pain stitched through his side. Drenched in sweat, dirt and leaves stuck to his legs. And behind him, close in his wake, someone breathed heavy in their chase, loud enough to be heard over his sharp inhales and swishing of the corn. It was dark. So very dark. He grabbed at his chest, lungs begging for air, legs burning. But if he stopped, he'd be dead.

Lacing through towering stalks of corn, moving as fast as he could through air thick as sand, the leaves ended and the corner of an old shack began. Plopped right there in the middle of a maize field, a foot from the husks and silk, its front door was wide open. Thank God.

But he'd be cornered. It was a trap. Not like he had a choice. He ran inside and threw the door back, but it crept back open. He threw his back against the far wall, where he could watch the door, chest heaving while his lungs begged for cold air. The breathing came closer.

It was at the door. Neither man nor any beast, it had no shape or form. It was hot breath and anger, and it was going to chew his toes off.

Kyle jolted up in bed, covered in sweat. Jacques took up three-quarters of it, his nose pressed against Kyle's foot.

He grabbed his phone off his nightstand. Four in the morning. He scrolled through the internet and let his heart rate return to normal, watching cats push things off tables, and he did his best not to laugh and wake up the dog.

He opened a browser window, looking for dream interpretation advice about Distorted corn and abandoned cabins.

The search results were disappointing.

*… because you are avoiding an issue or person, and you must confront it to move on.*

He closed the browser and pushed up in the bed, careful not to disturb the puppy who snored at his feet, tongue lolling from his open mouth.

*Gee, what could I be avoiding? Everything? Just get out of bed and make some progress. You're already awake.*

The laptop was old and slow to boot. He sat at the kitchen table and watched the progress bar inch across the screen. Typing as quietly as he could, he checked in on his savings account. It wasn't much, but there was enough to afford cleaning supplies and some fixtures. He'd be able to pay his bills for a while, especially since rent would be free. He hated to touch it, though. Every time he got a cold or needed new clothes or just wanted to splurge on fresh foods his savings account shrank.

He ran a few numbers, something he should have done before he even met with Adelle, but he hadn't been serious then. Maybe he'd get lucky and start-up costs would be so big his dream would be unattainable. It would take the edge off if all hope was lost. Then he could safely back out without risking any regret. But even overestimating, start-up costs were reasonable. With rent that cheap and utilities included, he'd be dumb not to take a chance.

Maybe she was right. Maybe there was hope for him yet. He was a smart, capable guy. He learned how to fix a tractor or ten. He did all kinds of labor at the farm that he never went to school for. And it included a place to live, so it's not like he'd lose the roof over his head.

It would take a lot of elbow grease. He only had five thousand dollars in the bank. It was all that was left from the meager fortune he moved home with, after paying for his mother's funeral and caring for his dad. It wasn't much to live on, and not much wiggle room to make mistakes.

He'd have to turn a profit pretty fast. Half of his income would have to come from cooking classes to make ends meet. All of his rent and utilities would come from classes, his inventory expansion and living expenses would come from merchandise sales. And he'd have to turn that profit in the third month.

*That almost never happens for a new business.*

Kyle scratched at the stubble on his chin, caught in a limbo between his safe reality, however small and endangered it was, and the vision he could bring to life if only he had the resources. The inner turmoil of whether or not to take the next step wasn't worth all the aggravation. Especially if it gave him nightmares like that.

His father would have hated this, Kyle digging more roots in. After all the times he pounded the table and insisted Kyle get out of town and never look back, he'd been less than pleased to see his son come home with a moving truck full of furniture. His father had sat on that rotting porch, the roof falling in and steps decayed, and told Kyle it better be temporary. He expected his son to pack up and get back to something that resembled the real world. This place, he said, was a trap.

Kyle ran a hand over his face and cleared sleep from his eyes with the heels of his hands. It was almost a relief his father was too far gone. He wouldn't have to justify his decisions out loud when he could barely justify them to himself.

*You mean you don't want to tell him you made a mistake.*

His father's voice boomed in his head. "You ruined everything. What's wrong with you? Why can't you get it together? Stop screwing around and get back to work."

His father was right. He'd always been right; nothing good came from being lazy, sitting idle.

He opened his email and slid from the chair, moving as silently to the kitchen as he could, avoiding the creaking floorboard while he filled a glass with water. If he woke up Jacques, he'd have to take the dog for a walk, and he just wanted some alone time. Leaning against the counter, he waited for the browser to load, the soft glow from the monitor the only light for miles.

*Okay. When you sit back down at that table, you have to write an email to Adelle and make a perfectly good case for not opening a store, even though these are the best possible terms that any retailer could hope for.*

The water did nothing for his dry throat. He dumped the rest in the sink and slipped back into his seat without a sound.

There was an email from Adelle.

*Hi, Kyle. The board was unanimous. The store is yours whenever you'd like to come by to sign the paperwork. And I just wanted to say that, though they aren't tasked with judging the store, they were very excited about a kitchen shop. There's nothing like that anywhere around, unless you count the old dishes at Penny's Loft. Pet Jacques for me. ~A.*

Unanimous. Everyone on the board loved it. If he backed out now, the whole town would know he was a coward. Every time he walked down that street and saw other stores opening, he'd be reminded that he was too afraid to try.

And then there was Jacques. The puppy snored and whined in his sleep, content in his puppy dream world. Kyle had responsibilities now. He couldn't just rush into some financial trap and not be able to feed his dog. He swore his kids would never go to bed hungry, not like he did when he was little.

But the spreadsheet wasn't wrong. It was possible.

*It's not like I'm doomed to failure. I was never going to stay in this weird barn apartment pretending I know how to fix tractors forever, anyway. It's not like I'm abandoning Zeb in his time of need. He doesn't want to take my advice anyway. And if things get worse here, I won't have this job to lean on much longer.*

He stood and shook the tension from his hands.

*But the last time I took a leap of faith, I ended up stuck in this weird barn apartment. There's only one way to get out of this place, though. Leave it.*

He hunched over the laptop and hit the Reply arrow.

*Thanks. That's great news. I'll be by first thing in the morning.*

The email moved from the Drafts folder to Sent.

*That's it. I did it.*

He opened a blank document and typed *Dear Zeb.*

* * *

"Stupid, stupid, stupid. What's this garbage letter for?" Zeb spun to face Kyle, waving his resignation in the air. The fury on the man's bearded face sent him reeling back through the years, back to the showdown with his old boss who begged him to stay on, not to abandon his clients.

"I've taken care of everything. You have a full maintenance schedule for every piece of equipment. I finished that grant application I told you about. All you have to do is keep up with your receipts and file your taxes. That's it."

Zeb combed his beard with his fingers, his eyes narrowed in rage. "You can't face me with this? You gotta write it in a letter?"

Kyle shifted his weight and stuck his hands in his pockets. His jeans weren't as loose as they used to be. Stress eating and bad food choices added a layer to his gut. It was one more thing he needed to fix, one more part of his life that unraveled over the years.

"Two weeks' notice in a written letter is a professional way to leave a job. I didn't mean it as an insult; it's a matter of respect."

Zeb threw the letter on his desk. Ashes fluttered from the ashtray onto the floor, and his voice shot through the roof. "Respect is you not leaving me hanging. I did your dad a favor. Don't you need an income to help him?"

"I can't afford to help him now. He's already taken care of, anyway. I can't keep treading water for other people, Zeb. I have to live for myself." He winced. It was a superficial claim, facing a man who couldn't afford to have a dream. Tucking in his elbows, Kyle looked past the weary old man, out the window and across the fields. He never spent much time in them, but he loved them all the same, the way little shrubs and rocks made borders between the plots. The way summer clouds cast shadows and made an ever-changing patchwork quilt of the land. The sensory overload of his city traffic past had been snuffed out by that blanket.

"What are you gonna chase a dream with? You ain't got no money."

As if he hadn't told himself that very thing for years. There was security in having an income, knowing someone else would sign your check after you worked for two weeks. It wasn't easy to turn his back on the objection that kept him safe and sane for decades.

It was a rash decision, signing that paperwork. He'd only gone to look. He hadn't made a decision to open the store or incorporated a business or set up funding. He had no capital. Everything he knew about the business he was starting stemmed from his business knowledge and a running list of protests he'd told himself for years. *You can't afford to buy inventory. You can't afford liability insurance. You know nothing about managing a property.*

And now he was quitting his job. He was making the biggest mistake of his life.

"Zeb, if I don't try, I'll never know. What if you told yourself you could never run this farm and you sold it. Where would you be?"

"This ain't about me. I know what I'm doing. I grew up here. You don't know nothing about running a store. How are you gonna sell kitchen crap to people who can't afford to eat? People ain't got money here. There's no expandable income."

"Expendable."

"See? You book smart learning types are just too dang smart for your own good. You know all the business ways, but you can't see the field for the corn. If people had money for stuff like that, the businesses that used to sell it wouldn't have left to begin with. Where you gonna find people to buy fancy plates and copper-bottom pots?"

Kyle threw his hands up. "Here. Passing through. The town is changing. People love to come to small towns to relax and shop. Look at that art festival. It was fantastic."

"It was a mess. There was traffic everywhere."

"Exactly. People came and spent money, and the town is all the better for it. There's no other small town between all that mess out there and...Canada. Ramsbolt is the perfect place for people to stop, rest, and do some shopping."

"But they won't. Because they can drive an hour to a fancy mall and spend all their money on better stuff there. Why not go there and avoid Ramsbolt entirely?"

He couldn't argue with the man. He liked him too much, and felt too much gratitude to continue. And maybe he didn't feel strongly enough about the argument. Ramsbolt had been a distant thing to him as a kid, and when he went off to college, it was nothing more than corn fields and potato farms that he left behind.

"I don't know. I don't want to fight about it. All I know is that I really want to do this." He was too far along to turn back now without losing all his momentum and a bit of his pride.

Zeb fell into his desk chair. It sank six inches, and he threw his hands on the desk. But for the outrage tinting his ears red and coloring his cheeks, the man would have looked ridiculous. "Now I gotta hire somebody else and train them not to be a darn fool. Two people, probably. Who the hell is gonna fix tractors *and* balance the books?"

Kyle shrugged and looked out the window while Zeb fiddled with the sinking seat. "You did it for years before me. You don't need me to do your finances. I know I was a convenient hire, and you did it as a favor to my dad. I don't mean to seem ungrateful. This place... You saved me when I needed to come home."

"What did you come back here for anyway? You had it made out there." Zeb dumped his ashtray in the trashcan and flung open a desk drawer. Kyle stepped back, toward the door, in case the man was lighting another.

"What you have and what you need aren't always the same thing. You know that."

"I *do* know that. That's why I'm saying I need you. I needed you before, dammit. Didn't want to admit it. Outta smokes." Zeb slammed the drawer shut, and Kyle jumped.

"You don't need those either."

"Don't tell me what I need." He leaned back, and the seat sank again, sending him plummeting. He jabbed a finger at the monitor. "The landscape ain't what it was. This internet don't make no sense. Everything is in that box, and I can't file my own taxes now. I gotta know the tax laws and the new programs. I don't know what to write off and what loses me money."

"You'll figure it out. It's not that hard. I'm writing it all down for you." He stopped short of offering to come by and do the man's taxes for free. It wasn't all that complicated, but time was money, and he had no idea how much of it he'd need.

Zeb braced himself and heaved out of the chair, sending it flying into the windowsill. "Don't do me any favors."

Kyle stepped out of the way when the man launched past him. Zeb held the edge of the door and nodded down the hall; Kyle's cue to leave.

"Get on, now," Zeb said. "Good luck figuring out your own mess. Book smarts don't give you common sense, and I can't talk any into ya."

Kyle took small steps back into the hall. He gave the old man a small nod. All he could do was hope the man's mood tempered, that with time, he'd understand.

"I'm really sorry," he said. "This isn't personal. I'm not leaving you or being ungrateful. I just need to do this...for me. I need to find myself again."

"Find yourself? That's what you wanted when you got here! That's what I gave you, a place to find yourself." Zeb gripped the door, his knuckles white. "Good luck. If you can't find yourself in the city or at a farm, and if you ain't saved enough to move out of this dung heap already, you may just be so dumb you can't find yourself in an empty room. Clear outta here as fast as you can. You hear me? No more. No more patience while you fiddle around out there. No more hoping you can fix this mess. I want you out of here."

The door slammed in Kyle's face, sending a blast of sour, acrid air over him and down the hall. It wasn't the type of slam that said Zeb would get over it any time soon. The message was clear. He wasn't welcome there anymore.

"I will still help you, you know. I'll fill out every grant application I can before I go, and I'm still around."

From behind the closed door, he could hear Zeb tug open a desk drawer, pens and business fodder being stirred around. With the strike of a match, Kyle knew the old man had found his smokes. It was a terrible habit, but at least someone had a crutch.

He checked his phone one more time to be sure the email was real.

*The board was unanimous. The store is yours...*

# CHAPTER ELEVEN

Kyle hunched over the steering wheel of his Saturn, staring blankly at the back porch falling off his new store. Or what could be his new store. His stomach growled, reminding him that he hadn't eaten all day. He was early for his appointment with Adelle to sign the lease papers, but he never knew whether the damn car would cooperate. The last thing he wanted was to show up late again.

"Looks like a sinking ship." The ramp was rotten and boards were missing. Deliveries would have to come through the front, if he could afford any. His hands shook as he reached for his phone to check the time. It was still too early to walk to the flower shop. He squeezed his eyes shut and tried to think happy thoughts, but a tight band constricted his chest. He sucked in shallow breaths. A cool breeze pushed through the open car window, but he was boiling inside. He wiped his hand across his sweaty brow and prayed it was stress and not the flu.

"Don't panic."

His legs wouldn't let him sit still anymore, and the car was sweltering anyhow. He grabbed a pen from the glove box and paced the sidewalk in the alley.

*Focus on the positive. This is my best chance at a solid future that makes me happy. Plus, I'll look like an utter fool in front of her if I'm a nervous mess.*

They were great words to tell himself, but renting this building was the dumbest thing he'd ever done. It was a drastic, rash step, hardly a reasonable reaction to his plight in life. He tried to tell himself that a bold leap was the only way to move forward, the only way to fight complacency. The future was bound to start off a little soupy before he found solid ground. He just had to get through it. The bridge that connected him to the farm had been burned to the ground, anyway. There was no going back now.

*This is supposed to be one of those days you'll remember forever. Enjoy it.*

Two minutes early wasn't technically early, so he plunged into the street and flung open the flower shop door. Adelle stood at her counter, sticking Black-eyed Susans in a vase of ivy. Her hair was tied back, but a piece had strayed in front of her face like a delicate ribbon. It stopped him dead in his tracks. Suddenly, he was enjoying the day immensely.

"Sorry, I'm early." He was surprised to hear his voice steady.

She locked eyes with his, and he held his breath to keep her gaze. Everything within him said to look away, to stare at his feet, to look at the wall, at anything but her. His heart was already racing enough. But he squeezed his pen with his sweaty hand and returned her smile.

"Pull up a stool." She pushed the vase aside and wiped the counter with a rag. "I have everything here in a folder for you. This part is easy."

He pulled a stool up to her counter and laid his pen down. "It's everything after that hurts."

"You were in finance, right?" She dropped a folder in front of him and sat, leaning forward, hands folded. They looked soft. That stray piece of hair fell in front of her eyes, and she brushed it away, tucking it behind her ear. She smelled like flowers and captivated him like coming face to face with a famous work of art. He knew her by heart, like he'd seen her everywhere, but the presence of the real thing, the brush strokes—the scent of her soap and hints of gold in her hair—called him closer.

The folder opened to a few pages of legalese. He'd already read it in the email she sent. It was nothing new, but his stomach clenched anyway, seeing it on paper. He should have eaten something.

"Yeah, finance. For big companies, not little things like this. I managed money that already existed. I'm a little out of my element here." He signed the pages and nudged the folder across the counter. It was safer than risking a touch.

Adelle stacked the pages and stood, her stool scraping on the wood floor. She went to a copier on a shelf a few steps away. Kyle hadn't noticed a thing about the shop, captivated by her hair, her eyes, her scent, the flowers, the necklace she wore with the five-leaf clover. He would have to go through his books after he moved and find the clovers he'd stashed there over the years. Maybe they could bring him some luck.

Moving. He needed boxes. A truck. He ran a thumb across one eyebrow.

"I just think it's remarkably brave of you." She handed him the folder with his copy of the signed forms and he smiled his thanks. "You look so confident and happy. I was thrilled to inherit this place, but I was young and dumb. I don't have your financial chops, and I would be terrified to do this today."

Years of putting on a mask for clients, wearing the uniform and pretending to like golf must have paid off. "Too much knowledge can create fear. It's not lost on me how hard this will be. And what I could lose. At least I don't have *much* to lose. The best I can do is plan for the obstacles I can predict."

Adelle grinned down at the counter. "Ah, the *ignoring negative thoughts* phase. I've been stuck in that phase for years. I think it's part of my DNA now."

"Want to know a secret?" He wanted to tell her how beautiful she was, how kind and comforting her company felt. "I don't have a business plan yet."

Her jaw dropped. "You're kidding. The proposal you sent yesterday was so thorough."

"I wrote that in the middle of the night. I've been thinking about this store since I was a teenager. It's called Kitchen Concepts. I even know what the sign will look like. Maybe I'm dumber than brave, jumping in without a plan. I never would have let a client sign a mortgage without a plan." Saying it out loud, how dumb the whole thing was, made it seem even dumber. And telling the town manager, who happened to be gorgeous to an intimidating degree, that he had no confidence in his own idea seemed dumb, too. "I dunno. It's either brilliant or stupid. I guess I'll have to dig in and see for myself."

"I'm sure you'll be fine. Martin went through the place to make sure everything was okay. He ran the hot water and flushed the toilet. Everything checks out. The unfortunate thing is that any repairs are on you from here, but you should be fine. There's three-quarters of a tank of oil to get you started."

"Good to know. I hadn't considered that." And he only had five grand to live on so every penny mattered, and dreams wouldn't keep him warm at night.

"I wouldn't think of it either. I admire you for doing this. You have a great background, and there's no reason it won't work. Ramsbolt is lucky to have you." She reached over and grabbed a set of keys on a bent and rusty keyring. "And these are for you."

The way she looked at him, he wanted to crawl under the counter. He didn't deserve the admiration. The keys landed in his outstretched palm, and he pushed away from the counter, clutching the folder to his chest and the keys in a tight fist. He had to get out of here. "I should run. A lot of cleaning to do."

"The water and electric are on, so you can jump right in. If you need anything, don't hesitate to ask. I mean, I'm not great at construction, but I know my way around town resources."

"Great." He pushed the stool in and it clattered on the floor. He couldn't meet her eyes. "I mean, thanks. That's good. I should…I should go. Lots to do."

"Of course." She stuck out her hand. He almost missed it in his rush. He accepted just as she pulled away and his hot, sweaty hand grasped hers. It soft but for the bandage on her right index finger. His eyes met hers, and the room began to spin.

"What happened?"

"What do you mean?" she asked.

"Your finger. The bandage."

She pulled her hand back and squeezed her finger with her left hand. "Silly thing. Cut it on a thorn. Roses can be deadly."

"I believe it." He nodded and turned to the door, pausing with his hand on the knob. "Thanks for everything."

"No problem. Good luck, and don't be a stranger." Behind him, he heard the vase scrape across the counter. She was getting back to work.

He needed to go.

Crossing the street was like treading through pudding, and there was nothing sweet about it. He felt like a kid compared to her, not like a businessperson prepared to start a new chapter. He was reduced to explaining himself, making excuses for his failures. Not that she asked him to. If anything, failing to match up to her expectations and being years behind her in terms of success made him feel even worse.

He kept his head down, his eyes fixed on the pavement outside of his control, and shoved the key in the lock. After a bit of jiggling, the door opened on his responsibility. Cleaning it up would be the easy part. Filling it with things was a major challenge. He had no capital, but plenty of vision. So much vision that he was bound to let himself down with what he couldn't afford.

His footsteps echoed in the empty space. There was nothing there but potential for collateral damage. He could ruin his credit, destroy his future, run headlong into bankruptcy with no way to restructure. It was nothing but mess, bills, dust, and this twisted knot in his stomach that wouldn't go away. He clutched the folder to his chest and tried to catch his breath.

*Maybe I should clean first. Go home and get my vacuum, a broom, some cleaner and a lot of paper towels. Where do I even start?*

He tried to clear his throat but the air was thick and his throat was dry and closing up. He shuffled to the back of the store, dodging a broken chair, and turned to face the room, to make a sketch on his folder of what it could become. With a shaky hand, he wiped sweat from his forehead.

*How am I going to keep this together? What if the windows all break and the walls cave in? What if the plumbing is bad and the wiring is faulty? What if there are major problems I can't see?*

He drew a line, a wall, on the folder, but the pen wouldn't work, so he shook it.

*No negative thoughts, like Adelle said. Only the obstacles. The real ones. Feed on the stress, just like the old days.*

His stomach roiled, and his legs went weak. He slinked backward into the corner, rubbing his neck, his back against the wall. The ink wouldn't come out of the pen, but it didn't matter. His peripheral vision was gone anyway. *Why is everything so dark, and why are my ears ringing?*

Bile surged in his stomach, and he ran for the bathroom tucked under the stairs. On his hands and knees on the dirty floor, he hit the flush and thanked Adelle for having the water turned on. He wiped his hand across his clammy forehead and crawled from the bathroom, to sit on the floor with his back against the wall, one butt cheek resting on a fallen ceiling tile.

Slow breath in, slow breath out. *Hold it together, you idiot.*

The walls were closing in, and his wobbly knees were too weak to carry him to his car, back to the farm, so he could curl up in bed. Wallowing in his own self-pity and letting fear take control was no way to live life, anyway. Lying in bed was no way to save yourself. He pushed to his feet, and found the pen and folder he'd tossed to the side.

"You jumped in the ocean. Now you gotta swim." He patted the old candy table and leaned on it for stability, hoping it was strong enough to hold his weight. "You're just a big test, aren't you? One big test of my will to be successful. If you weren't, it wouldn't be so stressful."

He inched to the battered chair. It didn't look safe for sitting, but Kyle gave it a try anyway. Head in his hands, he searched for answers.

"I'll have to get creative. I wonder if that antique store will let me borrow some furniture. I can get shelves at discount stores pretty cheap. All I need now is some money."

## CHAPTER TWELVE

Kyle stood in the bathroom of his new store, lifting his chin and tightening his tie in the cracked mirror over the old porcelain sink, careful not to touch anything and get plaster dust on his jacket. He couldn't remember when he last wore that dark jacket and bland tie, but it was no doubt in some stuffy room, choking himself in the name of conformity. He smoothed his jacket, and his heart raced. This time, finance was personal. He hated that outfit, but after half a day on his hands and knees scrubbing the floor and making the bathroom presentable, it felt good to wear something clean.

He spun to face Jacques. "What do you think?"

The puppy's tail wagged his body.

"I'm sorry, buddy. I can't play right now." Jacques tugged on his pant leg, and he bent to smooth the crease. "I know, it's just another day to you, but it's a big day. Today is the day we get our small business loan, so we can order the stoves and inventory for the store."

He ruffled the puppy's ears and looked around. Old nails and thumb tacks, splinters of wood and peeling lead paint. Jacques could get himself into trouble in no time.

"You can't come with me. And you can't stay here." Kyle peered down his nose at his furry friend. "Would you be a very good boy if Adelle watched you?"

Jacques let out a bark. He sat, his front paws prancing, his tongue lolling from his wide grin.

Kyle slipped the leash on his collar. "Let's give it a try."

Across the street, Adelle was at her counter, making a floral arrangement of something white and floofy. She mouthed the words to some tune he couldn't hear, her head bobbing with the music. He knocked on the glass, and she looked up, waving him in.

"I hate to ask this," he said as he opened the door. "I lost track of time. I have an appointment at the bank, and I don't want to leave Jacques alone in the store with all that mess. He could get hurt if he's unsupervised."

Jacques looked up at him with sad eyes, the ones that said he shouldn't go to work.

"I would be happy to watch him." She wiped her hands on her apron and fell to her knees, scooping him up off the floor.

"I really appreciate it." Kyle let the leash go, and it dangled at her side. The radio picked up a classic rock station out of Canada. Something from Styx faded into a commercial in French. "I'll be back in less than an hour, I guess."

Adelle had no eyes for him. He could have said he was leaving for a year, burning down her store, or starting a cult in her kitchen. Jacques was licking her nose, and she was lost in a fit of giggles.

"Don't worry about a thing. He'll be just fine."

Kyle checked his watch. "I gotta run. Thank you!"

He bolted down the street and skirted the park, heading down Main

Street. He slowed to catch his breath and straighten his tie in the newsstand window. The suit was tighter than it used to be. Or maybe he was just out of breath and out of practice. At least his reflection looked the part.

He stepped into the bank, and a blast of cold air caught in his throat. After signing in with a cheap blue pen, he circled a black lacquered coffee table. The vinyl chairs in the waiting area sagged, their stuffing beaten by anxious and weary customers. He stood by the water cooler, skimming the contents of the bulletin board. A happy couple from the land of stock photography dangled a key in the foreground of their new McMansion. In a town that hadn't seen new construction since before the Korean War, it seemed strained and artificial. It definitely didn't line up with most of Ramsbolt's aspirations. Most of the people who walked in here looking for a loan were probably trying to get out of town. He ran a finger along his collar, under his tie, looking for air.

"Are you Kyle?"

He turned to face a woman in a cardigan with an outstretched hand and gave her a firm shake. She looked familiar in a small town way, someone he saw in the market or walked past in the hardware store, a neighbor who he hoped he hadn't offended in some unintended way.

"Yes. I'm Kyle. Nice to meet you."

"Shall we?" With a nod, she gestured to an office, and he followed.

The office was small and cold, with an exposed brick wall. Paintings of landscapes clung there. The desk was bare, but for a photo of a smiling family.

"I'm Emily. It's nice to meet you, too." She gestured at the empty chair with her glasses, then laid them on her desk. "So you're the first resident to take on one of the old stores. I heard through the grapevine that you used to work in finance."

Kyle smoothed his tie as he sat. "I did. I had a decent portfolio of clients when I was down in Boston."

She folded her hands on her desk. "What made you come back to Ramsbolt?"

"Home. You know how it is." He leaned back, relaxed, hands folded in his lap. At least one part of the process felt like slipping into an old sweater. It was almost comforting being back in an office, talking about money, even if he was on the other side of the desk.

"Well, this should be easy then." She pulled a stack of papers from a drawer and laid them before him. "Just the usual disclaimers and bank info. It's nice to work with someone who knows the language, to be honest. We don't often get to work with people cut from the same cloth. So many people in Ramsbolt come in looking for help we can't provide, so you're a nice change of pace."

"I totally get it. Small business is a lot easier than personal loans."

"Very true. Strong, profit-driven goals are easier to monetize."

*At least they want to deal, and this won't take all day.*

There was no sense wasting time. He dug his wallet from his pocket and pulled out his license and social security card. "You'll need these, I guess?"

Her smile was broad and kind. "I'll copy these into the system and be right back."

She left him alone in the tiny room, and he adjusted his tie. Two women walked by, talking about their kids, the conversation fading in and out until it muffled behind a shared wall. A cash-counting machine kerchunked its way through a stack of bills. He ran his finger under his collar again. That shirt was definitely getting tighter.

Emily reappeared, and he returned his cards to his wallet.

The keyboard swung from a tray beneath her desk. Keys clicked as she pounded them, her eyes fixed on the monitor. "So tell me a little about your needs."

"I need to cover some initial expenses. Inventory. Appliances to start some cooking classes. That kind of thing."

"Most small business loans require at least six months in business, which you know. There are a few that can help you at the start. Do you have any accounts that aren't held here with us?"

"One retirement account. I have the last statement here." He slid it across the desk, and Emily pounded her keys.

"How much of your own money have you put up?"

"It's a sole proprietorship right now, so every penny I have, it has." Kyle leaned forward, hands on his knees. "I'll open a second account once the doors open. I expect money to roll in from the cooking classes first. They have a higher profit margin, too. After the first year, I'll split it off into an LLC. For now, I need to keep things small."

"That's a reasonable path for a business of your size, especially starting out."

"I have no employees, so it keeps things simple."

She returned to her monitor, clicked with her mouse, and a printer behind her churned out a page. She snagged it and stood. "I'll be right back."

"I know my capital is low, but I'm willing to make the commitment, and I'm determined to exceed expectations here."

"I'm sure." She waved the page. "I just have to take this over to my manager so they can run the numbers. Shouldn't take long."

He leaned back and ran his hands through his hair. He knew plenty of bankers who liked to make people squirm. In a world where money was the ultimate power, there was no wielding it without some satisfaction. Altruism was the only miracle in banking. But his dues had been paid ages ago, and all it came down to was his interest rate. It made the wait more bearable to know he wasn't being judged.

Shaking his sleeve and adjusting his cuff, he let office white noise wash over him. A copier hissed and rattled, spitting out paper.

He hated to take the hit to his credit, but a small business loan looked better than maxing out credit cards.

He drummed his fingers on the arm of the chair and jumped when Emily's footsteps padded behind him, muffled on the thin carpet.

His phone buzzed with a text message. It was Adelle.

*Couldn't resist taking Jacques for a walk. Meet me at Diane's across from the bank for tea after to celebrate!*

He tapped his foot to discharge the static. His fingers teased his phone.

*Thanks! Will do.*

Not excited enough. He should have used an exclamation point.

His energy rippled across the room, and the cup of pens on Emily's desk jiggled. What was taking her so long?

Emily scooted into her chair and leaned forward, her hands folded on the desk. Kyle's fingers tingled, and he rubbed them against the chill. "I am so sorry, Kyle. It's just not going to work out."

His breath hitched in his throat. Hunching in his seat, he lowered his eyes, focusing on his jagged thumbnail.

"We can't do a small business loan without any assets or collateral. Your bank accounts aren't sizable enough, and a 401(k) can't be used as collateral against a loan. Which you know."

He did know. He'd known all along that his risk was high, that he wasn't the type of small business owner that banks saw as a good investment. That's why his internal organs had been coiled and tangled all morning. He wasn't successful with a strong track record. He didn't already have a string of wins. All he had was a lot of hope, a lot of wishful thinking, and tenacity. He wouldn't fail, because it wasn't an option. But that didn't matter on paper.

His heart squeezed. He'd become one of them, a hopeless dreamer plopped in a bargain chair to wait for an inevitable no. They'd watch him leave with his tail between his legs, click their tongues and lament that they couldn't do more for their community. Others would laugh behind his back.

*What do you care? You've never belonged here anyway.*

He forced a stony expression to mask his embarrassment at being rejected by the smallest rural bank he'd ever done business with, and he settled his gaze on a painting of a pastoral farm. It could have been anywhere. Midwest or Northeast. A pale blue sky kissed a field of golden grain.

*If I had a dozen pigs as collateral, they'd give me a loan and some chickens, gift with purchase. Stupid rural banks.*

How could someone who once managed the investments of a Fortune 500 company not be able to get a small business loan? Why didn't anyone have confidence in him anymore? What changed between Boston and Ramsbolt? He'd been too provincial for the city, too nice to be worthy of a corner office. Now he was too poor to make it in his own hometown. He didn't belong. Never had.

There was no use hanging around, hashing it out. Far too proud to beg, he placed his hands on his knees and stood.

"Thanks for your time. Sorry for wasting it."

She accepted his shake and settled her glasses on her nose as she returned to her monitor. "You're quite welcome. And keep us in mind in the future. Once things improve a little, we'll be happy to help."

It came off like a script, but it wasn't one he wanted to let play out. He slipped through the bank, quickly and quietly, and stepped onto the sidewalk. There had to be another way that didn't involve the Ramsbolt Savings and Loan and their misguided impression that the only people worthy of money were people who dangled keys in front of McMansions. He only needed some short-term capital, a little infusion to get the ball rolling. But if he couldn't get a loan in Ramsbolt, was there any use ruining his credit by checking with every bank in the country? His insides felt like a shaken-up snow globe. He needed to sit and think, let the debris settle. He needed some time alone to figure things out.

*Just go have tea with Adelle. Put on your best poker face, thank her for watching Jacques, and we'll figure this out later.*

Diane's Tea House sat across the street, in the house where his father grew up. The window was open, the one where his grandmother had sold her pies to an eager town. The woman had raised a child and kept a home based on a business plan that involved nothing but flour and blueberries, and he couldn't get a store up and running to teach people how to cook.

He'd never been inside before. But then, it had been someone's home until a decade ago. And he'd never been in the market for tea.

*Wonder if it still looks like the house my father grew up in.*

He plodded across the pock-marked street. Inside, the tea house smelled like Earl Grey and things he couldn't afford. A woman whose name tag declared her to be Diane stood behind a counter draped in a floral cloth. On it sat an old-fashioned register and a mason jar of feathery pens. Baskets of tea bags and cellophane-wrapped cookies shaped like teacups sat to the side. Tables for two and four were crammed like ill-fitting puzzle pieces into every nook and cranny. Two women nursed tea by his grandmother's open window, hunched low in a gossip session. A bell rang out as the door closed behind him, and the women snapped to attention, sending withering glares in his direction.

He whispered to Diane, "Is Adelle here?"

Her nose wrinkled when she smiled. "You must be Kyle. She brought your dog. She's out back."

The two women at the window scowled. He shrugged and gave them a weak grin, but he didn't mean it. As if not being welcome in a tea parlor were the epitome of life's worries. He had to sit with a woman much more put together, a woman who had her life in order, and pretend like he wasn't on the verge of a heart attack.

Diane stepped from behind the counter and waved for him to follow.

"It's a lovely day out. Come. I'll show you the way." It was more a demand than an offer. He followed her out the door and around the building, to a table beneath a string of darkened lights. A woman with a book sat at the farthest table, smearing white cream onto a scone. Adelle sat, skimming a menu, Jacques snoozing at her feet.

She looked up and smiled. "I really wanted to take your dog for a walk. I hope you don't mind. And the weather is so nice. I figured tea would be a great way to enjoy it."

"Of course." Kyle smiled. It felt unnatural. He thanked Diane and fell into a dainty cast-iron chair. "Jacques loves walks. And this is…nice.

Unexpected."

Unexpected cost, no matter how small, was giving him heartburn. Trying to pretend he belonged in this uncomfortable chair and that this was all okay—the bank, the tea, being in his grandmother's house which reminded him of his father, and the anger his father would have at his string of failures if he wasn't too ill to feel it—was making his stomach burn.

Trying to keep a stiff upper lip in front of this woman who intimidated the hell out of him because she was so damn perfect was too much. He didn't want to let her down, because she was so excited about leasing this building, and he was the first person to try. Not only was he a total failure, but he was about to become the symbol for just how much of a failure her plan could be. He didn't belong here with her, in this town, around these people. And he couldn't let it show. He had to hold it all in.

Letters swam on the slip of paper Diane placed before him. He shook his head to clear the fog. It looked more like summer reading assignments than a list of teas. Jane Austen had lavender and vanilla. Charlotte Brontë had hints of peppermint and lemon. He flipped it over to more of the same. Every cup was four bucks.

He dropped the menu. "What would you suggest for someone who prefers regular tea?"

Diane lifted her chin. "How about Earl Grey. It's a standard."

"That sounds perfect."

"A pot to share?" She aimed one raised eyebrow at Adelle, who nodded.

"That sounds perfect." Adelle handed the menus back, and Diane retreated. "My treat. Congratulations are in order."

Kyle lifted a shoulder. He transitioned a shrug into a nonchalant dismissal, rounding it off with a weak grin.

"It's a big climb. I can't even imagine. And taking out a loan must be so scary."

Done with formalities, he ripped off his tie and threw it across his knee. Holding himself up required too much energy. He stared down at his empty hands. "Yeah. It's scary, alright."

All those years of endless work and late night calculations, negotiating deals, and bending over backward to give clients confidence in him and help them balance their feelings against their books were worth nothing in the end. He'd worked hard enough, he should have had the money in the bank to build an empire. How would he explain this to Adelle? She had her whole life together and was so excited to have a first tenant.

He couldn't call Cadwalladr for advice. He felt too small in the shadow of his old mentor for that. Besides, he seemed to be the only person left in the universe who had confidence in him. Why spoil it?

Diane placed a tray between them with saucers and teacups, a teapot, sugar, and milk. Adelle placed a finger on the teapot's lid and let tea cascade into their cups. Thank God she was competent, because he was a mess, and his hands were shaking. That dainty cup was doomed.

Before she picked a topic, he changed it.

"My grandmother used to live in this house."

Adelle's eyes widened. "No way. Really?"

"My dad's mom. She sold blueberry pies from her living room window. Apparently it was a thing. Everyone would come here to buy her pies."

Brow furrowed, she collected the porcelain cup in her fingers. She made it look easy. "My dad loved pie. He used to talk about Blueberry Window Pie, like it was a thing he used to be able to get."

"That was it." He nudged the cup on its saucer, lacking her courage to grasp it.

"I haven't thought about that in years. I always thought it was just some brand they had in the market. That was your grandmother? Are you going to sell it in your store?"

"Sell it? No. I can't bake. Never could." He shook his head. He hadn't even considered trying to make his grandmother's pie. He'd experienced enough defeat to last him a very long time. "And I wouldn't want to step on the bakery's toes. That's a bad way to start a business." If he could start it at all.

"Speaking of starting, how did the bank go?" Adelle sipped her tea. "You look a little…distracted."

"Oh, good." He lifted the cup to his lips, but it was too hot to drink. "I'm petrified. So if I only come off as distracted, I'm doing a good job of hiding it."

She rested her elbows on the table, the cup perched in her gentle fingers. "It's only natural to be petrified. I'm not good at change at all. I can barely stand redecorating my living room. Thank God I inherited the flower shop. I'd fall to pieces changing jobs, never mind starting my own store. I've been through some hard times with the flower shop, though, that's for sure. You'll survive. I promise."

Tea swirled in his cup. The saucer wobbled on the uneven table. "How'd you get through it?"

"One inch at a time. You'll figure it out. Tea is for everything in between." She nodded at the tray. "You want sugar?"

A shrug and a nod were all he could muster. "Thanks for watching

Jacques for me today. I hope he wasn't any trouble."

Adelle cocked an eyebrow. "He's no trouble. I can't wait for him to be a neighbor. I'd dog sit any time." Her cheeks grew pink, and she grinned into her cup.

Jacques stirred beneath Adelle's chair. The puppy stood and shook his head, his tags jingling, then curled up in a ball and yawned, returning to his nap.

Kyle admired the ease, considering his insides were on fire. It would take a lot more than tea and Adelle's kind words to put it out. It didn't matter how scared or poor or hungry he was, nothing but a miracle would fix it. Cadwalladr and Adelle had fate on their side. They started with assets. All Kyle had was an empty stomach, an empty wallet, and a dog that was eating him out of house and home.

What would he tell a client? Patience. Take it one step at a time, and face the consequences every time you fall. Of course, it was a lot easier to tell a client that things would work out, to have a little faith, than it was to believe it himself. It was hard to see the daylight in the middle of the forest.

Tiny bits of brown tea settled in the bottom of the cup. It took three tries to grasp the dainty handle in a way that didn't make him feel like a giant. Lifting it to his lips took all his effort. When he set it down again, the leaves floated back to the bottom, sediment of his contentment.

"My mom used to joke about reading tea leaves." Adelle peered into his cup.

"See anything interesting in there?" A small fortune perhaps?

She leaned back in her seat. "I wish. I have no clue how that works."

"Me either. My mom swore by tea in times of trouble, but my dad found hope in a different kind of beverage."

"Ah." She licked tea from her bottom lip. "False hope."

"That's the truth." It was the worst kind. The more his father chased it, the further it got. At some point he stopped looking. It was almost like looking for hope made it impossible to find.

Kyle didn't see any hope in the bottom of that cup, no vision of his future. He couldn't imagine what the future looked like at all. He couldn't picture himself living in that building, working in that store. Living across from Adelle. His chest ached.

"So what kind of foods are you going to teach people to cook?" Adelle's eyes sparkled over her cup as she sipped. At least someone was keeping the dream alive.

He straightened his shoulders and cracked his neck. It didn't make him feel any better, but judging by Adelle's reaction, she bought into it. "I guess I'm going to start with classics and regional foods with a twist. Seafood. Pot roast. Fiddlehead ferns in a hollandaise."

*I have to get the kitchens set up. That's the next step. Then inventory. If I can't find a way to buy ovens, I'll never get this store off the ground.*

Nothing had ever seemed so insurmountable.

Adelle set her empty cup on its saucer. "I have plenty of time to talk you into selling pie."

"You really don't want to do that," he said. "I can't bake to save my own life."

# CHAPTER THIRTEEN

Kyle's bedroom flooded with a snap of light, and he gripped his teddy bear, trembling as thunder rolled across their little house. Little fingers dug into the fur, clutching at matted hair. The once-plush bear had been dragged around for most of its life and scrubbed in the laundry tub more times than Kyle could count. One eye had gone missing, found under the couch and glued back on. But it was more security blanket than companion since he started first grade. Big boys didn't need such things. Except maybe they did when lightning made monsters in the shadows.

"There's a storm coming, Beary." Kyle stroked the matted fur. "Don't worry. It'll be over soon."

Another crack and thunder rumbled through the room. Kyle clamped a hand over his mouth to hold in the squeal and pulled the cover tight over his head. His breath was hot and smelled like chicken and boiled veggies, even though he'd brushed his teeth. He always brushed his teeth. Nobody had to tell him anymore.

His parents' muffled voices scraped down the hall. He peeled back the covers from his head to hear the argument that had been swelling in the kitchen since he went to bed.

"All I'm saying is that I can't cook food that's not in the fridge." There was an icy edge to Mom's voice, like she was tired of repeating herself. Like his dad hadn't cleaned up his toys.

"What happened to the damn garden? Huh? What happened?" His father wasn't angry; he was sad. Kyle could hear it in his voice. The tight wad of emotion in Kyle's gut unraveled, and fear swelled up in its place. It was hot, and it made him sweat. He kicked the covers off his feet and fixed his eyes on the darkness over his bed, eyes straining to find some small detail in the darkness, one light in the darkness.

"The garden died, Sam. We don't have a hose, remember? You ran over it with the lawnmower. You said you'd get another one, and you never did, so don't blame me."

Kyle couldn't see his mom, but he knew she had her hands on her hips. She always did that when he forgot to do things.

"You couldn't find some other way to water the garden? All those cucumbers and tomatoes just dried up. And what about a part-time job. You said you'd get one, and that was years ago. Where's that?"

"It's not out there." Dishes clattered in the sink. The water ran. Kyle could feel her fuming. Her angry mom vibe could pass through walls. "There are no jobs downtown, even if I could get there. Not at the farms, and not in the kitchen where I scrape together whatever I can with what little food we have because you were supposed to support us. You, Sam. *You* were supposed to support our family. I was staying home with Kyle, and you were going to support the family."

A fist slammed into something wooden, and Kyle jumped. He clamped a hand over his mouth again to hold in a yelp. He couldn't hear his father's words over his own breath, fast and shallow and hot in his hand, but the scrapes and taps told him that the contents of the lazy Susan were being put back in their place on the table.

His mother's words were hard to make out. "Don't…noise and scare him…finally went to bed."

"I work as hard as I can." His father was loud and steady. "If only you'd find another job…"

"If only you got a better one. If only. If only." The water shut off, and the pipes banged. Kyle strained to hear what was happening as rain outside started to tick against the roof. It sounded worse than the usual rain. "Thank God. No rain all summer, and now that the plants are dead it's finally gonna pour outside."

Kyle peeked his head from under the covers in search of fresh air. Light seeped into his room from under the door. If his mom got a job, he'd be alone when he got home from school. No one would be there with snacks or help him with his homework, and the teacher said homework was very important. But worse, they had no money for things. Dinner got smaller and leaner. More vegetables from their dying garden with the rotten bits cut out and less meat from the store. His mother tried to get a job, she really had, and she bargained with the local farmer's wife—a chicken in exchange for sewing.

Kyle hated to see her beg. She deflated every time they walked to that farm and handed in mended shirts and clean laundry. Just that afternoon, when he got home from school, they took a long walk through summer humidity to trade her sewing for a chicken that wouldn't lay eggs anymore. She stuck it under her arm for the long walk home, and Kyle carried the bag of rags, skirts, and pants that needed hemmed and patched. They rushed home under a darkening sky to beat the rain and Dad, so he wouldn't worry. And mom sat in the chair by the window and mended his own worn-out socks that he still had to wear even though they were too small.

The fight didn't start until after Kyle went to bed, until the storm was bearing down.

"Did we just eat the chicken you got from sewing? We needed that for eggs." Dad's voice dripped with rage.

"It didn't make eggs no more. We had to eat it. That was the point."

They'd eaten some with the icky broccoli, the gray kind without the yellow cheese he liked, and the rest went into the freezer.

The calculator clicked and clacked and little gears inside added up whatever his father was counting. "We're gonna have to sell more stuff."

"I'm doing everything I can. I treat every penny like it matters."

"No more hot showers. Period. And ration the soap."

Down the hall his mother mumbled, her words dimmed by the rain on the roof. What else would he have to say goodbye to?

"Not you, bear. You get to stay. I already asked. So don't you worry."

Kyle's throat tightened, and water welled in his eyes. His nose burned. He fought the urge to cry. Big boys never do.

"Imagine how much easier it would be if you would just get another job," his father said.

"Listen to me. There are no jobs. No one wants to hire a woman who got no skills anyway. There ain't no opportunity for me out there, and there sure as hell won't be any for him. You were supposed to take care of your family. You were supposed to work hard so we didn't have to raise our son in this town."

The wind picked up. Trees scraped the window outside Kyle's bedroom. He clawed beneath the blanket and stroked his bear.

"It's okay. It'll be over soon."

"Supposed to." His father was calm, his voice quiet. "What does that even mean?" Someone was ripping paper, like they were opening envelopes or tearing up junk mail. Dad liked to rip up the mail. "All the stuff we were supposed to do was nothing but a dream. Some of it comes true, but most of it don't. It's not supposed to. It's just a dream."

"Nobody owes us anything, Sam. I was supposed to marry the handsomest boy in school and have the best life. You were supposed to marry the prettiest girl and get a great job."

"And you were supposed to inherit your parents' house so we could sell it and leave this town. I could have made more money if we were somewhere else."

His mother's voice rose. "My parents weren't supposed to get sick. They weren't supposed to sell their house to pay the bills. What about your mother's house?"

"It was the same thing! I didn't inherit no house."

"Then it ain't all my fault," she said. "Nothing worked out the way it was supposed to."

"None of that happened. Kyle happened."

"Shh. He'll hear you." It was the tone she used about Christmas presents. "You were supposed to find a way to pay for childcare so I could find a job."

"When did we get so old, Birdie? When did things get so hard? Shouldn't they have got better by now?"

"My grandma used to say that *should* was just an opinion about someone else's obligations. Life's a lot better without any *should* in it."

"That's the sad thing about it, Mel. What if this is the way it's supposed to be? What if Kyle is supposed to live this life? What if it never gets any better for him?"

"If he's lucky, he'll stay a kid forever. Like Peter Pan. Boiling chicken bones for soup and freezing leftovers? Maybe we'll win the lottery, and he can inherit the whole world, but the best we can do is make sure he gets an education so he can get out of here. Otherwise, he'll be busting his ass and getting nowhere just like us."

Kyle peeked out from beneath the covers but another crack of lightning lit up the room. He dove back between the sheets, his trembling hand clutching the clumped hair of his little brown bear.

"We're never growing up, bear. We're gonna stay small forever."

# CHAPTER FOURTEEN

"Jacques?" Kyle snaked through the path between boxes cut into his loft apartment. Mounds of puffy trash bags spilled into the trail like shrubs overstepping their bounds. The dog had to be in there somewhere.

"Jacques?"

A yellow head popped up from behind a box, and a pillow tumbled from a stack of books, startling the dog. Jacques leapt into the path, his tug-of-war rope in his mouth, and tumbled to a halt at Kyle's feet. He dropped the rope and looked up with a broad grin.

"Sorry about all this, little guy. We'll be out of here soon." Kyle tossed the pillow in a trash bag and hurled it aside. "If you think this is bad, you should have seen the mess when I moved in."

He'd downsized before he moved from Boston, but it hadn't made cramming all his furniture into that tiny barn loft any easier. It had been more than just a bed, a table, a bookshelf, and some nightstands. It had weighed even more saturated in failure and coping and settling for less. Packing it all up and taking it to downtown Ramsbolt should be the exciting start to a dream, but it was like someone loaded the starting pistol to kick off a fun run then pointed it straight at his heart.

"I'm never gonna fit all this in my Saturn."

Jacques wagged his body, hanging on every word.

"I need to borrow Zeb's truck. That means I gotta go talk to Zeb."

Jacques spun and bounded down the path. He pulled his leash from the hook by the door.

Kyle bent to rub the yellow lab's ears. "Sorry, buddy. Not this time." He placed the leash back on the hook. "In a few days you won't be stuck inside alone anymore."

Asking Zeb to borrow the truck was the last thing he wanted to do, but he kissed the top of Jacques's head, closed the door, and crossed the gravel path to the farmhouse.

The kitchen was quiet—no sign of Dan or Bern. The Sunday newspaper was still strewn across a midweek table, coffee ringed and mustard smeared. The refrigerator motor shuddered to a halt, and down the hall, papers shuffled behind a closed door.

Kyle paused at the end of the hall. He folded his arms across his middle to keep in the warmth. The acidic reek of smoke leeched under the door. There wasn't enough viable oxygen to make sighing worth the effort. Standing in the hall and breathing in Zeb's noxious fumes wouldn't get him off the property any faster.

"Zeb?" He rapped at the door with his knuckles. Zeb grumbled. "Can I come in?"

"Come on! Get it over with." Zeb coughed and hacked, his voice like gravel scraping on pavement. Kyle inched the door open as Zeb spit into a tissue. Vile habit.

"Sorry to bug you. Can I borrow the truck for a few hours? I need to move my stuff out of the barn. Can't fit some of this stuff in the Saturn, and I can get out of your hair faster."

Zeb waved one hand, and the other clutched a cigarette. Blueish gray smoke ribboned into the air. Kyle assumed that was a yes.

"Keys are by the door?"

Zeb swatted again. Kyle turned away, grabbing the handle to close the door.

"You're really doing this thing?" Zeb sputtered the words and coughed.

Kyle clung to the doorknob. "Of course. You know I am. I have to."

"That bank didn't give you a loan. How are you gonna get started?"

Kyle's mouth went dry, and the room got a little colder. He folded his arms. Word traveled fast; he wondered whose. "I'll figure it out. How'd you know about the bank?"

"You're just as bullheaded as your mother was. She'd walk a mile in one direction for pennies when she coulda walked half the distance for a lot more."

"What's that supposed to mean? We didn't have a car. She had no skills. She sewed and washed people's clothes by hand, and she walked their clean laundry back to them year round. She worked hard enough."

"What I'm saying is she coulda worked smarter, not harder. Old man Brouse offered them that old hunting cabin on his potato farm. Said he'd give her a job. He told me so. But she didn't want no part of that."

Kyle balled his fists and folded his arms. Zeb didn't have to attack his mother just because he was pissed. "So what if he did? What's that got to do with me?"

"Your daddy busted his ass here. Did more'n Dan and Bern and all 'em put together. I paid him as good as I could. People tried to do for them, and she would pick and choose her work. You're as hardheaded as your mom was. Pride makes you soft in the wrong places, hard in the wrong places."

Fire burned within Kyle, hotter than the day he left Boston. He laid his hands down on the desk and leaned down to meet Zeb's leering gaze. "If my mom didn't want to work at the old Brouse farm, she must have had a reason. And it had nothing to do with pride. And it's got nothing to do with you and me."

"It was about pride, but that ain't the point." Zeb stroked his beard. A cough rumbled in his chest. "You're not living up to your daddy's name."

"Are you kidding me?" Kyle stood and folded his arms. "My father wanted me out of here. I did exactly what he asked. I went to college and worked my ass off for people who don't care about anything but the label on their tie."

Zeb blinked back at him. The man would never understand, and Kyle didn't care anymore either. It was all a waste of time. "You know what? This is stupid. Thanks for letting me use the truck. I'll be out of your hair by the end of the day."

He stormed down the hall. The truck keys dangled on a nail by the door. He snagged them on his way out. The gravel slowed his charge across the drive, but it gave a satisfying crunch. The earth was too wet to do anything but slosh as he made his way to the barn.

*How dare Zeb judge someone else's decisions? Questioning my mother and using my parents against me?* Deep down he knew Zeb was just lashing out, that he'd say anything to get in one last dig. The farm got harder to run every year and he'd blame everyone but himself for it. It was fitting that the man would project his own problems onto Kyle's mom in a parting blow.

*I should have told him if he'd cared that much, he could have hired Mom or paid Dad double. If he spent all that energy worried about himself instead of what my mother was doing, he wouldn't be in financial trouble himself.* The good zingers always came too late.

His legs ached from stomping through mud, and his mind still reeled with angry retorts when he reached the barn. Bern leaned against the wall, picking dirt from his nails with a pocketknife. With his hat pulled low, he looked like one of those plywood cutouts people propped against their sheds.

"If you need something, I'm not working today." Kyle trudged past him toward the stairs that led to his apartment. The truck was already parked in the barn. Boxes of books and dishes, bags of clothes lined the wall inside.

Bern didn't budge. He wiped the knife on his jeans and dug under his thumbnail again. "You're not working any day, the way I seen and heard it. I'm waiting on Dan."

"No, I mean I'm moving. I'm packing my stuff in the truck and moving to town. I won't be back. Can you give me a hand getting a few things down the stairs? I'll be out of your life faster with a little help."

Bern pushed away from the wall. "Wish I could, but I'm just too tired. Parts aren't here yet. I don't have a manual to read."

Kyle was already on the stairs, facing away, so rolling his eyes was purely for his own gratification. "Thanks, Bern. Means a lot."

"I'll help ya." Dan yelled up to him, and Kyle turned.

"Yeah? It's just a few things." Kyle shoved his key in the door. Jacques barked a greeting from inside. "I really appreciate it."

"I ain't doing it out of the kindness of my heart. I'm just doing it to piss off Bern."

* * *

Every muscle in Kyle's body ached. He pushed open the door to his new home with the last cardboard box and let it fall on a stack. Sweat dripped from the ends of his hair, and his lower back ached.

"I don't remember moving being this hard. Of course, I didn't have to walk a mile to return a truck last time, either."

Jacques spun and twisted, doing his little jig, almost knocking over his water bowl.

"Want to see what's in this back room?"

Double doors at the back of the shop opened to a narrow office. Kyle had ignored it until now, and the second he inched it open, he wished he'd kept it closed for eternity.

"You stay out here, okay?"

It looked like an old construction site, with sawhorses, old doors, and broken shutters covered with layers of white dust. The wall was newer sheetrock than the rest of the plaster. Clearly this little addition had been made to hide unsightly things from shoppers. It would come in handy once it was cleaned up. Jacques sniffed at the air, tail wagging.

"We're gonna need a shop vac."

A door led to the porch outside, where the delivery ramp rotted away. A small window by the door looked out to the yard, a crack stretching across one pane of glass like an arching creek across a map. No wonder the air was so chilly back here. He could see the oil drum outside, and the barrel gauge read three-quarters of a tank, just like Adelle had said.

"We should flip this thing on and see how it works before it gets too cold outside."

A thermostat clung to the wall above the light switch, next to a red emergency shut-off switch. It's round metal dial was a relic of a time before digital thermostats.

"This seems like a stupid place to put a thermostat. I guess I can add this to my list of improvement pipe dreams, moving it into the store."

He toggled the switch with his thumbnail, turning on the heat and holding his breath. The boiler beneath his feet rumbled and heaved. Radiators pinged, and water rushed through pipes.

"I have no idea how any of this works. I need to make a list."

His eyes traced the ceiling, and the intimidating maze of water lines hidden within.

*BANG!*

A massive boom from the basement shook the walls. Jacques ran into the shop, his nails scraping on the floor. Kyle covered his head, a useless instinct when the offending blast was beneath his feet. The sound of water spraying came from the basement. With a shaky hand, not even sure if it was the right thing to do, he flipped the red emergency shut off switch, and the boiler fell silent.

Heart pounding in his throat, ears ringing, he placed a hand on the basement door and pulled it open. Cold air blasted up from the cellar. The stone walls and unpainted steps made it seem like a cave. A light came on when he hit the switch, buzzing as it warmed. Black dots of heater sludge splattered the stairs and the wall, and the boiler hissed from somewhere below.

He ran a hand through his sweaty hair and bounded down the stairs. The concrete floor was rough and pock marked where walls or shelves were once anchored. The basement was empty but for a hissing green boiler, like an angry dragon ready to spit fire, and a growing puddle of water on the floor. Water sputtered from a valve sticking from the side.

He traced the lines to find the main shut off, and he twisted the knob until it was tight. At least it was labeled.

Upstairs, Jacques huddled in a corner, back against a wall. Kyle went up to comfort him and rub his ears.

"It's okay, little guy. It was just a scary noise, that's all. I'll fix it." *I think.*

The papers Adelle had given him were in the front of his old briefcase. A list of emergency numbers, Martin's at the top, was tucked in with his copy of the contract.

The number rang. Kyle made comforting sounds to Jacques while he waited to leave a voicemail.

"Martin. Whatcha need?"

Kyle snapped to, his mind searching for words. "My boiler exploded. I think that's what happened. I'm Kyle. I have the old general store."

"I know it. What did the boiler do?"

"I turned it on, and there was a loud bang. Black water went everywhere, and I—is this a thing? Does this happen all the time?"

"Nah, it's just old. Flip the emergency switch off and turn off the water." Martin sounded weary, like he was tired of reading the same script.

"I did that. I don't know how I knew to do that, but that's what I did."

"These old boilers get cracks on the inside. Pressure builds up and kerblamo! They up and die on ya. You'll need a new one."

"But, how? I just got here. I'm not even actually here yet. I mean, I guess I am, but my clothes are still in bags, and I haven't even found my bedroom yet."

"Boilers don't care about your clothes," Martin said. "I'll be by in the morning with a new one. Gotta go get one from Colby. I don't guess you want the fancy machine?"

"Fancy?" Kyle ran a hand through his dusty hair. "No. No fancy. The cheapest machine that functions and doesn't explode. How much is this going to cost?" He winced and braced himself. "Do I want to know?"

"Long as nothing else broke, it'll run you six."

*That's a relief.* "Six hundred is easy. I can pay you with a check?"

The laugh through the phone was full-bellied. "Six thousand. Check is fine."

Kyle threw his head back and growled at the ceiling. Damn pipes. He couldn't go long without heat in Maine. The water pipes would freeze, and he'd only end up with more problems. But six thousand dollars was out of reach. He had less than five thousand in his savings account, and he needed it to live on.

"Do you finance?"

"I don't do payments. I don't barter, either. No chickens or deer meat. I take cash. I'll see you tomorrow first thing."

Kyle slammed the door to the office, shutting away the mess.

He hauled his body up the stairs. Jacques bounded past him, sniffing at boxes and plastic bags full of clothes he hadn't unpacked. His pajamas were in there somewhere with his towels. Too weary to start a shower, and too drained by the heater carnage to face more problems, he ripped open the bags looking for sheets.

He found them with a thin blanket and his favorite sleep shorts, threw them on his mattress, and curled up next to his headboard.

Assembling the bed was for another day. Jacques curled up at his side, his puppy body swelling with a sigh.

The room lit up with a flash of distant lighting.

"There's a storm coming, Jacques. Don't worry. It'll be over soon." His voice soft, soothing, he stroked the dog's fur. "Do me a favor and don't ever grow up. Stay small forever, okay?"

# CHAPTER FIFTEEN

Kyle juggled his cell phone and a bag of groceries, half of it dog food. He squeezed the bag as he switched ears and winced at the soft crush of his bread, but it didn't matter. Peanut butter and jelly would taste just as good on smashed bread. It would have to, because once Martin replaced the boiler and the invoice came, it would be all he could afford for a very long time.

The on-hold music offered by the retirement account people could have put him in a coma, it was so slow. He willed his feet to pick up the pace, turning at the end of Main and aiming for his store. At least it wasn't a long walk. The way things were going, he wouldn't be able to afford gas anymore. The line clicked, and the music stopped.

*Thank God, I was about to fall asleep standing up.*

"Kyle?"

"Yeah? I'm here." He switched arms again, trading the bag for the phone.

"Thanks for holding. We did receive the form you faxed. Your 401(k), minus the ten percent penalty fee, will be transferred to your checking account within a week. It usually takes five days, but give it a week to be sure."

*Thank God.* Martin seemed like an amenable guy, but the last thing Kyle needed was to build a reputation as a guy who couldn't pay the bills.

"Thanks. I appreciate it."

"Just a reminder, though, that you'll have to pay federal and state taxes on the disbursement."

"I know. I'll set it aside."

"Is there anything else I can do for you today?"

*A million dollars? Six functioning ovens and inventory for my store? A pill I can take that will make me feel like I've done the right thing?* "No, thanks. I'm good."

That was it, his entire retirement account closed and gone in the blink of an eye. It was the last piece of his old life, the one gear in the machine that still held on, and now it was gone. It was an empty feeling, like a giant void that his heart and his head didn't know how to fill. He'd been slowly slipping backward since he left that old life, his savings dripping away, but he'd never taken such a giant leap back before, and he'd always had that retirement account to hold onto. He shoved his phone in his pocket and fought his key into the lock.

Jacques greeted him, tail between his legs, with four paws wet to the knees.

"What did you get into?" He dropped the grocery bag on the counter.

The faint hiss of running water filled the room.

Jacques barked and took three prancing steps toward the bathroom under the stairs, as if trying to tell him that the giant puddle of water that flowed from under the door was definitely a problem.

"Shit." Kyle rushed to the bathroom and flung open the door. A small wave of water gushed from the room, soaking the wood floor. Water spewed from behind the toilet. He fell to his knees, soaking his jeans, and twisted the shut off valve until the water slowed to a sputter, then a drip.

He stood, hands on his hips, knees soaking wet. Jacques blinked from the doorway.

"This is a lot to absorb. Literally. This is going to cost a fortune. I don't have the money to waste on this."

He ran a wet hand through his hair and cringed.

Jacques whimpered.

"I'm pretty sure this isn't your fault."

The puppy pranced, splashing in the puddle. Beneath his feet the unfinished wood floor grew dark, soaking up water. The wood would swell. Mold could form. Water was probably dripping through into the basement

Kyle wiped his forehead with the back of his wrist and pressed the heels of his hands against his eyes. It was too much. All of it. Zeb and his money and the groceries, and the dog was wet, and the store was falling apart, and he hadn't even ordered any inventory yet. He held in shallow breath after shallow breath, letting them out slowly, until he could breathe deep and his heart stopped trying to pound its way out of his chest.

"Well, now that I've cashed in my 401(k), I guess the whole universe wants a cut." He kicked a toe at the water and made a tiny splash. "I can't ignore this. I need a toilet down here, and all this water has to go somewhere. Two bath towels with holes in them aren't going to solve this one. What's that plumber guy's name? Blue?"

Kyle splashed across the store and pulled Adelle's papers from the shelf beneath the counter. There were receipts and notes, catalogs from vendors. "Grey. The plumber's name is Grey." He dialed. "And voice mail. Of course."

He left a message with his address and number, and he rushed upstairs to get his towels and put the groceries away. Crouching on the ground for half an hour, his knees aching on the hard floor, he soaked up the water that hadn't seeped into the wood. Back against the wall, two wet towels by his side, his stomach lurched, and the room spun. He needed a break, for one thing to go right.

Jacques's nails ticked on the floor. The puppy dropped his tug-of-war rope in Kyle's lap. Kyle grasped one end. It had been spared by the flood.

"Imagine if I'd been gone for a whole day. This floor would be ruined, and there'd be mold everywhere. I'm gonna have to seal this floor with some kind of varnish."

Loud exhaust rumbled to a stop outside. A large vehicle backfired before its engine went quiet. With any luck, that would be Grey.

Jacques spun around and barked. Kyle tossed the rope, and the puppy scampered after it.

Kyle scrambled to his feet and unlocked the door. A guy in a knit cap with wavy dark hair pulled a bag of tools from the back of the truck, and Kyle held the door open.

Grey dropped his bag on the floor and straightened his cap. He pointed at Jacques. "Who's this little guy?"

"This is my dog, Jacques."

"That's a big name for a little dog."

"I named him after Jacques Pepin." Kyle scooped him up and turned his face from the slurping tongue.

"That guy from the public TV. I watched him all the time. Odd name for a dog. Cute, though."

"Thanks for coming. Sorry about the short notice." He let Jacques tumble to the floor, where the dog sniffed Grey's work boots.

"Emergencies are usually short notice. I wouldn't do this for fun or anything, but I get paid for it most of the time, so it's worth showing up for." He bent down to pet Jacques and let him sniff his hand. "Except for Helen. She always tries to pay me in food. I don't mind it. She's a good cook. It doesn't look like you have much to barter, so I figure you're a money customer. What is this place?"

"It used to be a general store."

"I know that. I mean, what's it now?" He picked up his bag and walked to the dark stain on the floor. Jacques followed like an obedient assistant. "Other than a mess. You really oughta seal these floors."

"I know. Might take a while."

"Uh huh." Grey pulled a flashlight from his back pocket and shined it at the wall behind the toilet.

Kyle stayed back, Jacques at his side. "The light works in here, if that'll help."

"Nah. I never turn on the electricity while standing in a puddle of somebody's water. 'Specially if it's poo water, which this isn't. Congrats on that, by the way."

"Thanks. It's what I always wanted. Not poo water. Does that make it cheaper?"

"Nothing makes plumbing cheap. Poo just makes it cost more."

"Good to know. Hey, is this a disaster, by any chance? Because I'm trying to open a store here, and I don't have a lot of money, so if good news is cheap, I could use some."

"The news is free." Grey crouched, the thick soles of his work boots sloshing in the water. He pulled at something attached to the toilet. "What kind of store are you opening? Is it a secret?"

"Kitchen supply. Cooking things."

"Yeah? My girl's thinking about opening a liquor store, but it costs a lot to buy inventory. We're still saving up for it. Maybe someday. You might know her. Logan? She works at the bar."

"I haven't been to the bar." He couldn't afford the bar. He knew the place, though. At the end of the street on the way to the farms, across from the motel and the gas station. It burned to the ground a few years before, and the woman who worked there won some contest to fix it. The drinks were supposed to be good, but any drinks were too rich for his blood. Even tea, apparently.

"What you got here is a cracked supply line." He stood and nudged a floor tile with his heel. "Water got under these. You'll have to pull 'em up and fix it. You could get mold if you don't. You definitely need to look at this subfloor, because it's spongy. The sheetrock over there is wet. I don't think you have to replace it, but since it's a bathroom, you should have greenboard, anyway. And this trim needs to be dried out. It could cost a bit."

"How much?"

"Won't know until I get started. About two ten for the supply line. More for everything else."

Kyle ran a hand over his face. "How much including everything else?"

"Could be thirteen hundred or so. Hard to say until you get started." Grey scowled at the toilet. "You want me to? Get started?"

Moving money around used to be fun. Like one of those video games with falling pieces that would fit together. But the pieces kept falling faster and the music was getting more frantic, and it never seemed to get any easier.

He chewed the inside of his lip and did some mental math. If he paid Grey with his credit card, he could pay it off when the retirement money went into his checking account. That would clear his balance to help him buy appliances. He'd have less money for inventory, but he could cut back and stagger product lines to keep people coming back to see what was new. It would take a little creativity and some positive thinking, but he could make it work.

"No reason to wait, I guess. Might as well get it fixed now. I can't open without a working bathroom down here."

"That's true. Town code." Grey scratched at his forehead. "I think I got what I need in the truck. If not, Carol will have it. I'll be right back."

Kyle followed him to the door, leash in hand, Jacques prancing at his heels.

"I'm going to take the pup out for a walk while you work, if you don't mind."

Grey pulled his hat down over his ears before stepping outside. "Not at all."

Jacques waited while Kyle hooked the leash to his collar, and they walked around the side and down the alley. The air was still and cool, crisp on his cheeks. He rested his back against the wall and let his breathing slow while Jacques did his business.

It had been a long time since he had to fix something of his own that broke. His condo had a maintenance guy on site. The farm took care of his loft. But here, every brick was his responsibility. Every drop of water that made its way into the store from God knows where could be his undoing. Toxic mold could be inside all the walls. Termites. Electrical gremlins.

Jacques kicked at his deposit, and Kyle shook the negative thoughts from his mind. He cleaned up and took the bag around back to the trash can.

"Kyle!" Penny sat in a pink plastic lawn chair, a glass of lemonade in hand. "How's Monday treating you?"

"Hey, Penny. Not so great, to be honest."

"Saw Grey's truck out front."

"The water going to the toilet exploded." Jacques pulled on the leash, aiming for Penny. Kyle gave him some slack.

"Good times. Adelle is coming over this evening for a drink. Wanna join us?"

"Tempting, but I still have a lot of cleaning to do. Have to order stoves for the cooking classes and buy inventory. I hope to have the store open as soon as I can. A week maybe."

Penny swallowed her sip, eyes wide. "That's fast."

He shrugged. "It's easy to set everything up."

And the sooner he could start cooking classes and generate revenue, the sooner he could upgrade from squished bread sandwiches to something with more substance.

"That's exciting. Let me know when you have a grand opening date. I'd be happy to spread the word."

He coiled the leash in his sweaty palm and squinted at the leaning porch. A week, maybe. It was actually happening. His store was in there, behind that dilapidated deck. The words had fallen out of him without any real plan. He hadn't even solved all his disasters yet. He opened his mouth to take it back, but his breath hitched in his throat, and the words threaded and knotted. He didn't want to take it back.

He'd weathered financial embarrassment, cleaned out his retirement account, fixed the heater and the plumbing, scrubbed every inch of the place by hand. It felt like years had passed since he first saw the place, and he barely had a moment to come up for air. Why slow down now, when his dream was on the brink of happening? The store was finally real, or it would be soon. A small fire lit within him, feeding on the kindling of his education, the student loans he'd hustled to pay back, the corner office, the clients, the stress of working at a job he hated just to climb a ladder that he never wanted to climb.

He had to use that retirement money wisely, to fill the store with cooking ranges that reflected how Ramsbolt cooked at home, so people felt like good food was attainable. He needed beautiful pottery and classic porcelain. He needed a grand opening. It was everything he ever wanted, and it was here. Behind that broken porch.

"What the hell. Thursday." He was tired of treading water, looking for dry land. "Grand opening is this Thursday."

Penny hoisted her lemonade. "Great news!"

He tugged Jacques back toward the store "Come on, Jacques. We got a lot of work to do."

## CHAPTER SIXTEEN

Excitement from the night before burst like water balloons as Martin banged on pipes in the basement, booms and clangs slinging up through the floorboards. Jacques slept through it in the front window as only an exhausted puppy can. Kyle was grateful for shelves to assemble, simple as they were, and boxes to unpack.

The Kyle from ten years ago wouldn't have blinked at a heater repair bill. He would have celebrated as he unpacked his first boxes of inventory, checking his phone for a call from the oven people to schedule delivery. But this Kyle, the one whose insides were solid steel braids of potential regret, tangible fear, and unbridled hunger wanted them unpacked, organized, and the cardboard shoved in the recycling can so he could get on to the more exciting work of setting up cooking classes. He ripped the packing tape off a box, unstuck it from his shirt, and wadded it into a ball that he lobbed at the bathroom door.

"Damn thing."

The box held clear glass pie plates with fluted edges. He lifted one with the shaking hand of a man who'd skipped lunch, and the clatter of Martin slamming the basement door sent a quake through his body. The plate slipped from his hand, and his heart leapt into his throat as it crashed to the floor. Jacques roused from his nap in the window, head cocked to the side.

Kyle snatched the plate from the floor and ran a hand across the cool porcelain, wiping away bits of packing dust. At least it didn't break.

"Sorry, buddy. Go back to sleep." He placed the plate on the shelf.

Martins' footsteps got his attention. He turned to find the man covered in oil, clutching his tool bag.

"You're done already?"

"Already? It's been six hours." Martin reached into his back pocket and pulled out a plastic-wrapped packet of papers. He waved it until Kyle caught up with it and snagged it from the air. "Here's your stuff."

Warranty. "There's a warranty?"

"Ayup. Call me if you get trouble. Should be fine though. Might need a tweak if you like your water hotter or colder, but other than that, you're all set." He aimed a thumb at the back of the store. "Whatcha putting back there in that empty spot?"

"Huh?" Kyle ripped open the plastic bag and thumbed through booklets and slips of paper. "Oh. Cooking classes."

"This town could use that. I can't cook for nothing. Not that you can tell by looking at me." Martin adjusted the waist of his pants. "Nowhere to eat around here either, unless you go out to that old log cabin place. It ain't half as good as it used to be, if you ask me. "

"I should have classes open soon. Happy to take requests for things to teach, too." Kyle flipped pages of a warranty booklet with lots of small type. "What does the warranty cover? Like, problems?"

Martin hoisted his bag to his shoulder. "Yeah. Five years of free repairs. After you pay me for today, that is."

*Money might not buy you happiness, but it'll buy you security, and that's pretty much the same thing. No trouble for five years. Heat without interruption. I might run it in the middle of summer just to enjoy the peace of mind.*

He felt a ton lighter, like someone had just lifted a piano off his chest. Or a giant boiler. A slow smile spread across his face, and he was buoyant. He could have floated out of the store, down the street, and into the clouds.

"Ahem." Martin's mouth was twisted into a grin, one eyebrow raised. He held out his phone, a white contraption plugged into the top. "Payment?"

"Oh. Right. Of course." Kyle dug his wallet from his pocket and pulled out his credit card. He slipped it through the card reader and scrawled his signature across Martin's phone.

Martin yanked up his pants and tossed his phone in his short pocket. "Thanks for doing business."

"I didn't have a choice. You're the only guy in town."

"All the same." Martin nodded and slipped out of the store.

"You hear that, Jacques? The heater can't cost us any more money. If the shit hits the fan, it's free."

Jacques swelled and shrank with a sigh of consent.

"You'll appreciate that in January."

Kyle emptied the last cardboard box of its pie plates. He tossed the empty box on the pile of others, a chestnut mountain in his untidy landscape.

A stack of unpacked boxes leaned in a daunting tower, inventory for his shelves. It was happening so fast. All for the better. If he stopped to think too hard about all of it, he'd only make time for regrets. Maybe it was dumb to blurt out a date and declare a grand opening four days away, throwing away extra money on rush shipping. But with work to do, an aching back, and an empty stomach, he didn't have time to worry that he'd rushed into it. He didn't have time to worry that every penny he was spending came from a nest egg that should have been sacrosanct. Every cheap metal utility shelf and every box of gorgeous kitchen art he had no clue how to sell was only there because he hadn't worked hard enough to get it any other way. And now that account was almost gone. Between plumbing and heating and inventory, and the stoves he still had to pay for, he had just a few months to live on. Those classes had better take off, fast.

He stretched his lower back. He just had to make it through opening day. Then he could focus on business instead of the future he couldn't picture and the money he didn't have. But he didn't have time to think about that. He just had to keep moving.

"Where are those mixing glasses?"

His phone rang in his back pocket, and he accepted the call without looking.

"This is Kyle."

"Christa with a C here. I'm calling from Grogan's. About the order you placed for six electric ovens?"

"Yes!" He wiped the back of his hand across his forehead. "I'm really excited. This is a big part of my plan. You're calling to schedule delivery?"

"Well, we got your online order, and we can have them out to you and installed on Friday. We do have rush delivery options, if you—"

"No." Every cent mattered, and he didn't need to start cooking classes right away. "No thanks. Friday is fine. My grand opening is Thursday so people will expect a little mess."

"Good. We'll ring you on Friday when we're on our way, then. For large orders, though, I need to verify the three digits on the back of your card. We do this for every order over a thousand dollars."

"Of course." He dug his wallet from his back pocket and read off the numbers. "Thanks for checking. I used to work in banking, and fraud is—"

"No problem." Her keyboard clicked through the phone, and the tone of her voice said she was disinterested. "Your order is being processed now. We'll be in touch on Friday. Have a great day."

She hung up.

"That was abrupt." He shoved his phone in his back pocket and turned to face the mountain of empty boxes. So many empty boxes. Inventory stacked on shelves and sitting unpacked that he had to sell.

He tossed his phone on the counter and grabbed his box cutter as his stomach grumbled. There wasn't time for lunch. Not now. Not while the place looked like a disaster zone.

"What am I going to do with all this cardboard? This is not gonna fit in my can."

"You can put some in my recycling, if you want."

He jumped at the woman's voice and spun on his heel. Penny leaned in the door with a broad smile, her mop of flame-red curls trying to break free from a hair tie as wind whipped in behind her.

"Hey, Penny." Kyle waved her in. "Cold out there."

She pushed her cat-eye glasses up her nose and stepped inside. "Yeah. Winter's gonna be brutal this year." She smoothed her hair as the door closed behind her. "The wind really whips around in that entrance, doesn't it?"

She tightened her ponytail.

Kyle nodded, grabbed a box, ripped the tape off, and squeezed it flat. He threw it on the floor, starting a stack.

Penny shoved her hands in her back pockets, scanning the room. "This place looks amazing. You must be really excited."

"I'm trying to be. It comes and goes." Maybe all those years of keeping his dreams safe in a box, holding onto aspirations because it was more comforting to dream them in the dark of night than to chase them in the light of day had dulled the shine for far too long. Excitement was hard to hold onto these days. It came and went with the bank balance.

"This place looks great, though," Penny said. "It's light and airy. You have a good eye."

Kyle grabbed another box and hugged it flat. "Thanks. It's the store. Good bones. For a while I thought it would have white walls and bright lights. Then I thought maybe dark grays and spotlights. I need more lighting in here, but that's for later."

"No, this is perfect. The exposed brick and unfinished floors are a great nod to what it used to be." She tilted her head back. "And that ceiling. Oh my God, that's gorgeous."

"It was like that. Someone painted it white at some point. Haven't seen any paint falling off, and I like how the copper shows through, so I left it."

He scanned the room. She had a point. Nostalgia seeped from the walls of the old general, tinting everything with a simpler time sentimentality. Hopefully it would rub off on his sales. "You don't think the shelves look empty?"

"No way. It makes things stand out." Penny ran her finger over the pattern of a diamond cut mixing glass.

"Good to hear. I'm a little cash-strapped so inventory is sparse."

She moved down the shelves. "I had the opposite problem when I got started. Not the cash-strapped part. I'll be poor forever. I mean the inventory. I had a billion of everything and nothing anybody wanted. Anyway, I came to see if you needed any help with anything, but everything here is perfect. It makes me want a bigger kitchen. It's gorgeous, and I'm not just saying that. This place feels...glamorous. Like something—"

"That doesn't fit in Ramsbolt?" He shoved his hands in his pockets.

"I was going to say expensive."

"It won't be, though. I want it to be affordable. We should love what we eat, you know? And your kitchen should reflect that. It shouldn't cost a fortune."

Penny grabbed a pepper mill and turned it over in her hands. "You're really lucky you get to pick what you sell. I inherited all of my inventory, and the place was packed to the gills with old, dusty garbage. I hated being in it."

If only she knew. There might not be a lot on the shelves, but it was still too rich for his blood. Was it too nice for Ramsbolt? The guys at the farm said he was arrogant for keeping his old sneakers clean, and they called him condescending for not putting prepositions at the ends of his sentences.

Kyle rubbed his temple and swallowed hard. "You were lucky to start with inventory. I'll expand the product lines later, when I can afford more stock. It'll get people to come back anyway, to see what's new."

Penny placed the pepper mill back on the shelf. "Good point. It's really easy to fall into debt buying things."

"Speaking of which, there is something I've been meaning to ask you. It's kind of a big favor. I imagined having a big table in the front of the store, all decked out to set a tone for the store and show off the products. Until I can buy something more permanent, I wondered if I could borrow something from you?"

"You'd be doing me a favor." She rocked on her heels, lips pursed, eyes narrowed as she took in the space. "You definitely don't want something too stately. Something with a rustic feel, comforting, but not something that stands out too much. I have a few tables that might work."

"That would be kind of you. I'll keep the price tag on, of course. And if someone wants it, I'll send them straight to you."

She offered him a gentle smile. "That's a very nice offer. We can probably work something out. Like a finder's fee. Things are still cramped over there, and I'm happy to have some storage that could lead to a sale, especially if it's in a setting like this. Besides, if your first few months hurts as much as mine did, every bit will help, right?"

"Rough start, huh?"

"You could say that. I was on my way to being a surgeon when my grandmother died. I'm not sure which was more exhausting, medical school or learning to run a store. Not like I'm an expert, but I've got the hang of it now. Steep learning curve. It'll be easy for you, though. You were a finance guy, right? That's what Adelle said."

"Investments, but yeah. I worked with money. I don't have a lot of experience with managing money that doesn't exist, though, or running my own business. This is all new."

Penny shrugged. "You've got a good start, though. You're selling aspirations. Running an antique store in a place like this is a losing proposition. They sell their crap to me in the first place. No one wants to pay twice as much to get it back."

A small laugh escaped, and Kyle fell back against the wall. "Makes a lot of sense when you put it that way."

"The tourist season does okay. People stopping for a potty break before they wait in line to get into Canada. People buy little things. But winters can be hard." Red curls shimmied when she shook her head.

"Like, how hard are we talking?"

She raised an eyebrow. "Like, I hope you enjoy putting puzzles together and wearing sweaters in layers hard."

A lump formed in Kyle's throat. The bricks were cold against his back. He swallowed and shifted his weight, looking for some comfort. He couldn't afford to start a business just at the start of the worst season. He could barely afford to start a business at all.

"Of course it didn't help that Ramsbolt didn't want me here," Penny continued. "I didn't belong."

*They don't want me here either.* "I'm sure that's not true. You seem to fit in great."

"I do now. Not then. Everyone loved my gran. Then I came along, expecting everyone to help me out by extension and boom—opposite, and I wasn't very nice about it, either. I didn't grow up here. I didn't know anybody, and I didn't even want to belong in this stupid little town. I just wanted to get back to my life. It took a lot of work to prove myself."

Belonging in Ramsbolt was all Kyle ever wanted. He wanted to belong when he was a kid, living on the outskirts. He wanted to belong in college with classmates who arrived with pedigree names. He wanted to belong with his kitchen colleagues, but his classwork kept him apart. He wanted to belong in the office, but he wasn't cutthroat enough to fit in. He never belonged anywhere. Not at the farm and certainly not back in Ramsbolt where they thought he was pompous for having left in the first place.

And here was Penny, a woman who never wanted to run and store, someone who never wanted to belong here at all, picking up where her grandmother left off. She made it look easy.

Kyle wrinkled his nose. "Have you ever heard of Blueberry Window Pie?"

The slow spread of bewilderment on Penny's face made him regret asking. He was starting to sound like a crazy person.

"No. What's Blueberry Window Pie?" she asked.

He waved a hand. "Never mind. Forget I mentioned it. You fit in just fine here. I've seen plenty of people coming and going from your store. Gives me hope they'll accept me, too. I'm just some kid who grew up here, ran away to get a fancy education, and came back home when he couldn't hack it."

Penny shimmied onto a stool that wobbled as she settled. "Couldn't hack it? It sounds like you accomplished something to me. But you grew up here, right? So people remember you. They'll support you. This place'll be packed."

If they didn't show up for the granddaughter of a woman they loved, they sure weren't going to show up for Kyle. Every time someone raved about his grandmother and her pie, they turned away as soon as they found out he'd moved. It didn't matter to them that he'd returned.

He shifted his weight, but it didn't shift his mood. Brick shards cut into his shoulders. "If this place is packed, it'll be a miracle."

She clasped her hands and offered him a smile that hinted at comfort. "Nah. Opening day jitters. It's only Tuesday. You have two more days to panic, then you'll see. I didn't mean to bring you down.

There's a lot to be excited about in here. How did you end up back in Ramsbolt, anyway? If I had financial skills like that, I sure as hell wouldn't choose this lifestyle."

"It was supposed to be a pit stop. My parents were aging, and I figured I'd help them before moving on to the next thing. That was years ago."

"Years?" She furrowed her brow. "Why didn't I ever meet you before? I mean, this place is so small."

He nodded to a point beyond the far wall, up the street, around the circle, and a mile away to the land that bordered the town. "Worked out at a farm. Kept to myself mostly."

"Ah. Well, now that you're in town, word will spread."

If stomachs could wince, his did. It didn't matter how good it looked. If being *one of them* was what it took to get people in the door, it would be more than just a rough winter. It could be the end of him if he couldn't break that barrier.

Penny leaned forward, concern etched on her face. "Are you okay? You don't look so good."

He rubbed his eyes with the heels of his hands, willing his stomach to settle. "Yeah, I'm fine. Just nerves. This store's been my dream since I was a kid. It's just…there are a lot of challenges. It's not how I expected to start."

"I know that feeling. Where I wanted to be and where I belonged turned out to be two different things."

The words hit him across the chest like a baseball bat, and his breath tangled in his throat. That's what it came down to, really. Everything hinged on whether or not he belonged, and it always had. What if this dream, this store, wasn't where he was supposed to be? What if he never found his place and never belonged anywhere at all?

He painted on a grin. "It's cool you had a legacy."

"What about your family. Were you always in farming?"

"Not always. My grandmother sold blueberry pies from her living room window. My dad was in farming. Mom did odd jobs around town."

"From blueberry pie to a cuisine empire. Not bad for two generations. Are you going to sell her pies?"

"No way. I'd step on Marissa's toes. And I can't bake. Not my thing."

Penny shuffled off the stool. She crossed to the shelf and picked up a pie plate. She held it up to the light. "Says who?" She put the pie dish in his hands. "I never got to be a surgeon, but I spent a lot of time in the ER. A lot of patients told me that they couldn't do it. Couldn't walk, couldn't stand, couldn't make it to the bathroom. Most of the time, they did. The only ones who were bound to fail were the ones who never tried."

The glass warmed his hands. "I cashed out my retirement account. Major tax penalty. I've destroyed my financial future for this place, and I have no guaranteed return." He shook his head, his eyes fixed on the fluted edge of the dish. He'd chewed the inside of his cheek raw the last few days. The pain of prodding it with his tongue was a small release. "If a client told me he was spending his retirement on inventory, I would have put him in a straitjacket and locked him in an empty office to save him from himself. Cashing out that account was rough, and it's hard to reconcile that against chasing a dream. I guess it's not a real leap of faith if your parachute is open."

Penny's eyes widened. "That's some heavy emotional weight to carry around."

"Yup." Kyle chewed his lower lip. "I'm okay if I keep busy, but when I slow down, it catches up with me. Know what I mean?"

"Hell yeah, I do." She shifted her weight and folded her arms. "You definitely have the support of your neighbors. You can vent to us any time. And you need to find outlets for the stress, cut loose sometimes. You should hang out and drink wine with us—me and Nate and Adelle."

Adelle. The one person he should stay away from most. But she was also the person he wanted to be around more than any other. Wine with Adelle was dangerous territory, but it was the kind of terrain that begged to be scaled. He rocked on his heels. "That's a great offer. I'm definitely up for wine. I'll take you up on that sometime."

"You'll find joy in small things, 'cause for a while, small things are all you'll have. Sense of humor is important around here. And learning how to rest."

He shook his head and folded his arms across his middle. "Rest doesn't pay the bills. I have five and ten year plans, my goals are on paper. I just have to tread water until I make it. Things will get better."

*Once those stoves are installed on Friday, I can breathe a little easier.*

Penny grabbed the doorknob and offered him a broad smile, which he took as vindication. No one could argue with hard work as a path to success. "Good for you. I don't know what five and ten year plans look like, so I might pick your brain about that someday. In the meantime, come on over whenever you want and pick out a table. Nate and I will help you bring it in. He's my…boyfriend? Partner? Whatever the adults call it these days. He'll love this place. He's artsy." She took a step toward the door and examined a shelf of handcrafted pottery and coffee mugs.

"There's a lot of people around here I haven't met."

"Two hundred and twelve Ramsboltians now, I think. Ramsboltarians? Don't hold me to that. I'm not sure that's what we're called." She pointed to an open box, its flaps bent back exposing a white serving platter with an embossed turkey. "That would look gorgeous on a Thanksgiving table. I think I have just the right one. Anyway, I'm gonna run. The store's open, and lunch is when I do my best business."

"Can't wait to be able to say that." He waved and watched her go, her path crossing that of the mailman. Riley's head was down, his hand deep in his bag.

"Penny." Riley stopped in the doorway. At six feet, six inches, he made the doorway look small. He shuffled envelopes in his bag and pulled out a small stack. "These are for you. Saved me a trip. Anything outgoing?"

"Not today. Thanks for these." Penny took the bundle and swatted the mailman's arm. She thumbed through the stack. "Nothing but bills, as always."

With a wink she was gone. Kyle stepped over broken-down boxes and held out the pie plate. Riley filled it with a pile of mail. The dish felt hotter than the surface of the sun. A scary looking envelope from his credit card company was on the top, and he drew his fist around it, letting the sharp envelope dig into his fingers with satisfying measure. His desire for lunch passed. The mounting bills would save him a ton on groceries, and knowing he was almost out of cash and his credit card was nearly maxed out, he wouldn't be able to afford the sign he'd always dreamed of. He'd have to paint it on the window instead. If he was lucky, he'd be able to afford paint.

He locked the door behind Riley, dropped the mail on the counter, and carried the pie dish up the stairs. Somewhere up there was his mother's box of recipes and in it, the formula for Blueberry Window Pie.

# CHAPTER SEVENTEEN

Fruit soup.

Kyle squinted at the recipe. He'd followed it to a T. Lemon juice. Cinnamon. Four hundred degrees for twenty minutes, then he'd turned the temperature down by fifty degrees for another half hour. Letting it sit hadn't helped at all. It was thin, like generic maple syrup with globs of doughy flour caked to the berries. And the crust was a soggy mess.

*The rest is Ramsbolt magic. Only a truly worthy Nolan from Ramsbolt can figure out the secret of this pie. Once you do, share it with no one.*

The last line of his grandmother's notes didn't make him feel any better. He'd lain awake all night thinking about what Penny had said— how she didn't want to belong in Ramsbolt. It was funny how much they had in common. Both of them from beloved local families, both of them trying to make sense of what their ancestors left behind. Though she never wanted to belong here, she did. She just had to accept it. No amount of longing could make Kyle belong in Ramsbolt or anywhere else, for that matter. And no amount of longing was going to make that pie edible.

He dumped it in the trash where it oozed over crumpled plastic wrappers and an empty toilet paper roll.

Jacques sniffed at the can.

"Sorry, buddy. Even if you could eat pie, you wouldn't want that one." He grabbed his jacket from the back of a chair and paused to scratch the dog's ears. "I gotta go see Dad. You hold down the fort, okay? Opening day's tomorrow so I won't be sad if you sweep up one last time before people show up."

Driving past the front door on his way to Colby to see his father, he told himself that taking some time away wasn't a betrayal to the store. There was nothing left to do but pace the floor and wring his hands, worrying about things he couldn't control. Sure, his father never knew he was there, but he'd made a promise he planned to keep. His weekly visit wouldn't be interrupted. As he pulled into the parking lot of the senior center, his mind flooded with a tide of tasks. He needed to order a breakfast tray from Marissa and paint his sign on the window. There was a fine layer of dust that never seemed to lift no matter how many times he cleaned. He still hadn't sealed the floor yet. And he needed to figure out a menu for cooking classes.

He tapped on the door to his father's room and let himself in. He couldn't stay long, not with the growing list of worries that pushed at the boundaries of his patience.

He knew better than to address the man as Dad or introduce himself. For all he knew, he was an acrobat that day, a circus performer perhaps, or a thief come to steal the batteries from the remote. Whoever his father thought he was, he had to play the role. He never came for himself, but for the memory of the man who raised him. But this time, he had to play the role and shift the tide, tell his father the truth about the store. It should be an easy win, one that his heart needed. He'd never get easy approval from his father, but the shell of the man might lend him support, pat his knee, and tell him he was proud.

This time he came for validation.

As the man in the bed with the wisps of white hair turned his head and lowered the volume on the TV, Kyle waited to find out what role to play.

"What's that? In your hand?" Dad waved the remote in the air.

Kyle hovered in the doorway and held up the newspaper. "News. Figured I'd read it to you, if you're up for it today."

His story was the headline.

"*Wheel of Fortune* comes on at six." His father's eyes narrowed. "Where's the guy who usually comes?"

Kyle let out a sigh of relief and held the door open with his hip. Visiting his father was never easy, but the best days—the easiest to get through—were days like this. His heart twinged; his stomach fluttered, eager to share the news.

"I would never interrupt *Wheel of Fortune*. I don't know where the other guy is. Can I come in? I brought the paper. I know you like to hear it read." The cue he waited for was long coming. His father smoothed a blue knit blanket over his lap, his knuckles knurled and nails yellowed.

"I guess. Probably nothing good. Bunch of whiners and thieves."

The door closed behind Kyle, shutting out the beeps and whirrs of medical monitors and the guy yelling a few doors down about lettuce. He moved a stack of magazines from the vinyl visitor's chair and settled next to his dad.

The newspaper was coiled tight from its time in the car door pocket. He smoothed it over his knee.

He hadn't looked at the paper since he picked it up for a quarter, digging it from the box by the post office. The headline snagged his breath. "One Less Vacant Store. Kitchen Concepts signs lease to own agreement."

The chair scraped the floor as he scooted closer. He couldn't contain his smile.

In his father's most lucid moments, when he remembered their house and his wife, when he believed his son was still little or away at college and that everything would go back to the way it ought to be if someone would just help him out of that bed, Kyle had held his breath. He'd bit his tongue and pushed back his fears. He'd gnawed holes in his lip to keep the truth from his father that he'd moved back home and was there to stay. But this man wasn't his father. This man would be proud of him. This man would slap his shoulder, beam with pride, tell him he'd done a good job.

It might not be the acceptance he wanted from his father, but he wouldn't be holding in the lie anymore. The regret would be gone.

Kyle cleared his throat. "Kitchen Concepts will open in the vacant General Store, next to Penny's Loft, in the coming weeks. No word yet from the owner." Kyle put the paper down. "This is my store. I opened a store in Ramsbolt. I'm going to sell kitchen supplies. It opens on Thursday."

"What kind of damn fool idea is that? Kitchen supplies." His eyes rolled to the ceiling. "Nobody needs that. You don't know the first thing about Ramsbolt, do you?"

Kyle dropped his head. He winced down at the paper and clenched his jaw to relieve the sting. It wasn't a dumb idea. Ramsbolt wanted nice things just as much as any other town. He tapped a foot against the floor and water on the bedside table rippled in its cup.

*They didn't want Penny's antiques either. I haven't done any research at all on this town, on what they'll buy and where they'll shop. The woman at the bank was right. Dan and Bern and Zeb are right. Why did I come here hoping for support from a man who doesn't remember me? If he were himself today, he'd only tell me the truth.*

What if his father was right and no matter how affordable, no one wanted a nice kitchen or a new look for their dining room? His only customers would be people cruising through town in the summer, their sights set on Québec or New Brunswick. He had to figure out how to stay afloat, so he wouldn't crash and burn, destroy his savings, and end up back where he started, sleeping in a broken bed under the leaking roof of a borrowed shack.

Kyle shook the negative thoughts from his head. He was starting to sound like Zeb, all absolutes.

His father plucked at the blanket. "Kitchen store in Ramsbolt. That's the damn dumbest idea I ever heard of."

He cleared his throat and blinked over at the man who couldn't hear the truth any more than he could tell the time. He couldn't risk his financial future, his dreams, his entire fate on the rejection of someone who didn't know him anymore. He couldn't lie down and give up like that. People wanted cooking classes. The woman in the store said it. Martin said it. It had real potential.

"I disagree. Ramsbolt is ready for an upswing."

"Not on Main Street, it's not. Dead-end road nobody goes down. Can't afford nothing. My mom used to sell pies from her living room window."

Not this again. The smell of failure was a burned yet somehow still undercooked blueberry pie.

But the memory was closer to the past than his father usually went. It was closer to something real, nothing like the tall tales he usually told when he talked about his family.

"Do you remember anything about the stores that were there when you were a kid? There was an antique store, right? And a florist?"

The man's eyes searched the ceiling, looking beyond the walls to another time and place. Kyle expected another made-up story about life in mansions, being waited on by servants and fawned over by the town, but he braced himself for the possibility of a sober memory.

His father spoke slowly, eyes narrowed in on a scene that formed in the fog of his mind. "There was a florist. Around the corner. Wasn't on our street. Didn't go in there, though. Couldn't afford it."

Adelle had said the store was her family's legacy. "Do you remember the people who ran it?"

"Some guy." His father waved a hand, his face contorted. "Some bigwig guy is all I remember. What are you asking me this stuff for?"

"What about a furniture shop with antiques? You sold some of our furniture there when I was a kid. You and mom borrowed a truck and drove it into town and sold furniture for money. Do you remember the shop? Or the lady you sold it to?"

His father's face twisted with anger. Kyle scooted back in his seat, out of arm's reach. He'd been a victim of the man's powerful swat a time or two, but he'd never tried to grab his father by the arm and drag him to the surface before. All he wanted was a few memories, something to anchor his store to the town's history from the man who kept it from him, and him from it. Approval was out of the question, but he thirsted for recognition.

Kyle flatted the newspaper on his lap.

His father drew the blanket into his fists, knuckles white. His bushy white eyebrows low over his eyes. "Stop asking me dumb questions. I can't remember nothing."

Just one more. "The antique store was full of junk." That's what Penny had said, anyway. "Do you remember it?"

"No." Eyes shut tight and lips lined in a scowl, his father hunched his shoulders. "I don't remember none of that shit."

"What about the woman who ran the antique place. Do you remember her?"

"Why are you asking these dumb questions?" His voice boomed in the concrete room. "What do you want from me, huh? I thought you was reading the paper."

If he kept ranting, the nurses would come. They'd make him leave and give his dad a sedative. Kyle didn't want to face their pitying stares while his father had a meltdown. He was dumb to think he'd ever get anything from the man who raised him but anger and dissent.

"Don't worry about it. Just forget I asked, okay?"

"No! I'm done with this." His father pointed a shaking finger at his chest. "You want to know what that town was like, go ask my son. That asshole lives in Boston in some fancy-pants job, and he's smart enough not to come back here. Thinks he's too smart to be seen visiting his old man in this dump, and this place ain't good enough for him, and he's right. It's just fine with me because at least I did one thing right and raised a kid smart enough to get the hell out of here. Want to know what it was like? Go ask him."

Kyle's face flushed hot at the distanced remark. He knew better than to give his father's words any weight, not to take him seriously. The man's perception of reality was just as warped as his memories of the past. Pushing the man to take responsibility for either was futile. Kyle's insides went hollow, like someone took a spoon and scooped them all out. All that was left was a cavity, a cold cavern where his feelings used to live.

Kyle reached out a hand to touch the man's arm. "I'm sorry. I didn't mean to upset you. I thought you might…you'd like talking about the past. Some people do."

His father flung out an arm and struck him in the shoulder hard enough to leave a welt, knocking him back against the chair. There wasn't any use trying to salvage the visit. The damage was done. The sooner he left, the sooner his father would calm down, and he could spare the nurses any lingering outrage.

"I'll go. I'm sorry. I didn't mean to upset you." Kyle stood, the chair scraping against the tiled floor. His arm stung, but he refused to acknowledge it. Crossing the threshold and stepping into the hall, he paused to look back at his father, whose face was turned to the window, to his view of the sky and the tree that obscured it.

He wanted to believe that his father had sacrificed to give him the best life he could have. He wanted to believe that the man did everything he could to provide for his mother, to give their family security. Zeb might have been right; his parents could have worked smarter instead of harder. Maybe his dad would have saved enough energy to patch the roof that leaked when it rained. His mom could have been happier with a stable job. Maybe his father would have had the energy to express some love once in a while instead of using it all up on blame and pride.

"Dad?"

His father's arm shot up, a hand raised in an emphatic no. "Don't come here no more. Send the other guy back, the one who actually reads the paper instead of asking stupid questions."

Kyle blinked back tears. Someday, when his father was clear and feeling himself, he'd tell him he loved him. He wouldn't ever hear it back, but it would be enough to know he said it. Forgiveness wouldn't be so easy.

He ran his hand along a scuff on the wall, taking shallow breaths of the antiseptic-saturated air while the knot in his throat untied. He nodded at a nurse pushing a cart of meds through the lobby.

"Feisty visit, huh?" she asked. "I heard through the wall."

Kyle shrugged. "He's like that sometimes. I don't take it personally. Sorry for the commotion."

She waved a hand. "It's okay. Better luck next visit, right?"

He managed a smile. "Sure. Next time."

His car was parked next to a stand of birch trees. It looked so lonely there, by itself, and he felt horrible for not being able to care for it. If he'd never left the world of finance, or if he'd kept up with his license and not turned his back on the past, he could have worked for Cadwalladr. He'd have the money to fix that stupid car when it broke rather than cut corners. Instead, he was selfish and didn't do all he could to fix things. To fix anything. But he couldn't go through the motions anymore, following a life path that had been dictated to him. It was his turn to earn his place in the world, to find the place where he belonged, even if it turned out to be the poor house.

He closed his eyes while the engine started, and he let it warm up for a moment, just until the engine settled, then he headed for home. For Ramsbolt. He had a lot of work to do to open the store in just two days. If only he hadn't wasted his morning on that stupid pie.

# CHAPTER EIGHTEEN

Penny's Loft smelled like old wood and earthy candles. Kyle stood just inside the door, a little orange cat weaving around his feet. His father might not remember, but Kyle knew his childhood furniture had ended up somewhere in this store, along with his grandmother's jewelry, the toys he grew out of, and their dining room table. All of it had been hauled to Eliza's second-hand store one piece at a time where his dad haggled over pennies with the woman for things she never wanted to sell and his mother sheepishly took what the woman offered. Penny's store was smaller than he remembered, and much less cluttered, if you could call what Eliza had arranged as clutter. It had looked more Tetris than a store when he was a kid. It had smelled like earth and rusty metal, not candles and lovely old furniture.

Penny had stripped much of the junk away. Chairs still hung from the ceiling, but you could see the walls and the floor. Shelves and furniture were easy to identify, though some were still stacked two high.

"You must be Kyle." A man in his forties, around Kyle's age, in a blue sweater smeared with paint emerged from a dark corner with a mug of something warm. Dried paint mottled his hands. He looked kind and unassuming in a blank canvas sort of way.

"You must be Nate. Penny mentioned you." Kyle waved and took a reluctant step, his hand outstretched, and the cat still winding through his legs.

"Jake. Stop. Don't trip the neighbors." Nate rested his coffee cup on the counter. He scooped up the purring cat and transferred him to a table. "Jake loves company. I'd shake, but I'm covered in paint. I've been working on scenes of town for next year's arts festival."

"I heard about that. I didn't come into town for it, but I heard it was great."

Nate nodded, his eyebrows raised. He gestured to the back of the shop and opened his mouth to speak, but Penny rushed down the stairs, her red hair bouncing in her dense ponytail. Jake leapt from the table to meet her on the stairs.

"Kyle! I've been looking at the tables, and I think I found just the thing. We dug it out yesterday." She pointed to a long table in the middle of the store. "What do you think?"

Kyle stood on tiptoe and peered over a desk. The table was thick, solid wood, with layers of white and cream paint sanded away, hints of it still visible over the time-worn wood beneath. Its legs were plain, unadorned, not turned wood spindles like the pristine glossy antiques that surrounded it. They looked hand hewn with saw marks and a gentle taper. It was a legitimate farm table that would look perfect beneath a simple place setting, decorated with greens at Christmas and gourds at Halloween.

It rendered him speechless. "It's...it's perfect. I almost hope it doesn't sell and sits in my store forever, it's so perfect."

"Great! We can help you get it out of here, if you're ready for it. I'm glad to have a little more room in here. Let me grab something to dust it off with."

Kyle grasped an end of the table and test lifted. It weighed a ton. "Don't worry about it. Really. I can clean it up. You don't have to do that."

Penny paused on her way to a sunny little back room. "No way. You have enough going on. You have a grand opening tomorrow! The least I can do is lend you some furniture that isn't dusty."

"Thanks for the help," Kyle yelled after her. "I really appreciate this."

Nate retrieved his mug and smiled over his sip. "You look really familiar. I don't suppose you've purchased children's toys from me at some point."

"Definitely not. No kids in my world. I lived out at Zeb's farm, about a mile outside town."

"Did you grow up around here?" Nate adjusted his grip on the mug.

*Not this again. I'm going to have to come up with a script.* Kyle tried to roll the tension from his neck. "Yeah. You?"

Nate shook his head. "Nope. I moved here as an adult. Bought the existing store. Thought this would be a great place to enjoy the quiet and make some art. The toy shop wasn't even all that old when I bought it. I think it was an appliance store or something like that before."

Penny tossed a roll of paper towels, and Nate caught them. "You and Adelle are the only natives on the street." She sprayed furniture polish on the table and held out a hand for a towel.

"And Sparky," Nate said. "He runs that small engine repair place. But no one ever sees him."

"I call myself a zip code native." Kyle crossed and uncrossed his arms, then shoved his hands in his back pockets just to keep them occupied. Standing awkwardly while someone else did something for him made him self-conscious. "We lived outside town and didn't come here for the shops that much."

Nate unraveled another paper towel and handed it to Penny. "You're in finance, right? Or you were?"

"I was. I worked for a big firm in Boston until a few years ago."

"I would have killed for that kind of education—to learn how to save and where to invest, even with the little amounts I have…it doesn't come easy."

"Good for you for trying. Most people don't."

Nate hugged the paper towel roll. "What made you get into finance?"

*If only I knew.* "It was probably a combination of things. I guess growing up without money made me want to learn to manage it. I figured that kind of knowledge would help me when I opened my own store one day."

Penny held out a hand for another towel. "I bet it'll be a huge help."

"I hope so. I hoped I'd have some cash on hand when I started the store, at least, but life throws you curveballs."

"I strongly encourage dodging them." Penny stood and collected paper towels into a ball. "With an eye like yours, you'll do very well." She turned to Nate. "You should see it. It's gorgeous."

"It still feels sparse to me," Kyle said. "Eventually I'll add to the inventory and spruce it up a bit more."

"Have you considered artists from the area?" Nate leaned against a curio cabinet. "Like potters and blacksmiths and furniture makers you could find online. You could offer to sell their things on consignment. You might make less profit on each item, but it would be good for inventory."

Penny's jaw dropped, and she swatted at Nate with an unused towel. "What a great idea. It's a great networking opportunity, too."

Kyle let the idea seep. He spoke slowly. "Like...if the artists are willing to tell people their items could be purchased in my store. I could even offer them a reception or something. The joint promotion could be good."

Penny nodded. "That's the spirit."

Why did these ideas come so naturally to everyone but him? It was hard to be patient with himself when the only lesson he was learning was how very little he knew.

"Do you have a place for this thing yet? We can help you carry it over." Nate knocked back the last of his coffee and set the mug on an old sewing machine table.

Kyle grabbed one end of the table. "Sure thing. No time like the present."

Nate grasped the other end, and they inched the table through the gauntlet and out the door to the sidewalk.

"Chairs!" Penny pointed back inside. "Do you want mismatched chairs? That's a really trendy look right now. I can pick out a few that would go with the table and clean them off for you."

Kyle peeked inside his store. Jacques was fast asleep in the window after a long walk. Knowing his dog was safe, he propped the door open. He didn't know how to say thank you to Penny for the table, or for the offer of chairs. Accepting kindness from others wasn't a skill he learned. Deep down he knew it was mutually beneficial, but it still felt lopsided, as if he should be bartering with her for the kind acts.

"Chairs would be really nice of you. Not if it's too much trouble. I can come over and—"

Penny smiled and shook her head. "Don't you dare. You have enough to do. Let your neighbors give you a hand."

"Think of us as the world's smallest chamber of commerce." Adelle shooed him to the side and grabbed a corner of the table. He made room for her. Her closeness sent electricity through his skin, into his veins, and through his chest. It pounded in his ears, and his hands went clammy when her elbow brushed his.

"Let's get this thing inside," she said. "I wanna see the store."

They edged the table through the door, and Kyle caught his reflection in the window. He'd inherited a lot more than his jawline and nose from his mother. He also got her refusal to accept help, her inability to take something without strings attached, and the kind of pride that kept her isolated so no one would know that she needed anything. He went out into the world to do better, to conquer those things, but instead he learned to nurture his own sense of wanting, to hold close to his chest what he needed from the world. It was almost as if fulfilling his needs and chasing his wants would only lead to more needs and wants. It was easier to accept the shortcomings of money, security, comfort than it was to make new ones. And the only way to ease those shortcomings was to work harder and dig deeper.

"How about right here?" Kyle paused and lowered his end of the table. "Then people will see it when they come in, but it won't be in their way."

"Whoa." Nate stood back and took it all in, the brick walls and the industrial shelves, the ancient paint on the tin ceiling tiles, the wide-plank floors. The old candy table was polished and filled with brightly colored napkins and linens. Plates and mugs and drinking glasses rested on shelves, elegant in their simplicity. "Penny's right. This store is incredible. This looks like something out of a catalog."

Penny dropped a chair at the head of the table. "What about this one? I like the classic windsor chair look."

Adelle studied it, hands on her hips. "Looks great to me."

"I have more where that came from." Penny wiped dust from her hands to her jeans. "I meant to apologize for the other day, too."

"What for?"

"I didn't mean to be such a Debbie Downer. You're going to do great at this. Running a store isn't all that hard. It's not magic. If anyone can do it, you can. It's not magic."

Magic. Where had heard that before?

"No kidding." Adelle spun and in one spot. "This is lush. This is way more than we deserve."

She was wrong. Ramsbolt deserved it just as much as any other town. Maybe even more. Kyle ran a hand through his hair. "Thanks. I think it's gonna take more than magic. I definitely appreciate the support."

* * *

Evening light limned the store purple. Kyle ran a rag cut from an old T-shirt along Penny's old table, but it came away clean. He'd finally won the battle against the settling dust. He brushed packing peanuts from a thick ceramic serving platter, and set it on the table. It wasn't one of those dainty white dishes with a gold band that spoke of unattainable generic elegance. This was a dense platter that called for turkey legs and lakes of gravy. Standing back and taking in the tablescape, he couldn't deny that he'd made the right choice.

Jacques rested in a stream of sunset, chewing on a duck-shaped squeaky toy nearly as big as he was. Little did he know that tomorrow would be a flurry of customers, and the lazy days of unpacking deliveries and setting up shelves were behind them. Jacques shook the toy, and Kyle embraced the chirps and squeaks. They were his only reprieve from the inner dialog that threatened to upend his confidence.

*What if I can't sell anything and I get stuck with inventory? If I can live on seven dollars a day, my food money will run out in five months and three weeks. What if I can't catch up? Where will I go when the money and the luck run out?*

"At least we're staying busy, right?" Kyle wiped sweat from his brow. Jacques lifted his head and barked his assent.

Kyle gathered the last empty boxes and packing materials into a pile. It was worth holding onto some of it, in case someone bought everything, and he had to repack. He carried them to the back of the store, Jacques prancing behind him with the squeaky toy in his mouth. *Chirp. Squeak.*

*Bang. Bang. Bang.*

Jacques jumped to attention, head tilted, an ear flopped over one eye. Kyle brushed packing peanut debris from his sleeves and ruffled the puppy's ears.

"Could be the Publishers Clearing House people with a hundred balloons and a check big enough to solve all our problems. Let's go see."

Jacques bounded after him, ears flopping. Kyle sidestepped a pile of cleaning supplies and wove around the table. He expected Penny or maybe Adelle, but the wind died from his sails at the sight of Zeb at the door, and his chest filled with the heavy swell of dread. They hadn't spoken since that bitter exchange at the farm. Nothing uplifting would drive that man into town on a weekday evening.

"Definitely not good news, then. You stay here, pup. I'll get the door."

Zeb shielded his eyes and peered into the store. He waved as if nothing more foul than acrid smoke had ever passed between them. "Kyle. I see you in there. Open this door up. Let me in."

Kyle fiddled with the toggle until the door released from the jamb. He stood back and ran a hand through his hair. "What's going on? I left the apartment key on your desk and put the truck key back on the nail. I got out as soon as I could, like you asked."

"Calm down. I ain't here to pick at ya. I had business at the hardware store. I came to say it worked." Zeb stroked his beard.

"The engine swap? Of course it worked."

"Not that. The grant you put in for. I ain't got every penny I need. I'll need extra financing to buy better hybrid corn for next year, but that grant got me back most of what I lost so I can pay people and keep things moving."

Kyle had no intention of meeting the man's eyes, let alone give him a tour of his shop and let him pretend to be supportive. He had plenty to be proud of. The store, his future, how far he'd come, and, if Zeb was right, he'd saved the farm from another disaster. He wasn't making room for Zeb to cast shadows.

Jaw set, one eyebrow raised, Kyle faced him. "That's all you came for?"

"I lashed out at you." Zeb's mouth twisted into a gnarled grin. "I do apologize for being hurt."

Kyle folded his arms. "You apologize for being hurt? That's an interesting way of putting it."

"I ain't good with words. You were a valued employee to me. More than that. And it hurts when someone who rescued you leaves you. I ain't vulnerable or whatever kids say these days, but when you get to be my age the only energy you got left is the emotional kind."

Kyle dropped his arms to his sides and shoved his hands in his pockets. "It wasn't a personal attack, me starting this store. I'm sorry I hurt your feelings when I left, but I have to do this, or I'll never forgive myself for not trying. What you said about my mother, on the other hand. That was a personal attack."

"All I was saying is that stubborn runs in your family. Just be stubborn 'bout the right stuff." Zeb took a step into the room and craned his neck to see around the clutter. "Mess in here. I'm surprised you're not begging to come back."

Kyle cleared his throat. "Everything is going just fine. If I can rescue you a hundred times, I can certainly rescue myself."

The arched eyebrow said Zeb didn't believe him. "Yeah, well I got more faith in you than you think. You'll be fine in the long run, but I'm not buying it just yet. How bad is it?"

Kyle threw his head back and looked to the ceiling for respite. "It's fine. Everything's fine."

"Bullshit. Your daddy told me to look out for you, and I've been looking. You ain't fine."

"This is fine. I got turned down for a small business loan, but I got the money to stock the shelves and maybe the only reason the lights are on is because utilities are included in the rent, but I'll get by."

"That sounds more like the truth." A shine of satisfaction lit Zeb's cheeks. Kyle shot a look at Jacques, who examined the scene with his trademark inquisitive tilted head. "I wish I could help, but a long time ago I learned that advice and experience are more valuable than money. The best I can do for you is this: When you think you're at your lowest, look down and see how much lower you can get. Then, look up and see where you fell from. You've fallen before. It don't matter how you get up, you just gotta do it, son."

Zeb had never called him that before. Son. It hung in the air with the last of the sunset and the faint aura of Zeb's cigarettes.

Kyle probed between his teeth with the tip of his tongue and nodded. "I suppose you're right."

"I got one other thing to say. Your daddy and I were good friends. He might not have been the best at working out his problems, but he was a good man."

"*Is* a good man."

"He is. I couldn't help him no more, but I could help you. You being around was like having my friend there. You left, and it was like losing him a second time. You tell him I said hi, even if he don't know me no more." Zeb turned to the door. "Don't be a stranger."

The tight bind of wounded pride within Kyle stretched and snapped, and warm resignation spread through him. All the trials he'd seen Zeb endure, all the walls the man had thrown up against modernity and the choices he'd refused to make for the sake of not letting go...maybe they weren't the senseless avoidances of an old man. Maybe they were sentimental binds.

"I won't be a stranger. I don't get out that way very often, especially with my car being the mess that it is. The store takes up a lot of time."

"I don't expect to see you much." Zeb looked back over his shoulder, scanning the room. "This ain't what he'd have wanted for you, but I reckon if you're happy, he'd have let it go." The door fought Zeb. It nearly flung the man into the wall when it let go. Leaves and an empty chip bag flew in with a gust of air, just one more thing to clean. Zeb turned to him one last time. "I never thought you were much for farmland, anyway. I coulda used you as a scarecrow. Stuck out like a sore thumb. That's how I know you're gonna make it out here. If anyone can, it'll be you. You got one last check coming to ya. It'll be in the mail. And you gotta clean up that ceiling. That paint's gonna fall on somebody and give 'em lead poisoning."

With that, he was gone. Those were the kindest words the old farmer had spoken to him, and if they were the last, they'd be good enough. Jacques bounded across the room, pounced on a leaf, and tore it to shreds. His whole body wagged with his tail.

Kyle scooped him up and carried him to the display window. Jacques licked his jaw.

"We're gonna be okay, little guy. We have no choice, because you eat *a lot.*"

Jacques leapt from his arms to the ledge and scratched at an itch on his neck. Kyle leaned his head back. Zeb had a point. The old ceiling tiles were flaking. They were horrible for his cell phone signal, too.

"What do you think? Ten foot ceilings? I'm five foot ten, and they're…"

So high up. He'd fallen a long way over the years. He'd taken many little leaps of faith and never once truly landed on his feet. If only he'd taken one big leap earlier, he wouldn't have wasted all that time and money, and he'd have something to show for all his energy. Now his uphill climb was even steeper.

"No more messing around. I have to throw all my cards on the table. I have to get these classes off the ground. And I have to ask Penny if I can borrow a ladder, but that's for another day. We have a grand opening tomorrow, and we're gonna need some sleep."

# CHAPTER NINETEEN

Kyle laid awake, one leg dangling to the floor, one arm flung over his eyes. Every minute that passed felt like weeks. He needed to sleep but excitement for the grand opening kept his synapses firing. When he reached for his phone to check the time, the light fell on boxes and bags, reminding him that he hadn't unpacked a thing. More worried about the store than his clothes, his entire life was still packed away. His skin frizzled with anticipation, and he itched to move.

He flung the sheets to the side, blanketing the snoring puppy.

*If you can't beat 'em, join 'em.*

While coffee sputtered into his mug, he unpacked bags of shirts, grease-stained jeans, and balls of holey socks. He'd need a new wardrobe. At least something that didn't belong in a barn. All that worrying about whether the store would fit in town and all those fears about not belonging, and he hadn't even bothered to dress himself for the part.

The coffee maker beeped, and he strained to his feet, stretching over bags and twisting around boxes to reach the kitchen. Coffee warming his hands, he leaned in the doorway. The damage spread out before him like a scene from a cop movie after a shakedown, clothes and books and bags strewn everywhere. He resisted the impulse to throw it all away. Starting over again would be more expensive than his wallet could bear.

"I'm forty-two years old, and I can't afford to buy a new pair of jeans. For now."

Jacques raised his head, and his jaw widened into a splitting yawn. Kyle blinked into his coffee cup, dark and bitter.

"We're gonna slay this thing."

The puppy blinked up at him, clearly annoyed at the interruption.

"You might not care right now, but you will when you have fifty toys and a dog bed the size of a castle." Kyle set the coffee cup on a box of CDs he couldn't bear to part with, even though he didn't have a CD player. "Seriously, Jacques. The people of this town are gonna love this place. But I could really use an omen right about now."

He fell to his knees and pulled a box close. The sweet musk was his childhood, huddled under blankets with a flashlight, sneaking off in the night to other worlds, wrapped in a cloak of old ink and yellowed paper.

*Treasure Island.*

He flipped through the pages. Just after page 131 was the five-leaf clover he'd found as a kid. The memory of finding it was long gone, lost in the ether with trillions of other moments. He'd forgotten he had it at all until Adelle showed up with a one around her neck. She'd been so excited when he signed those papers, and she'd had so much faith in him and his plan. She had said the town board loved his idea.

He ran his finger along the delicate stem, pressed nearly flat by years between pages.

*My omen.*

He smiled and closed the pages, careful not to disturb the clover. It was fun to think about, but there were no such things as omens and good luck charms. If there were, good luck would have started the day he found it. Adelle would be running a flower empire. The entire town would be rich beyond its wildest dreams for having grown two of them. He couldn't rely on luck. It would take hard work and sacrifice, and if this wasn't hard work and sacrifice enough, then Kyle had nothing left to give.

Adelle had said there was hope for us yet.

"I hope she's right."

He placed the book on the top shelf, and grabbed another. *The Sword in the Stone.*

"Maybe it'll take a little magic, too."

*Where did I see that?* Magic.

Jacques shook off his sleep, ears flapping. He padded into the kitchen for water, his bowl clanking against the linoleum as he slurped.

"It was in that pie recipe." Kyle pushed the box of books aside and sprang to his feet.

His grandmother's recipe was in the box, where he'd stashed it after his last failed attempt.

*The rest is Ramsbolt magic. Only a true Nolan from Ramsbolt can figure out the secret of this pie. Once you do, share it with no one.*

He tugged the freezer door open. A bag of icy berries sat on top of a brick of frozen bread. He threw open the cabinets. Sugar and flour. Salt and cinnamon. Cooking was art, but baking was science, and there was no room for guess work or dashes and pinches. He measured with care, making the filling first so it could rest and meld, then he rolled out the crust. While it baked, he unpacked the past. Childhood books and teenage CDs, textbooks and satin ties found their way onto shelves and into the closet. It wouldn't feel like home until the boxes were gone and he'd lived in it a while, but with his stuff put away, at least it looked like a place he belonged.

The timer buzzed, and he pulled the pie from the oven. As the steam subsided, he took Jacques for his morning walk. By the time they returned, the pie was cool enough to touch. Jacques tugged on Kyle's pant leg, begging for play.

"Not yet, buddy. Just a few more minutes."

Blueberry filling had bubbled up in the lattice, staining it deep purple. The edges were browner than he would have liked.

"Maybe I need to invest in one of those silicone pie crust shields."

He checked his phone for the time. Eight twelve, already. The store had to open in a few hours. He still had to get to Marissa's to pick up the tray of pastries he'd ordered. And he had to find something to wear that didn't look like he crawled out from under a tractor. His fingers itched at the utensil drawer. Only fifteen minutes had passed, but the pie had rested long enough that the crust didn't burn his fingers. He grabbed a knife and sank it into the pie.

Clots of flour clung to the berries, and the crust was a soggy disaster.

"What am I doing wrong?"

Somewhere in the bedroom his cell phone rang. Kyle dropped the knife on the counter and made for the bedroom, Jacques hot on his heels. The phone was tangled in his sheets.

"Hello?"

The puppy flopped and pranced across the floor, his duck squeaky toy in his mouth. He flung it into the air, his ears flapping, and chased it out of the room. Kyle raised the volume and followed Jacques into the kitchen to wrestle the toy from the dog's mouth.

"One second, Jacques. Sorry. Hello?"

"Christa with a C again, calling from—"

"The appliance store. Yeah. Everything is ready here for delivery tomorrow. I have a clear path to the back of the store." He could feel through the phone that she wasn't calling to confirm. The ominous envelope from the credit card company sitting unopened on the counter with the rest of the mail could have told him that.

"I'm afraid to say the payment was declined."

Heat rushed over him. His fingers tingled, and he began to sweat. He maxed out his card, and it bounced. He'd put off checking the balance because the reality was harsher than the avoidance, but the long-term damage would dismantle his credit score and make a loan even more unattainable.

*You never should have bought that inventory first.*

He kicked at the edge of the counter with his shoe.

*But opening a store without inventory would have been stupid, too. And it wasn't inventory that pushed you over the edge. It was the plumbing and the heater.*

He ran a hand over his face. "It's probably the expiration date."

"You said seven twenty-four, right?" Her words were slow and measured.

He swallowed hard, his throat dry. "Yeah. They've been glitchy lately. I'll have to give them a call."

"If you have another card you'd like to use, I can—"

"No! I'll give you a call back in a few."

Christa with a C sighed. "We keep quotes on file forever, but the price is only good for sixty days." There was a critical lilt to her voice, as if her time had been wasted before. He felt like enough of a failure without the help of customer service. He turned his back on the fruit soup pie.

"Good to know. Thank you. I'll be in touch. Right away."

He couldn't afford to have his day derailed with sinking feelings or knots in his chest. He had a grand opening to face and a tray of pastries to collect. He needed to keep his spirits high, accept that it would take some time to build the dream he'd fostered for so long. Hand wringing and problem solving were for tomorrow. Today was opening day. Looking pitiful in front of customers wouldn't win him any support.

He threw the phone down on the stack of unopened mail and tossed the toy back to Jacques.

"Sorry. I know you want to play. I have to go get this tray of food from Marissa, and—"

And what? Have a heart attack? Find a billion dollars in a crack in the sidewalk? All the words of support from Zeb and Penny and Adelle were nothing compared to the sound of his father's voice in his head, telling him how stupid he was to choose that run-down town over somewhere with opportunities. If he'd listened to his gut, he'd still be lying on the floor of Zeb's barn, but at least he would still have an available balance on his credit card.

That sinking feeling in his stomach was the snapping of his safety net, but there wasn't time to wallow. He changed into jeans and a T-shirt, threw on an old dress shirt with the buttons undone.

"No. You wore this one when you signed the lease. Adelle will think it's all you own."

His heart contracted at the thought of Adelle. It had been years since his insides fluttered at the thought of a girl, since he weighed the likelihood of running into her.

Adelle would definitely show up. She was the town manager, after all.

She'd want to be there to show support. Maybe.

He threw the shirt on his bed and pushed hangers aside in his closet. He grabbed a shirt just like it, but blue.

The puppy followed him down the stairs.

He pulled his jacket tight and paused at the door to ruffle Jacques's ears.

"Stay put, okay? Guard all our stuff. I'll be right back. I know you don't have thumbs, but if you get a chance to throw away that pie and clean the kitchen while I'm gone, I won't be sad about it."

Jacques barked and wagged as Kyle locked the door.

He rushed through chilly morning air down Main Street, happy to expel some energy. It didn't settle his nerves, but at least he wasn't sitting on a stool worrying about finances.

Marissa's bakery was every child's dream, with pastel-colored walls and candy-colored counters, and the smell of fresh-baked cookies hanging in the air. Marissa was somewhere in the back, banging metal trays together, but it was almost a joy to wait. His checking account was down to his last fifty bucks anyway and the pastry tray he'd ordered cost half that much. Chewing on his lower lip had become a new pastime, a stinging diversion from the boiling acid in his belly. He zipped his jacket and grabbed a magazine from the counter to flip through while he waited. A kid with a fist full of cotton candy grinned on the cover. Inside was a connect-the-dots picture that depicted a partial barnyard animal, a chicken plainly visible. What was the point if it was that easy?

Marissa hummed her way from the kitchen and dropped a tray of cinnamon buns on the counter. "You must be Kyle." She reached a hand across the counter, and he gave her a firm shake. "Adelle said nice things about you."

"She has?" His stomach filled with butterflies again at the mention of Adelle's name. Kyle passed his debit card across the counter, his hand steadier than he thought it would be.

"Yup. She says your store is going to be amazing."

Head down, eyes fixed on the magazine cover, he wanted to pry for more, but he focused his willpower on his debit card, begging the transaction to go through. Clenching a fist to hide his shaking hand, he rested his knuckles on the counter. He hadn't confirmed his bank balance before he left the store.

Marissa tapped her fingers on the register and gave him an impatient grin. He returned it, the start of a story swirling in his mind. Card trouble. Identity theft.

The register pinged, and she handed the card back with a flourish.

"I have the tray in the back for you," Marissa said. "One second."

His scalp prickled, and he ran his hands through his hair while she rushed back to the kitchen. He checked the time on his phone.

"Here you go." The plastic-wrap covered tray held two dozen danishes, turnovers, and strudels. "I hope you have a great opening day."

"You and me both."

"I'm stuck here all day, but I'll be down to see the store very soon. Penny tells me you have an eye for design."

"Thanks. That's nice of her to say. I hope she's right." He lifted the tray and slipped out the door.

Wind whipped down Main Street, ruffling the plastic wrap and pushing his hair into his eyes. Across the street, a woman climbed from a station wagon, and she paused to watch him pass. He shrank under her scrutiny, but he deserved judgment for being so stupid, for running out of money, maxing out a credit card, and not being able to afford a few ovens. This was not how he imagined it would be. Jumping into this dream had been one of the most irresponsible decisions of his life.

He picked up the pace, lungs straining against gulps of crisp air and his head lowered as he pushed against the wind. Every fiber of his being seemed caught up in a wind tunnel of doubt and dread.

At the store, he left the pastries on the counter and unzipped his jacket. Jacques bounded to his feet, doing a whole body wag, squeaky duck locked in his jaw. Kyle braced for the puppy's pounce and rolled the tension from his neck.

*Poor Jacques. He didn't ask for any of this.*

There wasn't time for play, but Kyle grasped the toy and sat on the floor, poised for a tug-of-war he couldn't commit to. His heart wasn't in it, and he knew the dog felt it. Despite the anxiety and negativity he'd spewed everywhere he went, Jacques still loved him, still needed him, and still wanted to play.

Jacques tugged with all his might on his end of the duck, his puppy muscles straining. The duck toy squeaked.

Everything looked different from the ground. The old candy table was massive. He imagined a tiny Adelle in pigtails, a dollar bill clutched in her fist and her eyes wide with delight, standing on tiptoe to peer over the edge. But instead of candy, it held cloth napkins folded in colorful waves, pillows of linen and silk. The walls looked a mile high, chipped bricks and crumbling mortar, reaching up to the ceiling, where light glinted from copper peeking through the old paint. His shelves were studded with glass, porcelain, stoneware, and copper pots. In the front window where a general store once showed off its wares, rainbow colored cast-iron stock pots hinted at cozy soups and summer clambakes.

Penny's table loomed just above eye level. An orange plaid table runner and the hint of eucalyptus dangled off the edge, hinting at the decor he'd scraped together. Dried hydrangea and sage tangled with the eucalyptus, with white plates and stoneware platters.

It was warm. Intimate. Personal. Nothing grandiose or implausible for even a simple kitchen. He'd made the best of what he could afford. Whether his decision to start a store was a good one or not, fate would determine. But he'd created the thing he'd wanted all along—restrained design, tasteful and classic, that complimented any palate and didn't talk down to any food it presented.

He tugged the toy from Jacques's grip and tossed it across the room. Claws scrambled on the hardwood floor as the puppy bounced after his prey.

"I'll have to cut your nails before bed. Don't let me forget." Kyle got to his feet and peeled the plastic wrap off the pastries. He lit a candle at the counter. "It looks great, but it still smells like my blueberry pie failure in here. And it's almost time to unlock this door."

* * *

The sun cast long shadows across the floor of his empty store. Nine hours had passed since Penny and Nate stopped by for donuts. Six hours and twelve minutes since Adelle waved from across the street and fire washed over his gut at the sight of her.

No one else had come.

All the planning, unpacking, and cleaning, had amounted to nothing.

A hot wave of reality washed over him, and his mouth went dry.

*Oh, shit.*

He hadn't made a single flyer. He hadn't put up a sign or an ad in the paper. He hadn't told the town he was opening at all.

He'd wasted precious dollars on pastries and limited energy on a deadline and done no marketing at all. He had nothing to show for all that effort. And he'd accomplished nothing with his day, but the unfurling of paperclips and meager attempts to bend them back into shape while counting up the list of things he didn't have as the hours ticked by. No money, no family, no marketing knowledge, no support system except for his neighbors and his dog.

"I can't sit here and look at this empty store." The floor creaked beneath him as he moved to the table. Slumped in a chair he'd borrowed from Penny, he rubbed his temples. Jacques dropped a knotted rope at his feet and nibbled at the cuff of his jeans.

"Ten more minutes, okay? I just need to think. Then we'll lock the door and go upstairs."

It took all his effort to heave himself out of the chair and plod to the shelf of barware. He pulled a rocks glass from the shelf and filled it with the Wild Turkey he kept behind the counter, but stopped short of taking a sip.

"Know what I like about this glass? It has a heavy bottom. It feels substantial. And it was handblown glass, apparently. That's why I picked it." He held the glass to the light. "It makes the whiskey look good, too. And no one will ever know about it, because I have no idea how to market a store."

He shot a glance at the door as he took a sip. His luck, ten people would walk through, catch him drinking on the job, and brand him the town drunk. But the street was empty. He locked the door, fell back into the chair, and knocked back the glass. All he wanted was to be alone, so his brain could rest.

"All those somber businessmen and all those boring dinners. You think I would have absorbed something about how to pretend like I'm not terrified while running a business." Jacques dropped the tug-of-war toy at his feet, and Kyle grasped the end. No match for the puppy, he lost his grip. "Am I being punished for something? What if Tracey was right, and I wasted my time? Maybe I'm too old and risk averse to put in the work, and I missed my chance. Do old dogs really ever learn new tricks?"

The puppy sat, tongue dripping on his toy.

Kyle paced, treading the floor in front of the shelves, letting the echo of his steps feed his audacity. "I have to do something. I have to get up, take something for this damn headache, and start thinking straight. Wallowing won't help."

A tapping at the door sent Jacques running.

"Are you open?" Adelle's voice was deadened by wood and thick glass. He squinted out the window, unlocked the door, and held it open for her. "How did your day go?"

Jacques lunged at her knees, and she dropped to the floor to ruffle his collar.

Kyle drew in a breath and let it leak out slow. He wanted to lie, to say it was great and soak up the glow that radiated from her, but she was across the street all day. He didn't want her sympathy. He just wanted her company and some of that blazing fever that shallowed his breath and sent his heart bolting when she was near. He gave her the truth.

"It was pretty terrible."

She stood and brushed dog hair from her hands to her hips. "It'll take some time. Penny struggled at first, too."

Her knowing smile was like drinking warm comfort, and he wanted more of it. "I'm glad you came by. I needed a beautiful distraction."

*Stop flirting with her.*

Adelle's cheeks flushed pink. It was a good look. "The place looks great. It looks like you've been doing this your whole life."

The laugh escaped him before his mood could reject it. "That's nice to hear, because I'm terrified of everything and only hiding half of it."

"Nah, you have to have faith. And figure out how to reach your audience. It takes time."

He glanced at the ceiling. Light picked up the shiny copper peeking from beneath the paint. "Marketing. Yeah. I suck at that, apparently."

"You could definitely collaborate with businesses in town, and even some artists, I'd bet. I'm totally up for putting together some kitchen herb pots even if you're not ready to start that cooking thing." She glanced at the dark and empty back of the store.

He rubbed the stubble on his chin. "We could do that. I could bundle them with some kind of little tray." Every little bit would help.

"See. You have great ideas. It'll just take some time." She rounded the table, running her fingers over plates and drinking glasses. "Everything is so pretty. You should try posting pictures on social media." She spun and turned to the old candy table. "Oh, my gosh. You brought this back to life!" She rushed to the table, and he followed. "This is great. I'm so glad you found a way to use this."

Her eyes glistened, and she turned from him. He swung to the counter and added to his drink, giving her space. Whatever memory the table dug up for her, it was one he couldn't visit.

"I know you cared a lot about it," he said. "I wanted to clean it up and put it to use. It wasn't all that dirty, really, just took a little wiping down and some wood polish. I mean, it weighs a thousand pounds so it's gonna stay where it is, but it was easy to incorporate into the store. I'm glad you're happy it's still here." He took a sip of his whiskey and rested his hip against the table. "Care for a drink?"

She waved a hand. "No, thanks. I'm a wine girl."

"Red or white?" He had a bottle of each upstairs, if they hadn't turned to vinegar in the years since he bought them.

"Either, really. But I'm good."

"I don't drink a lot. I don't want to give that impression."

"No, no you deserve to unwind after a big day. Especially this. A grand opening is a big…"

He followed her gaze to the counter where the pastries sat under plastic wrap on a stoneware platter. Her face fell.

"No one came? No one?" She offered him a raised eyebrow and a sympathetic look. He accepted.

"No one. Well, Penny and Nate came by. Maybe I went a little overboard at Marissa's. Want one?" He extended a hand. "Please. If I eat all these I won't fit in my store anymore."

"I love her croissants." Adelle peeled back the wrap and tugged one from the platter.

Her presence was an escape. Tension had become his closest companion lately, and it lifted like a fog when she was around. Everything seemed crisper. Cleaner. It wasn't just talking shop or making small talk. It was her. Her voice, her eyes, her smell.

"It might not be healthy, but these'll keep you busy for a while." She lifted the croissant. She was close. Close enough to touch. To take the croissant from her hand and pull her closer.

He scooped Jacques into his arms. "Staying busy is definitely the plan."

"Things will look up. Everybody thinks so. Penny. Nate. It just takes a little time. There's no magic to it, just experience."

He craved proximity. How did she have this much hold over him? The squirming puppy licked his face, and he let Jacques jump to the floor.

He took a step and stopped himself, holding in a breath of her. He would definitely let down the town manager and prove himself a failure if he made a move. The distraction of her was too great. He'd lose track of everything. He'd lose control of the store. His whole world would fall apart.

"Dinner. I'd love it if you would come over for dinner." Words formed, sentences fell from his mouth without any concern for his wants or needs. "Let me cook for you."

The last time he cooked, he set the smoke alarm off with an egg.

Adelle lowered her head, chewing the last piece of croissant. He couldn't give her a chance to say no.

"I love to cook. I don't get to cook for people often enough. Let's do a test run of a recipe for my cooking classes."

*Cooking classes you can't have?*

"What do you say? Dinner?"

A slow smile lit up her face, and her eyes met his. "You could write it off as a business expense."

"Three for one. Time with you, recipe practice, and a smart business decision." But it wasn't. Nothing about spending time with Adelle was a good business decision. "Tomorrow?"

Adelle chewed her lower lip. "I'm in."

# CHAPTER TWENTY

Kyle rubbed sleep from his eyes while coffee sputtered into the pot. He drummed his fingers on the counter, impatient for the bitter fuel, but he didn't really need it. His entire body frizzled with anticipation. With everything going on, how had he ended up with a date tonight? With Adelle?

Jacques dropped the squeaky duck on his foot and looked up, expectant. Kyle grabbed it and flung it toward the bathroom door, and the yellow lab puppy clambered after it, feet scrambling for purchase.

"We have a date tonight. Are you excited?"

The slobbery toy landed on his foot, and he lobbed it back into the hall. He was as ready for playtime as Jacques.

"We have a lot to do around here."

His little table was carpeted with recipes on scraps of paper, notes hastily scrawled as he tried to pull a menu together for a cooking class. Pulling them into a tidy stack, he threw them in a drawer.

He flung open the refrigerator door and dumped creamer in his coffee, Jacques under foot with the toy in his jaws.

"What do I cook for Adelle?"

He had everything he needed to make a good soup. Bread was doable. A salad. He had a few potatoes and vegetables. He could pick up a small roast and make pie for dessert.

"How does blueberry pie sound? Think I can get it right this time?"

Jacques wagged his tail and spun around.

"It's worth a shot." He pushed bags of freezer-burned vegetables around, but there were no blueberries. "Looks like I'm out. I'll have to swing by the market for some."

He slammed the drawer and a thundering crash rose beneath his feet, dying with a crescendo of broken glass, a shattering pitch that sent Jacques scurrying for safety under the bed. Kyle's heart leapt into his throat, pulse pounding in his ears, and hair raised on the back of his neck. He shut the door to keep Jacques upstairs, raced down the steps in his socks, and spun around the newel post to face a nightmare of broken dishes and ceiling tiles.

Slabs of his beautiful copper ceiling had crashed down on Penny's farm table, crushing the table setting. Shards of broken plates and glasses shot across the floor creating a glittering minefield.

He brushed glass from a chair and slumped into it, head in his hands, waiting for the adrenaline wave to wash over him and the tide to turn and his heart to slow. Stress was supposed to be rewarded with momentum, money, or some sort of progress, but this was ridiculous. All this effort should be bringing people in the door, not bringing down the ceiling. He grabbed a dented ceiling tile. It was cold in his hand. A few old nails had given way. Jacques running around upstairs must have loosened a few.

Pulse steadied, he pushed out of the chair, grabbed a broom and a dustpan from the back, dragged the trash can from behind the counter, and swept up the floor. Broken pottery jingled and clanged as he emptied it into the can.

The tiles weren't damaged, and Penny's table was unscathed. His inventory was a write off. At least it wasn't the table or an artist's plates he'd offered to sell on consignment. *It wouldn't be a loss if I had insurance, but who can afford that?*

A knock at the door made him jump. A man in his thirties with dark hair and an athletic build peered in at him. He wore a green jacket with a messenger bag slung over his shoulder. Kyle unlocked the door and flung it open, leaning on the broom.

"I just had a small disasters, and I—"

The man adjusted the strap of his bag and pushed through the door. Kyle stepped out of his way.

"Nice store you have here."

Kyle closed the door and glanced over his shoulder at the debris. The table was still a mess, but the floor was mostly free of broken glass. A pushy customer was still a customer.

"Welcome. Feel free to browse. And excuse the mess. Had a bit of an incident with some ceiling tiles. Let me know if I can help you find anything."

"Thanks." The man peered into the old candy table. He examined a napkin ring. "You're Kyle then, right?"

"Yup." Kyle dragged the trash can to the table. He lifted a giant shard of platter and let it shatter in the can.

The man turned to him. "Where do you find the things you sell here?"

*Strange question.* He shook a placemat over the can and glass shards glittered like winter flurries. "Lots of different places. Some come from larger vendors and others, like those platters, come from artists."

The man raised an eyebrow. "Are they Maine artisans?"

Kyle cleared his throat and straightened his shoulders. "Most of them. Some are from further away. The inventory will change over time, so we…I may have more local artists represented at some point. Maybe even do some kind of artist meet and greet."

The shopper tore his eyes from a blue-glazed ceramic coffee mug and leveled them on Kyle. It was a scrutiny that peeled away layers and questioned his authority. Kyle's insides twisted in a knot. He hadn't had enough coffee to prepare him for the test. He wasn't even sure it was a test.

*Who is this guy?*

"What made you choose to open this store in this town?"

Kyle layered broken shards of dinner plates in his palm and threw them into the can harder than he needed to. The splintering shatter wasn't satisfying enough.

He spun to face the man who'd intruded on his morning. "I don't know what you're trying to imply. Do you think Ramsbolt doesn't deserve a store like this? Or do you think the store's not good enough for Ramsbolt."

Both hands raised in surrender, the shopper winced. "I'm just trying to put a story together here."

Kyle rolled his eyes. "What do you need a story for? This isn't a bookstore. It's a kitchen supply store."

"I'm Stuart. Journalist. I run *The Ramsbolt Reader.*" The man's words were intended to cut with sharp edges that dripped with scorn.

"How am I supposed to know that?" Kyle's mouth went dry. He wasn't prepared for an interrogation. He didn't have an elevator speech about the store, and every time he tried to describe the place, it sounded nothing like his vision for it. If he turned the guy away, he'd definitely make a bad name for himself and the store. Besides, this wasn't the first time he'd had to turn a bad start into profit.

*I can make this work. He's here, so I might as well talk to him. If I don't, he'll probably write a story about how the ceiling is caving in and the whole place is covered in broken glass.*

Kyle yanked a chair from beneath the table and brushed the broom across a seat. He gestured to it.

"Have a seat. Ask away."

Stuart shrugged his bag from his shoulder and eyed the chair before perching on the edge of it. He propped a mint green notepad on his knee. "Um." He cleared his throat. "What has your experience been like so far with the new lease to sale program? You're the first tenant, so people will be interested in your experience."

Nudging his chair with his foot, Kyle sat. He needed to form his words carefully. The truth was the last thing people wanted to hear, and it would be the last thing Adelle would need him to say.

"It's been full of unexpected moments, I guess you could say. The heater blew up. A supply line to the toilet failed, and the downstairs bathroom got soaked. The copper tiles just fell off the ceiling a few minutes ago. Old buildings are like that, I guess. Things go wrong, and you roll with the punches."

Stuart didn't look up from his notepad. "What was the application process like?"

"It was easy. I texted back and forth with Adelle a bit. I filled out an application and submitted a proposal. The town board voted, and I had an answer within a week."

"So the town took an interest in your business plan?"

Kyle shrugged. "I guess you could say that. They didn't ask for a full business plan, so I provided a basic outline of the goods and services I would offer."

"I see. Did they ask for any financial history or do a background check?"

"No, I—"

"And what has the town been like to work with?"

"It's been easy. Carol offers some discounts at the hardware store that take the edge off. Grey showed up pretty fast to fix the plumbing, and Martin was really helpful with the heater."

"Really? You don't think he was expensive?"

"I guess that's relative. I needed a whole new heater, and he's the only guy in town. So you just pay what he asks and hope you don't need him again any time soon, right?"

Stuart sneered. "Good answer. What's been the hardest part?"

*Everything.* He scanned the store. Affording inventory had been painful. So had being on his hands and knees scraping layers of dust off the old floors. Swallowing his pride and asking Penny for the table had created a lump in his chest that might be permanent. But those hadn't been the hardest things. "Managing my expectations, I guess. I know what profits I need to make to survive. I know what my bottom line needs and what I want for the store's future, but making all of those things happen isn't easy."

"And what advice would you give someone wishing to consider opening a store here?"

"Same advice I'd have given any client looking to expand when I worked in finance. Do your research. Know the consumer base, the demographics. Know how and where people spend. It isn't all about location. It's also about timing and giving people what they want."

Stuart looked up, his face blank. Slow narrowing eyes leveled their inspection, and Kyle sat straighter, refusing to bend under them. "And what kind of research did you do prior to putting *this* store *here*."

"This is a work of passion."

Stuart didn't jot down the answer. "So you're giving people advice you didn't take yourself?"

"I've wanted to open this store since I was young. That's why I opened it. The timing was right."

"Right for you. But is it right for Ramsbolt?"

He sat straighter, jaw clenched. "I don't understand the nature of the question."

Stuart gestured around the room, at nothing in particular and everything at the same time. "All of this. It's such a departure from everything else in town." He flipped pages of his notepad. "Here. I made a note. I looked in the phone book, and you're the only Nolan. I did some asking at Helen's Tavern, just to see how people felt about Adelle's plan, and some people said that you're new here. A guy—his name was Bern—said that you just moved here? Is that true?"

He let the ire etch on his face, glazing his eyes and knitting his brow. He wanted to ask Stuart why he hadn't done more himself, but he let moments pile up as the man squirmed under their weight.

Stuart tapped his notebook with his pen. "You haven't been here long. Where did you come from? Where did you live before you came here?"

Kyle stood. "We're done here."

Stuart scribbled in his notebook, and Kyle strained to read it, but it was some form of shorthand that made no sense right side up, let alone upside down.

"What are you writing?"

"My impressions. That's what I do." Stuart finished scribbling. He put the notepad and pen in his bag and stood. "I suspect people will be coming in here in droves to get it once your store is open."

"It is open."

"Is it, now?"

Kyle tugged the door open and gestured to the street, nostrils flaring as he choked back fire. "Thanks for coming by."

"Thanks for your time."

Stuart paused at the edge of the sidewalk and shot a look over his shoulder. "One piece of advice. Maybe rethink your employee dress code. The housecoat is a little casual, don't you think?"

Kyle yelled after him. "I'm not open yet. The store opens at ten."

# CHAPTER TWENTY-ONE

Kyle propped his macroeconomics textbook on the rack above the stove. He turned pages with his left hand, and with his right, he stirred a creamy pesto sauce into some gnocchi.

"I have never seen a college kid read as much as you." Seth whirled into the kitchen, straightening his tie. He picked croutons from a tub and popped one in his mouth. "Rush is almost over. Dining room's clearing out."

Kyle sneered at him. If he could finish his reading before his shift was over, he'd gain at least two hours to study for his business law test. Dr. Herbst was a tough professor, and she wouldn't tolerate less than perfect work.

"Thank God this night's almost over." Kyle dumped the gnocchi on a plate, topped it with shrimp, and pushed it down the counter for garnish.

"A couple of us are getting together after this. Wanna come?" Seth crunched through his croutons.

"Not a chance. I have way too much work to do, and I have a test tomorrow." Kyle squinted at a ticket. Lamb.

Seth was on his heels all the way to the fridge. "Come on, man. You never do anything fun. You cook at the hottest restaurant in town. You were on the cover of that magazine."

"It was a newspaper insert. About restaurant week. Hardly a magazine."

"Still. You should be out there schmoozing the girls. I'd kill for that kind of exposure." Seth took the lid off a tub of marinade and took a deep breath.

Kyle waved a wrapped lamb chop. "I don't want exposure. I want the opposite of exposure. Stop touching my food. And, no, I shouldn't be schmoozing. I should be getting my degree so I can get on with my life. Who says *schmoozing* anyway?"

"I'm just saying you need to cut loose. Look at you. You're all uptight and grumpy, and you're waving lamb chops at people."

"Not people. Just you. You're in my kitchen." Kyle let the lamb gently fall into a cast-iron pan to sear. "And you're interrupting macroeconomics."

Seth dodged a scampering food runner with steaming plates of crab cakes. He sighed and leaned against the metal counter. "That hot hostess girl who quit last month is gonna be there, and she was asking about you."

"I have no memory of any hot hostess girl." He could barely hear Seth over the sizzle, which was perfectly fine. He didn't want to end up in a downward conversational spiral, anyway. He'd already been called weird for not joining in on the locker room banter.

"How could you forget? She was in here every five minutes batting her eyelashes at you."

"Ah. Yeah." That jogged his memory. Fake nails and clumpy

eyelashes half an inch long. She bent across the counter with her top buttons undone, begging him to cook for her.

"If you're trying to motivate me to attend a party instead of studying, you're going to have to work harder than that," Kyle said. He flipped the lamb chop and tapped his textbook with the end of his spatula. "Look, I'm not trying to be ungrateful, but I really have my sights set on a much bigger prize. I do not have time for this."

Seth stepped between him and the stove. He closed the book and tucked it under his arm. "Buddy, I'm doing you a favor. Don't hook up with a girl if you don't want to, but you need to let loose. This book is mine until you do. Show up tonight, and you can have your book back."

* * *

The morning alarm was more obnoxious than usual. Kyle slapped it into submission and threw the covers back. His head throbbed. He could still hear the thump of the music and feel it in his feet. Whoever's house that was, they needed to shim the floorboards. It was fun, though.

His bed listed and an arm flopped across his middle, warm and distinctly feminine, and fragments of the night surfaced like popcorn. Dancing in a dining room. Laughing on a porch swing with feet tossed across his lap. Stumbling up the stairs of his dorm, hot breath, warm skin.

He swung his legs to the floor, and his foot landed on his macroeconomics book, a cold reminder of the looming test and how much reading he had to do before class. He nudged it aside and sat on the edge of the bed, head in his hands. He'd have to read twice as much to catch up from the night he missed. It may have been fun but it was hardly worth the headache. A pack of guys laughed and moved down the hall on their way to class. Water in the glass on his nightstand jiggled with their steps.

He downed two Advil with the rest of the water. Rubbing the sleep from his eyes, he focused. The clock said 9:02.

"Nine?" He jumped to his feet and turned the clock around, as if the reverse could confirm. He punched the remote and the television came to life, some local weather channel scrolling dismal news while classic rock music blared. 9:03.

"Shit." He dropped his pants to the floor, threw on a pair of jeans, ran his fingers through his unkempt hair, and grabbed a long-sleeve T-shirt.

There wasn't time to wake the girl. He scribbled a note on a piece of scrap paper. *Had to run. Late for a test. Didn't want to wake you.* It was all for the better that she wasn't up and ready to go. He didn't want to be that guy, a guy who hooked up with a girl and shoved her out the door in the morning, but his future was in peril, and there wasn't time to put the words together to let her know he wasn't into a long-term thing, that he wouldn't call, and he was sorry. For all he knew, she wasn't all that into him. Worst case scenario, she'd wake, find him gone, read the note, and steal all his stuff. He didn't have anything of value anyway.

He flung his book bag over his shoulder on his way out the door, closing it quietly. Better to let her sleep in.

Campus was freezing. Maine had thrown snow on the ground overnight. Kyle's T-shirt was inadequate, and his ears were ringing with cold. He slipped on patches of ice and blue rock salt as he crossed the campus on its brick walkways, his head down. Icy air froze his breath. Inside the building, students clustered in the hallways, clutching books and bags. He rushed between them, arms wrapped around himself for warmth, muttering to himself. Why did people block hallways when there were a dozen half-decent dining halls?

Outside his classroom, he paused, hand on the cold doorknob. His watch said 9:18. There was no way Herbst would let him take the test with only twelve minutes left. He'd be lucky to get an extension. It might not ruin his whole future, but it felt like it. He turned the knob. Locked.

Kyle slumped to the floor, back against the wall and knees bent, taking up as little room as he could. He'd been an ace student all year. She liked his work, called on him in class. She'd loved his paper about economic growth and unemployment rates. Without a doubt, she'd let him take the test later. He'd beg for extra credit. Ten minutes. He dug a book from his bag and tried to read, but the test he was missing, just on the other side of that door, was a magnet. It drew every thought, every wish, all of his attention and repelled everything else. Stupid Seth. Stupid party.

Clumps of freshmen moved down the hall, obedient and orderly, early for some 101 about psychology or algebra. He stood to make room. Beside him, the door flung open. Classmates filed out, shoving papers in their bags, eyes diverted. He caught the glance of a girl he barely knew, some fellow front-row student. She smirked and some competitive spark flared within him. He pushed past her and into the room.

"Professor?" As the last of his classmates filed out, he stepped up to the desk, but Patricia Herbst was stacking papers and gave her none of his attention.

"Professor. I missed the test."

She turned to him, eyebrows raised. "You did. Am I supposed to write you a sonnet? I don't do sonnets, Kyle. I teach economics."

It wasn't the greeting he hoped for. He didn't deserve compassion for missing a test. Concern, maybe. The benefit of the doubt. She turned to the window where her bag rested in a chair, and Kyle followed.

"I was studying at work yesterday and a coworker stole my book. He thinks I'm overworked and stressed out. He's not wrong, I guess. I had to go to a party to get it back, so I did, and I overslept. God's honest truth." Best to leave out the part with the girl. "I'm really sorry. I've never done this before. School has *always* been my priority. Can I take the test right now? For a penalty? Please?"

Professor Herbst slung her bag over her shoulder and turned to him. "No. You may not." She stepped past him and he followed.

"Please." How could she deny him the right to take a test? Was that even legal? Wasn't there some student bill of rights or something that said he could let off steam and mess up a little even if he hadn't meant to? "I have been the perfect student. I study constantly. I work five days a week."

Kyle followed her through the door and into the hall.

"Yes, I know you have split priorities. I've eaten them. You're a very good cook." She picked up her pace, and Kyle jogged after her.

"Thank you, but I really need to take this test. Please. Pleeease." He hated to beg. His father told him never to beg, to earn what he got and accept his consequences, to demand better for himself and plead his case, but never to beg.

The professor stopped at the door. Cold air rushed through the gaps and cold radiated through the glass. "I have rarely been this disappointed in a student. You will not take this test. You will accept the failing grade."

No. He simply refused to accept that he'd failed the test. He read while walking to work, spent holidays reading the books referenced in textbook footnotes. He was not the kind of student who didn't show up for a test.

"A good business person negotiates, right? What if I do an extra credit essay to make up for it? On the topic of your choosing. Twenty-five pages. At *least* twenty-five pages. And it's already late, so time is of the essence." He had no time to spare. "I can get it to you Monday."

Her feet were planted, her jaw set. Kyle knew that the response wouldn't be good. No one who glared like that was about to issue a ruling of compassion. "Second chances are miracles, not consequences, Kyle. If you want to be successful, you need to act like a successful person."

"Right. I couldn't agree more. That's why I'm willing to put in the work to right my wrong. No one's perfect—"

"I don't expect perfection. I expect hard work. Investors expect consistency from CEOs. You have demonstrated none of those things today. Therefore…" She waved a hand in the air. "Consequences."

"But I promise—"

"You have to walk before you can run. You may think that all the textbook knowledge in the world will get you far, but once you walk away from here with your degree, you'll be starting from the bottom like everyone else. And let me tell you something, Kyle. The unemployment rate is driven by a lot of economic factors. One of them is slackers who don't show up for work. What kind of macroeconomics professor would I be if I didn't teach you the lesson you begged to learn?"

"Message received." Kyle locked his jaw to hide his disappointment, but he heard her loud and clear. He'd been hearing that message forever. Life is supposed to be a hard climb to the top. And rewards are supposed to be hard won.

# CHAPTER TWENTY-TWO

Kyle scraped diced ham from the cutting board into the soup. He tucked the leftover meat in the fridge and paused to scowl at the trifle on the top shelf, layers of red and yellow and white. The market was out of frozen blueberries, so pie was off the table. He opted for trifle instead, but it was just a bowl of strawberries, raspberries, lemon curd, and whipped topping. It was a poor excuse for the blueberry pie he wanted to make for a first date, but given his track record trying to bake it, cardboard would be better than the lumpy soup his pies turned out to be anyway. The trifle, for all its failings, was still better than his attempts at pie.

He snapped a pair of tongs in the air, shooing the butterflies from his stomach, then plunged them into the pot of tuscan white bean soup. Snagging a cheesecloth bag of herbs, he dropped them on a strainer and let it rest on top of the pot. Steam spiraled into his tiny kitchen. It had been ages since he last made it, but it had always been a favorite.

Garlic and thyme drifted through the kitchen. Maybe she hated soup. Or garlic. It wasn't the most graceful thing to eat on a date, but it was too late to change the menu now.

The timer on the stove dinged, and he shoved his hand into an oven mitt shaped like a fish. Yanking a loaf of bread from the oven, the yeasty smell pushed the garlic aside. It smelled like what he wanted home to be, like it never was at the farm. The smell of baking bread was the kind of instant calm he needed to quell his sparking nerves.

He turned off the oven and tossed the roast back in to warm it up again with residual heat, leaning back against the counter, one hand growing warm in his fish mitt. He checked his watch.

"What if she hates all this? Soup was a bad idea. Beans and garlic are not good first date ingredients? Tracey hated garlic. Tracey hated everything I cooked, but she had a good point about garlic."

Having given up hope for cooking scraps, Jacques made his den beneath the kitchen table. Like all smart dogs, he knew that was his best perch for snagging a tasty morsel later. The puppy lifted his head, and his tongue rolled out in a wide, expectant grin.

"I know. Old demons, right?" Kyle spun and grabbed a clean spoon to sip the soup. Time was running out to make graceful improvements, assuming Adelle was prompt. "Needs lemon. I'll do that last. And cheese."

The block of parmesan cost him a fortune, but it was worth every penny. He pulled the cheese from the fridge and plated it with a sprig of thyme.

"Do I look okay? Should I change?"

Jacques tilted his head.

"Is this the wrong shirt? I'm trying too hard to make all this look easy, aren't I?"

The puppy lowered his head to his paws and closed his eyes.

"Thanks. You've been a big help."

He straightened the dish rag on the stove door. The sink was piled with dishes. He rolled up his sleeves and dove in with a sponge. People weren't welcome in his kitchen, not when he cooked for them. Dinner should be like an amusement park, where everything messy happened behind the scenes. He'd never cut it as a celebrity chef, people watching his every move. Everything needed to be perfect for Adelle and somehow, nothing was quite good enough.

Dishes dried and put away, he peered out the double windows to the street below while he dried his hands and the silence settled. She would cross the road soon. He'd rush downstairs, trying to play it cool, then he'd open the door and let her into his kitchen. He'd be ripping down the curtains to his inner sanctum. His mouth went dry as he pictured her there, among his things, judging his dishes. His life was far from perfect, and she was near perfection.

He rolled down his sleeves and opened a window to let in some fresh air. One pane was cracked, the rest old and warbled. He rested his forehead against the glass.

Adelle sailed outside, all grace and ease, and locked her door.

*Jeans. She's in jeans. I'm not underdressed.* The ache in his chest eased a little, though butterflies in his stomach mutated into grasshoppers.

"Okay. Don't touch anything, Jacques. Stay."

He rushed out of the kitchen and paced the narrow hall, heart thundering in his ears. He slammed his bedroom door to hide the pile of laundry on his bed. Clinging to the post at the top of the steps, he paused for a cleansing breath. "Play it cool. She already likes you. Just don't screw it up."

*Count to ten. Or twenty. Don't get fidgety. Don't beat her to the door like a creepy stalker.*

One step at a time, he descended the stairs, and swung around to face the entrance. His pulse throbbed in his neck, and it beat a cadence in his ears that he held in his breath to soften.

The door was unlocked, but he pulled it open, risking being creepy anyway. She smelled like summer, like some flower you'd pass on a gardened street, and she clutched a bottle of wine to her chest.

"Hey! We're eating in my tiny kitchen. It's easier than bringing food down the stairs. Hope you don't mind the mess."

"You're still getting settled," she said. "Nothing to apologize for." She tugged at her scarf, a silky drape with four leaf clovers. He started to stick out his hand to shake hers, but her head was down, so he ran it through his hair before motioning toward the stairs instead. "After you."

"I've never been upstairs here. When it was the General Store it was just stock, I guess. It feels like breaking the rules."

*Tell me about it.* He let her climb a few steps before slipping into the stream of whatever flower scent she wore. He wanted to ask, to imprint the name of it in his memory, but it wouldn't be right. It wasn't a date. Just a business meeting. If he could just get through the first course, his heart would sink back down his throat into its rightful place. His heart would go back to normal. This spell of hers would break.

"It smells amazing up here." The path to the kitchen was obvious; he didn't need to give directions.

"Can I take your coat?" He fumbled in the doorway, torn between the hook in his bedroom, with dog hair everywhere, and the one in the bathroom, presently occupied by a bath towel.

"Nah, this is good." She threw it on the back of a chair and headed for the stove. "What is all this?"

"Courses. Spring mix salad with a raspberry vinaigrette. Tuscan white bean soup." *Oh, God. She's going to touch the food.* He reached around her and snagged his oven mitt. "The soup has ham and garlic, fresh herbs. Sorry the herbs aren't from your shop."

"Smells amazing" She hovered over the pot for a deep breath, and Kyle held his.

"Fresh bread, of course. And a roast with potatoes and veggies. Trifle for dessert. No blueberries, though. There's a shortage of blueberries at the market, apparently."

"That's okay. I've never had trifle." She sniffed the air and smiled. "This is a lot of food. You did a lot of work."

"Not really." He inched to the stove. "Sorry—there's a roast in here staying warm."

He threw on his fish mitt and flung open the door. Adelle stepped back as warm, savory air filled the kitchen. The pan landed on the stove, and his stomach growled.

He swiped his forehead with the back of his hand, clearing away the heat of the kitchen but none of the fear that warmed his skin.

Adelle dangled the bottle of wine. "I brought this. I spent a long time trying to guess, red or white. I went with red." She wrinkled her nose, as if the question were still unresolved. "Have an opener?"

"Red is perfect."

He pulled a corkscrew from a drawer and took the bottle. The cork came out with ease. Adelle took two glasses from the first cabinet she opened, and he filled them.

*Everything about this is perfect.*

The table was barely big enough for two, hardly Kyle's ideal for dining, but form followed function in his tiny apartment, and the centerpiece of cheese would have to do.

"Sorry things are a little cramped and bare in here." He pulled two salads from the fridge, rested them on the table without making a sound, and slid into the seat across from Adelle. The table was too small for both of them and all the food. He shuffled plates to make things fit.

"We do live in tight quarters, don't we? Mine is about the same. It's laid out a little different, though." She settled in her seat, looking calm and comfortable.

"I'd like to see it sometime."

Eye contact sent tingles up his spine, and a fire ignited when she smiled and the corners of her eyes lifted.

"You're welcome to come by any time," she said.

He tore his eyes from hers and stabbed a candied pecan with his fork. It crumbled. He aimed for a cucumber slice instead.

"I might take you up on that."

She waved her fork. "Everything looks great. And you have a nice view of town from here. And this dressing, by the way… Did you make this?"

He nodded and swallowed. "Yup. You just mash the berries with a fork and shake it all in a mason jar. It's really easy to do. Do you need anything? Water? Juice? Napkins?"

She motioned to the napkin on her lap and finished her glass of wine, cheeks glowing. "No. Thank you. I should slow down on this. Too much could be a bad thing, huh?"

The narrow table left barely a breath between their plates. It wasn't a stretch when she reached out and touched his arm. Sparks snapped and burst beneath his skin, and his stomach whirled. He held in his shallow breath, lettuce cool in his mouth, half a cherry tomato tight between his teeth but not so tight it would burst.

"This is nice," she said. "Getting to know you."

She pulled her hand back to her salad for the last bite of lettuce just as ice rushed through his veins. Her touch was too much. Too soon. Too fast. He couldn't reciprocate whatever she thought this would become.

He chewed a piece of bitter lettuce as his belly soured. He chewed and choked it down. Letting his fork rest on his plate, soundless, he reached for his glass while panic shot through his veins.

"Have you stayed in touch with anyone from school," he asked. "Back in the day? People who moved out, I mean. I was trying to remember, if I could place you back then. We weren't in the same circles, but you used to hang out with that guy Tom, right?"

She lowered her fork and lifted her chin with the slightest of winces. He'd forgotten they dated. It was a million years ago, sure, but it was a careless thing to say, throwing an old flame on the table when it wasn't strong enough to hold a candle.

Eager to change the topic, he pushed away from the table. "Soup. I'll get the soup."

"No idea what happened to Tom. He thought he was too smart for all of us and ran off to conquer the world."

*Touché.* Kyle brought two small bowls to the table and slid back into his seat, savory steam billowing into the air between them. Kyle dipped his spoon into it, drawing up smooth broth, diced ham, and a white bean. "Having tried to run off and conquer the world myself, I'll say it takes a lot more than smarts. It takes a lot of luck. Besides, if he passed you up, obviously he doesn't know good in the world when *he* sees it."

His pulse was back in his throat again, too tight to swallow. Letting his imagination wander, he pictured himself sliding his chair around the table, sitting closer, touching her hair. She was such a distraction. A textured, soft, flowery distraction. But he couldn't afford it. Touching her, adding weight to the scale, would tip the balance.

"Why did you leave?" she asked.

"What do you mean?"

"After graduation. When you left. Why?"

He moved his spoon through his soup and gently sipped, his hand shaking. He was shocked any was left by the time it reached his lips. "To learn. And work. I figured I had to be successful at something before I could chase my dream. If I didn't work hard enough, I wouldn't be worthy of it. What about you? How'd you get stuck here?"

She smoothed her napkin on her lap, lips pursed. "Staying wasn't my only option. I wasn't stuck here. I heard that when I was running for town manager—that if I were smarter or braver I would have left for something better. I love that flower shop. I grew up in it. Running it *was* my dream. My dad was struggling a lot the year I graduated, and maybe leaving would have crossed my mind if he hadn't needed me, but that's love, right? I loved him, the store, the town. Nothing out there sounded better to me than being here."

Kyle rested his elbows on the table, wine glass in his hand. "I get that. I guess that's why I came back. It's just… It's home." His sip emptied his glass. He gave it a shake. "Okay, how about more of this and some roast?"

Her smile was broad. She threw her napkin on the table beside her plate. "Can I help?"

"Absolutely not." He cleared the table and turned to the roast. It held its juices after its rest, and his knife went through it like butter.

"I know you said not to help." She appeared beside him, flowers and wine, and gripped the bottle. "But let me. Please."

She refilled their glasses and lounged against the counter. The energy between them was static, connected, like one of those plasma globes he played with as a kid. The closer she got, the stronger the sparks. Her nearness was warm and light at the same time, but the knot in his stomach said it was not okay. His racing heart wanted to run for the stairs, to claw at the neck of his shirt and gasp for air. Wordless, he carried their plates to the table and had his fork in his hand before she sat.

It wasn't time for romance yet. Not now and not soon. He had too much to lose: his meager life savings and all the effort he'd put into the store. If he got distracted now and lost momentum, he could lose it all. He slumped in his chair, breaking the dynamic between then, and picked at his food. She was dangerous. Distance was wise.

"So where do you want to go from here?" Adelle sipped her wine.

His throat closed on a piece of roast. He wanted to go to bed, downstairs, into the street, back to Boston, to a tiny cot on the surface of the moon. Anywhere but here. "What do you mean?" His voice was stronger than he thought it would be.

"I mean the store. What do you want for it? What's your new dream now that you have this one?"

He hadn't thought about it that way, that the store was his dream come true. Maybe he would if he had more customers. "A chain of these, I guess."

"You never relax do you?" She smiled at him across her glass.

"I suppose I don't. Life should be a climb to the top. Rewards are supposed to be hard won. There's no time to rest."

Adelle tucked her lower lip into a frown. "But there's fun along the way. You're not punished for cutting loose sometimes, right? Having relationships?"

What is she asking? He shook his head. "No. There's no time for relationships."

His heart squeezed when he said it, like a part of him stood in defiance of his own needs. It was human nature to want all that, animal instinct. But nothing good came from caving to it.

"It wouldn't be fair to anyone. I can't put in the time. The last relationship I had—" It was forever ago. "I couldn't make her happy. My mind was always somewhere else. I guess that's just who I am."

"Well, here's to friendship then." She held her glass aloft for a toast, and he obliged, telling himself it was sentiment not courtesy. "We should do dinner again. My treat next time."

His glass hit the table with a thud, and a red wine sea tossed in his cup. "That's not necessary."

"I see. I get it." She bristled, her back straight, hands in her lap. "I suppose that was forward of me. I just…" She smoothed her napkin, the tips of her ears reddening. "I'll be honest. I was attracted to you. You can hardly blame me, right? But I can put that aside."

He returned her weak smile. What a terrible host he'd been. Lowering his chin and his voice, he said, "I can understand. I would be lying if I denied that a part of me felt something between us, but needs and wants aren't quite the same thing. I can't be tempted. Rather, I shouldn't."

She waved a hand and downed her glass.

In another world, she'd be just his type. She wore her hurt feelings like a queen donned a gown. It suited her, the rawness and realness of it. Most people would have been shaken, but Adelle let it be a part of her.

He wished that time could pass a little faster, that the awkwardness would dissipate like puddles after the rain.

He lost his appetite.

He went to the fridge and grabbed the trifle, hand-whipped cream and homemade lemon curd. In any other moment it would have been sweet and tangy.

He threw it unceremoniously on the table. An afterthought.

"That looks lovely. Of course it does." Adelle dabbed the corner of her mouth with her napkin. She pushed away from the table, her blank gaze fixed on the floor as she stood. "But I really ought to go."

Kyle rose, mildly grateful and grasping into the dark corners of his brain for a way to smooth it over and make it end at the same time. But his mouth moved faster than his sentiment. "Let me show you out. The door sticks."

"I know that. I showed you, remember?" Adelle fumbled, placing her fork next to her knife on her plate, straightening her napkin. She waved a hand in resignation, a universal sign she'd given up on fixing it, on making anything better than it was when she arrived. Kyle accepted the worsening of it, and the awkwardness of the future. He'd have to get used to it.

"I have this way of spectacularly blowing things up without trying." It wasn't the apology he wanted it to be, but he couldn't isolate any of the things he was sorry for. There were too many. "I hope you enjoy the rest of your night."

*Way to make it worse, stupid.*

Adelle's eyes were fixed on the door. "I like quiet nights. My favorite thing about Ramsbolt is how very small it is and how quiet. It's so easy to make time for myself. I think it frees up some of my emotions so I can focus on me. That's what keeps me going, anyway."

He nodded. He was out of words, even if his throat could have allowed them passage.

"Anyway, I do check in with myself sometimes to see if I'm happy or not. If I didn't, I wouldn't know exactly why my work is so fulfilling. If I don't follow that happiness, I shouldn't ever expect to find it. It works for me; you should try it. Thanks for dinner. I'll see myself out."

# CHAPTER TWENTY-THREE

A couple browsed the store. The woman carried a heavy jacket, far too warm for the weather. The man slung his coat over his shoulder, hooked on a finger while they spoke in whispers and poked at items on the shelves. Definitely tourists.

"Do you have a bathroom?" The woman passed her coat to her husband and set a stoneware spoon rest back on the shelf.

"Right in there. Help yourself." Kyle gestured to the door, but he couldn't pry his eyes from the newspaper. He'd found a stack, neatly tied with twine, on his doorstep, as if he were obligated to share whatever rancid news that Stuart guy dared to print.

The article was worse than he feared. "Brazen Abuse of Town-Owned Properties Brings Opportunistic Retailers to Ramsbolt."

Stuart claimed that Adelle was mismanaging public property, that Kyle's store was an eyesore, and that the board hadn't properly vetted his business before approving it.

*A teenage grocery store bagger has been granted the right to approve any business that seeks to profit off Ramsbolt's citizens. It's well known that the board was established to tighten the loophole that prevented the town from throwing a festival.*

*But the continuance of the board for greater purposes threatens the economic livelihood of our town.*

"Our town? Who is this guy?" Kyle crumpled the newspaper into a ball and threw it into the trash can so hard the can fell on its side, spewing bits of paper and an empty soda can on the floor. Kyle hopped off the stool to pick it up. When he stood, the couple was at the counter.

The husband dropped a hand-carved cutting board by the register, and his wife stepped to his side.

"Nice store you got here." The man dug into his khakis for his wallet. "We're just passing through. On our way to Canada. Skiing."

"I love small town newspapers." The wife reached out to take a newspaper off the stack, and Kyle swept an arm out, knocking the whole pile into the trash.

"Sorry. Misprints."

The woman pulled her hand back, pointing instead to the window display. "Do you have any of those cast-iron stock pots in blue?"

"Good thinking." Her husband wrapped an arm around her shoulder, one eyebrow raised and his eyes pinned on the trashcan. "To match the new kitchen."

His wife smiled up at him. "We try to buy useful things when we go on vacation. Is it five quarts?"

Kyle nudged the trash can with his foot, hiding it behind the counter. "Five and a half. The handle is phenolic, so it can go in the oven. I have a blue one."

The couple nodded to each other in hive mind agreement.

The woman whispered to her husband. "We should get one. It will look perfect on the stove." She nudged him with her hip.

Kyle slipped from the stool and grabbed one from the back room.

One less thing to unbox later. He scanned them and read out their total. The couple chattered while he waited for their bank to give him a few dollars toward his sanity.

"This is the cutest little town," the woman gushed. "We should definitely stay here next time we come through."

Kyle handed their card back. "Diane has some rooms over the tea house that she rents out. Definitely call ahead."

*As if Ramsbolt were teeming with tourists.*

"It must get busy here in the summer." The man returned his wallet to his pocket.

Kyle raised a shoulder. "Here?" He could play it up, pretend it was true. Plenty of small towns manufactured charm that drew tourists in droves. But he didn't have the energy to lie. "Not quite. It's never busy. But I'd call just to make sure she has a room ready with sheets and all that. We don't get many visitors."

The lady elbowed her husband as Kyle ran her card. "Do you hear that, Josh? That's just crazy. You have quite the little gem here. It looks like a postcard."

Kyle pushed green tissue paper into a paper bag. He'd practiced for days to get it right, so it looked like a natural motion. Nothing about tissue paper felt natural to him, but a nicely packaged bag was part of the experience. Or so the internet said.

"Thanks for saying so." He handed her the bag. "We love it here. There's an arts festival that happens over Memorial Day weekend. If you're ever in the area, stop back by."

"Thanks." The man nodded toward his wife as they stepped out the door. "She runs a travel blog. Always looking for cute towns to write about."

It was only as the woman waved over her shoulder, only as they left his store, that he realized he'd made his first sale. All that practice with the transaction software and ramming tissue paper into bags paid off. It felt like he'd been doing it forever, and for once, he'd helped someone, a real customer, and it wasn't about closing a deal. But any enjoyment he should have felt was stained by the stack of newspapers in the trashcan and the constant presence of Adelle's store across the street. He'd destroyed his store by not dealing with Stuart, ruined any chance of a friendship with Adelle by being a dick, and now she'd think he threw her to the wolves by slamming her plan to the whole town. The whole board would be pissed at him, too.

The street was quiet. Birds splashed in a puddle outside Penny's Loft and crisp leaves scraped the pavement, pushed by a cool late-September breeze. Across the street, a light was on at Adelle's. Yesterday, he'd have wanted to rush over and tell her the good news, to celebrate with her. But today, he wanted to avoid her like the plague.

"The pitchforks and torches should be here by lunch."

Jacques padded down the stairs, eyes heavy with sleep. He headed for his bed in the window and curled up for a nap. Kyle opened his laptop.

He flicked on the radio for the company, but the copper ceiling allowed for nothing but static. He turned it off and waited for his available credit card balances to load.

He'd avoided things for too long. Bills and credit, tracking his spending, and the stoves he couldn't afford. If he was going to avoid apologizing to Adelle for fear of what she had to say, wrapping his brain around one of his challenges was the least he could do. He'd parsed his finances a thousand ways in his mind, but dodged the reality. For some reason, it just wasn't as much fun to shuffle money around when there wasn't any to shuffle. He cringed as tiny available balances appeared on the screen.

His situation was worse than he thought. He had enough available credit to keep food on the table for another three months, but there was no wiggle room for emergencies, and something would have to change if he were to survive beyond that. Sitting around to see how much that story damaged his profits wasn't an option, either.

His relationships might be getting worse, but when it came to business, his leaps of faith were getting better. Opening the store was a great one, but the leap wasn't long enough or far enough. He pulled his phone from one back pocket and his wallet from the other. He threw it on the counter and thumbed through his cards, looking for the maxed-out Visa. Maybe if he called he could get an extended credit line. He'd been a good customer until lately. Maybe they'd raise his limit, and he could take the profit from cooking classes and apply that to the balance. Things would be lean for a while, but it was worth a shot.

Driver's license. Debit card. That little card that tells him where his voting district is, as if he'd forget it was in the basement of the church. The silver edge of an old credit card peeked out from behind an old business card. He threw it on the counter.

He forgot what it was like to be that guy, the one with the fancy credit card, the one who could use concierge services to get front-row tickets and backstage passes, the whole world at his fingertips. It had been easy once to throw money around. With a stupid high interest rate, this card was only for emergencies, and chasing this dream sure as hell qualified.

Jacques sniffed the floor and nudged at his pant leg.

"When did you get up? I know you want to go out. One second. I have one more leap to take, and then we can take the longest walk you can handle."

He pulled up his call history on his phone, found the number for Christa with a C, and hit the dial icon.

"Grogans. This is Christa. How can I help you today?"

"Hi, Christa with a C. This is Kyle from Kitchen Concepts. I have a new payment method for those stoves, if you still have that quote handy."

"I do. Give me one second to pull it up, and I'll take the digits from you four at a time."

The clicks of her keyboard echoed on the line. He was halfway through reciting the card number when his door flung open, and Adelle planted herself on his doormat. Jacques lifted his head, but rage came off her like heat from the road on a summer day. The dog curled tighter into a ball.

They locked eyes, hers on fire, his wide with fear, as he recited the rest of the digits from memory.

Christa rambled off some details he couldn't hear through the ringing in his ears.

"Thanks, Christa." His voice was barely above a whisper.

The line went dead with a faint click, and he lowered his phone to the counter.

Adelle's arms were folded over her green florist apron. "What the hell is that article?" She spit her words through clenched teeth.

The air in the store was suddenly thick and hot. "How long ago did you read it?"

"Before the sun came up. Why?"

"Just wondering if this is the originating anger or if you've cooled down at all, because I wouldn't blame you if—"

"Why didn't you tell me about this last night? And I don't think it matters one bit if I give you my opinion of you today, tomorrow, or twenty years from now, but I sure as hell hope that if I need to give you my opinion in twenty years, that you'll be a hell of a lot further away than across the street."

"I didn't mean to—"

"Oh, so you meant to say glowing things about this awesome opportunity you wouldn't have been able to afford otherwise? But you accidentally said terrible things about me, the town, the buildings, the street, the entire board, and your neighbors? Like it was just an accident?"

"I didn't say anything about—"

"You'd still be lying in a puddle of grease in Zeb's barn if it weren't for this place, and instead of being grateful, you have to bring down everyone around you."

He folded his hands in his lap, inspecting his nails as if the right words were embedded in his cuticles. "I didn't—"

"And you slammed the board! They voted to let you open a store here. You didn't have to apply if you didn't want to. It's like some elaborate long con. You went out of your way to come up with a half-assed business plan just so you could make my life miserable." She pulled the rolled up newspaper from her back pocket and hurled it across the room. It bounced off the old candy table and landed with a thud. "Just like dinner."

"No. That's not what happened."

"Like hell it's not." She spun on her heel and pulled on the door, but spiraled back to him. "That's exactly what happened. You're just so…"

She waved her hands. "I'm done with you. I gave you the courtesy you couldn't give me by waiting until you had no customers before I told you what I thought. That's more kindness than you've shown me or anyone else in this town. And one last thing. Are you listening to me?"

She pointed her finger at him, and he shrank.

"You can get out of this deal any time you want to, Kyle Nolan. You're welcome to leave whenever this place becomes unbearable. By the sound of it, it won't be long."

# CHAPTER TWENTY-FOUR

"All you gotta do is sign right here, and I'll be out of your hair." The delivery guy pulled a greasy pen from the pocket of his Grogan's shirt. "Remember, you gotta turn these stoves up to four fifty and let 'em run for half an hour. Make sure you got the vents on high. Clears the stink out."

"Will do." Kyle accepted the pen and scrawled his name in a rectangle. "Sorry I wasn't ready when you got here. I guess I wasn't paying attention when Christa said you'd be here today."

"Don't worry about it." The guy in the Grogan's shirt shoved the pen in his pocket. "I'm surprised you didn't get gas stoves. You pro cooks always like the gas ones."

"I had to compromise. No gas lines here. Plus, I think it's better for people to learn with the same equipment they have at home. Not a lot of gas stoves around here."

"That's true. Have a good one, then. If you run into problems, call the number on the card I left you." The man lowered his head in a departing nod, pushed out the door and hopped in his truck.

Six electric stoves lined two back walls, each with a stainless steel food prep table on wheels that made half the store look clinical, like at any second a doctor might show up with some terrifying tools to remove whatever was wrong with him. It might be half of what he hoped for, but a curtain or room divider could fix that. For now it was a work in progress wrapped in protective blue plastic.

Jacques tugged at his pant leg, leash dangling from his mouth.

"I know. We're going. I'm not looking forward to this, though." He grabbed the stack of flyers off the counter, hooked the leash on Jacques, and locked the door.

Jacques lunged down Main Street, choking himself at the start of his leash. Kyle lumbered behind. The puppy stopped at cracks in the curb to smell calling cards and leave some of his own at the corners of brick buildings. He paused to shake hands with the boy who tumbled out of the pet store, and half way down the street, Kyle was out of breath. Biting his lip and clutching the flyers, he detoured the puppy into Carol's Hardware Store.

He'd practiced his request a hundred times, while brushing his teeth, in the shower, and through two laps of the town park nestled in the roundabout. He had an answer for every objection. There was nothing left but to walk right into every store and for help spreading the word about his cooking classes.

He'd made a million pitches to people much scarier than Ramsbolt's shop owners, but he hadn't insulted them all in the local paper, either. With any luck, no one would mention it. But with his bad luck, he'd have a lot of explaining to do.

He'd never been more fragile than standing before Carol at the Hardware store. The door closed behind him, sealing him inside, and he lost his breath. The air was thick and stuffy, crowded with dust and wood and spilled paint. It was the smell of a million projects he couldn't start.

He threw his shoulders back, lifted his chin, and approached the counter.

"Hey, Carol. I've got a quick question for you."

"Everything going okay at the shop?" Carol leaned over the counter and peered down at Jacques, who scratched an itch beneath his collar, jingling his tag. "Seems like everybody has plumbing problems lately. I got a sale going on plungers."

"Everything's good, I guess. I'm good on plungers. I have a new thing I'm trying to promote, though." He flopped the flyers on the counter and bent down to disentangle Jacques's legs from the leash. "I'm starting cooking classes."

Carol folded her arms. "That's a great idea. I kinda get sick of Diane's cooking, to be honest, and I'm uninspired."

"I hope I can help with that. Would you be willing to hand out a few flyers? Maybe put them in bags with people's purchases for a few days?"

"That article…" In the split second of Carol's pause, Kyle's hopes for local support were dashed. Her eyes clouded over. "Why don't I put one on the community bulletin board, instead." Carol took one from the stack and stabbed it with a thumbtack, nailing it to the corkboard behind her. "You've always been kind to me. I have no beef with you."

"But other people do." It wasn't a question, and he didn't want an answer. He collected the stack of flyers with one hand and squeezed Jacques's leash with the other. "I didn't mean what that article said. It was all out of context. I never said anything bad about the town or any of you all. As neighbors go, I couldn't ask for better. That guy asked really leading questions, and he caught me before my coffee. It's no excuse, but..."

"Adelle." Carol raised an eyebrow.

A new wave of nauseating insecurity washed over him. Carol was friends with Adelle. Everyone was, as far as he knew. After everything he'd said to her and how he made her feel, he was blind to think the article would be his biggest hardship he'd created for himself. Adelle had probably told everyone he was scum before the article came out, and he deserved it. He held his breath waiting for something from Carol—some hint of anger or disgust. Anything he could refute. But Carol raised the corner of her mouth in a sad kind of knowing smile.

"Maybe someday, when this all blows over."

He didn't ask what she meant. He knew. His one-man sinning spree was costing him the support of the town. At least she was nice about it. "Yeah. I understand. Thanks."

"I hope it works out. Everyone goes through rough patches. Every pothole gets repaired eventually."

Jacques pulled him to the door, and he accepted the cue. "That's what they say. Thanks for posting the flyer."

Carol waved. "No problem."

Potholes might be fixed in some towns, but not in Ramsbolt. Jacques tugged the leash and dragged him farther down Main Street, past ruts in the road older than his Saturn. He paused at a trash can while Jacques sniffed the news, resisting the urge to toss the flyers in the trash can. Giving up wasn't an option. He had to prove that he wasn't the guy Stuart made him out to be.

"I don't know if you can come in here, buddy." He tied the leash to the leg of a cast-iron bench. "I'll be right back. You make sure everybody pets you on the head, okay. Two seconds."

He pushed open the door, and a bell rang out when he stepped inside. The place smelled of paper and old ink pens, and it hadn't changed a bit since he was a kid. Aisles of greeting cards and paperback fiction, racks full of magazines and yellowing packets of office supplies made a tidy grid for analog life. Kyle approached the counter, nodding to the two men who loitered at the register.

"Warren? I'm Kyle. I don't think we've met. Not since I was a kid, anyway." He handed over a flyer. "I run Kitchen Concepts, the new store next to Penny's Loft."

Warren slid his glasses down his nose and peered over them at the flyer. "I know it. Haven't been in yet."

Kyle braced himself for hostility. It was the newsstand, after all, where the grumpy gathered to moan about taxes. "Oh, don't worry about it. I'll be starting cooking classes next month, and I wondered if you would mind posting some information about it. Maybe sharing some flyers with your customers?"

Beside him, the two old men bristled, and one hiked up his pants. If he was trying to hide his ridicule, he failed. Kyle refused to meet their eyes as the men's crabbiness dissolved into laughter. If they weren't interested in cooking classes, he wasn't going to sway them with a flyer or some humor. Ramsbolt was stubborn that way. Kyle stretched instead, trying to crack some tension out of his neck.

Warren replaced his glasses. "Didn't you used to cook over at the old steak house when you were a kid?"

"Back when I was in high school, yeah. Before I left for college."

"You were a right good cook."

"Thanks. This kind of thing has been successful in other towns, having a cooking class to teach new skills and recipes. It brings people together, too."

Warren looked up from the flyer. "Soup? Really?"

Kyle pointed at the flyer. "There are other things, too. Something different every other week."

The larger of the two men hooked his thumbs in his belt loops and leaned back, his stomach protruding as if to prove his point. "Nobody here needs no cooking classes. You sure don't need cooking classes, do you Mack?"

The man who answered to Mack eyed Kyle with unfettered disdain. "Don't need cooking classes when you only cook for one."

Kyle shrugged. "I get it. I cook for myself all the time. You need a fast meal, easy to clean up."

Mack wagged a finger at him. "You cooking people make everything harder than it's gotta be. It's always a mess. It's hard on the knees standing at a sink for an hour scrubbing at a pan you ate out of for two minutes. Everything takes four hundred ingredients ain't nobody got in the cupboard."

Kyle shrugged. This was hardly the battle he expected to wage. "I can sympathize. Cooks are on their feet all day, and when they go home, they don't cook like that. What if I did a class on fast, easy dishes with little cleanup? I have plenty of one-pan meals I can offer. Or maybe a class on meal prep. You can cook for an hour on a Sunday and have food for the whole week."

Mack jabbed his thumb at his friend. "Lewis won't do it. He won't do anything that looks like a good time."

Lewis scowled. "That don't look like a good time."

Kyle folded a flyer and pushed it into Mack's hand. "Drag him along. I promise you'll have to work really hard to regret it."

"It's not a bad idea you got here." Warren shook his head. "But I can't help you."

Mack hiked up his pants. "Not after that story in the paper. I weren't the biggest fan of that girl's plan, and I love some good town drama, but that didn't make no sense, going after her like that."

"That's not what happened at all." Kyle took a *Ramsbolt Reader* off the rack and shook it. "This guy came into my store when I wasn't even open. I was in my bathrobe. He started asking all these questions. Never even introduced himself. I got angry at the line of questioning and, yeah, it didn't go well, but I wasn't being mean to Adelle at all. I'm very grateful for the opportunity."

Lewis let out a chuckle. "Sounded like it."

Kyle glanced at the door. Jacques blinked inside with sad eyes. "I should run. My dog's outside, and I want to catch up with Marissa. I would love to have your support someday. If you can't, I understand."

He slammed the newspaper down on the stack and rushed outside. Jacques leapt at his hands and gnawed on the leash as he unfurled it from around the bench. "Don't get too excited. I'm gonna do this to you again. On the other side of the street this time. Let's go find out how many people over there we've pissed off."

They waited for a car to make a U-turn at the end of the street, and they crossed, dodging the potholes. Stepping foot inside another store and asking for support was self-flagellation, but he needed to explain himself. He couldn't let the whole town think he wasn't grateful.

He tied the puppy to the lamppost outside the bakery. He exhaled until his lungs were shriveled, preparing to take a deep breath, and once inside, he filled them up with the sweet air thick with vanilla, cookies, and courage.

He'd thought he was saving his easiest request for last. He'd met Marissa a dozen times, and the overlap between the desserts he wanted to teach and the ones she sold everyday was minimal. But he approached the counter with short steps, sweaty hands staining the flyers.

Her back was to him, her head in a barrel where she kept plain bagels.

"Hey, Marissa."

"Yeah. What can I get ya?" She turned to him and wiped her hands on a pink kitchen towel. "This town can eat some bagels, let me tell ya."

"That's a testament to your bagels, I think, more than the town's eating prowess."

She snagged a spray bottle from beside the register and spritzed her counter, wiping it clean. "Well, that's kind of you to say. What are you in for?"

"I need to set the record straight. And I need to ask a favor." He put up a hand as she shot up an eyebrow. "I know what you're going to say. That article was horrible, and it made me sound ungrateful. That's not who I am at all. You know me better than that."

"Do I?" She folded her arms. "We barely know each other."

He shook his head. "That's true. But you have to know that I'm not the kind of person to say things like that."

Her eyes shot daggers. "Really? But you're the kind of person to flirt with Adelle for days, invite her to your house on a date, then shoot her down and make her cry? I just want to understand the distinction. You're *that* person, but not the person who told Stuart that the town is difficult to work with and generally unfriendly."

"I never meant to make bad will with my neighbors. That wasn't my intention with Adelle, and Stuart caught me off guard."

Her eyes rolled so hard she craned her neck back. "Oh, so that's just who you are when you let your guard down."

"No! No. That's not what I'm saying at all. Clearly. This has been really hard—"

"I'd imagine so. It has to be a big challenge to wake up every day and find new, creative ways to alienate yourself from an entire town. No one is obligated to shop at your store. It's just shocking to me, to all of us, that you'd want to kick off your grand opening with such fanfare."

He stepped forward and she stepped back, as if he had the plague. The flyers hung at his side. He was frozen in her chill.

"It doesn't matter what I say, does it?"

"No. It matters what you do." Marissa's back straightened, one eyebrow cocked in a sarcastic sneer. She pointed to the papers in his hand. "What's that?"

"The flyer?" He crumpled one. "I'm starting cooking classes. I was asking store owners if they'd help promote it. Maybe put some flyers in shopping bags or throw them on bulletin boards. But I got ahead of myself."

"I'd say."

"I need to put this right with Adelle."

"You probably didn't know that we talk to each other all the time so you'd have no way of knowing it, but by coming in here, you're asking me to choose between supporting a new business, which is something I believe in with my very core, or being disloyal to my friend. And I don't want to get *started* on that article."

He raised a hand, a white flag, and opened his mouth to acknowledge the mess, to promise to put it right, but she shook her head before he could say it.

"Don't. Don't even try it. If this is how you want to move through this town, that's just fine. But I'm not obligated to show up for every fight people invite me to. I have a bakery to run, and I'm just not that into the drama. You just stumbled into town, and you hurt my good friend. You don't get to come in here and make nice with me."

"I grew up here. But that's not the point. She didn't let on that she was hurt by what happened. She walked out with her head high."

"What did you expect her to do?" Marissa's voice shot up an octave. "Cry? Fall on the floor? Is that what you were aiming for? It was cruel and selfish of you, and if that's how you do business, you won't make it here."

The vanilla cookie air was sickening. He put a hand to his stomach. "I don't know what to say. This isn't who I am. I swear." His eyes darted around the room, unable to settle on anything. "I'll apologize. I'll fix it. I'll make this right."

"There's a big difference between doing right by someone the first time around and having to be told to do it." Marissa turned to the doorway lined with pink trim that led to her kitchen. "My loyalty will always be to my friends. If you want to fit in around here, you've got a lot to make up for."

Marissa disappeared into the kitchen, and shame fell on Kyle like a thick blanket, heavy and hot, pinning him to the spot. Half of him wanted to chase after her, to explain how mixed up everything got between his needs and his wants, how far out of reach everything was, and how much worse off Adelle would be if he hadn't rejected her. She deserved so much more than he could offer. But wanting to explain wouldn't make Marissa understand, just like no amount of needing ever made things turn out right. His whole life had been a storm of desire and deficiency, and just once it would be nice if he could come up for air instead of drowning in it.

Struggling for air, he pushed through the door and onto the sidewalk, directly into Stuart's path.

"You." Kyle exploded, stepping closer and forcing Stuart against the brick wall, finger to the man's chest. "That article was bullshit."

Stuart clutched the strap of his messenger bag. "What are you talking about?"

"Don't give me that bullshit. You know exactly what I'm talking about. You show up at my store when it's not even open, push your way in like you own the place." Kyle stepped back. "What the hell are you thinking?"

"All I did was ask you some questions. You never said—"

"Exactly. I never said any of those things. You took my words totally out of context and used them to frame your own narrative that this town is garbage. If you hated it here so much, why are you here?"

Stuart's eyes darted down the street. "I chose to live here."

"Oh, I see." Kyle flung his head back. "You're not even from here?"

Something lined Stuart's face. Whether it was fear or worry didn't matter to Kyle. He had Stuart where he wanted him. "Let me tell you something. I belong here. I grew up here. My parents struggled worse than anyone else, and all I wanted to do was make this store a reality and give something back. Make things better around here. Maybe it wasn't always clear to me, but I knew deep down I belonged here, or I never would have stayed. I could have gone anywhere, but this is where I belong. My grandmother sold pies to raise my father on her own in this town. Let that sink in. Her only income was from baking pies. In one oven. In her house. You don't get to tell me or anyone else in this town how we should get by. And running a newspaper doesn't give you the right to play gatekeeper or tell Adelle how she should run this town."

Kyle clenched his rage into a fist, letting his knuckles ache. Words he knew he'd regret burst within him, fireworks in the making. He spun on his heel, Jacques in his wake, and stormed down Main Street.

"Adelle called me," Stuart yelled after him.

Kyle paused by a bench, but he dared not look over his shoulder. "Did she call you an asshole? She should have."

"She said newspapers serve as a check and balance, and I cheapen my own value when I overstep my bounds."

"She's kinder than I am. She has good a point. You'd be a lot better off if you labeled it as fiction."

Jacques tugged the leash, and Kyle didn't argue. He followed the puppy home.

# CHAPTER TWENTY-FIVE

The door to his father's room was open, so Kyle took a chance and stepped in without knocking. The newspaper with Stuart's front-page apology and the updated review of his store was tucked in his back pocket. It crinkled when he walked. He braced himself for a hint of recognition, hoping his father had forgotten the last meeting when he earned the bruise on his right bicep that had faded to the yellow of a dying dandelion. But the inquisitive look on his father's face said he was far from recognized. It stung not to be known as the son that he'd been, the son that his father wanted him to be. Just once, just one more time, he needed it.

His father bashed the remote, and the TV went silent. "You the paper guy? The nurse said you were coming to read it today."

Kyle whipped it from his pocket. "Got it right here." He kicked the chair a few inches from the bed and settled into it.

"Can I ask you a question first? Are you any good at advice?"

The man smoothed strands of white hair across his head, plastering them in place. "I got opinions. That's as good as advice."

The logic was fallible, but he'd take it. "I met a girl. I really like her."

Eyes narrowed and lip curled, his father was either confused or annoyed. He plowed on. "I didn't mean to, but I led her on a little bit. I turned her down when she made a move. She didn't act like her feelings were all that hurt, but a friend of hers told me she was pretty upset about it."

His father rubbed at his snow-white stubble. "I met my wife in school. We didn't go to school all year back then, just when the farming was done. She was a year younger than me. Wore her hair in one long braid down her back. I sat at my desk and stared at it all day, and one time I asked if I could walk her home from school, cause that's what you do when you like a girl. You take care of her. You look out for her. I made sure she got home okay, and we walked every day after that. One day when the buds were on the trees, I knew we'd be back to farming soon, and I'd miss that girl, so I asked her dad if I could marry her, and he said we could."

Kyle held in his shallow breath. There weren't many lucid days, ten in the last year, perhaps. He didn't want to shatter it. "Go on. I'm listening."

"You younger ones don't get married as much. I see it on the TV and with these nurses. People live longer. I guess it makes them think they got more time to have fun. When I was young, we got married for security. It's just what you did. I loved that woman till her lights went out. When I say loved, I mean I took good care of her."

But they argued. And went hungry. And things weren't as secure as they could have been, not in the bank account and not in the fridge, if either of his parents had seen past their pride enough to ask for help and accept it. He couldn't say that out loud, though. Not unless he wanted another punch in the arm. Not unless he wanted another argument to add to the stack and carry around with him forever.

"Did you know right away that she was the right one?"

"I didn't. Not 'cause I was looking for someone, but because I didn't think she was looking for me. I never had a lot of…" His voice trailed off, and he examined the back of one hand as if it were foreign. "Words don't come so good anymore. What is it when you got a plan and you know you're good at things?"

"Strength?" No, his father had always been strong. "Confidence?"

"That. I never had confidence. I coulda done more, I guess. Put a better house together, got her more dresses and taken her out more. Whatever she wanted. But I wasn't smart or strong. I did what I could."

Kyle pulled in a sharp breath of nursing home air, iodine and alcohol tainted. He'd always blamed their need on pride. Zeb had said the same. He'd always thought his father was strong and pride held him back. To hear the opposite from his father and to see that fragility etched into his father's hands made him heavy. As his lungs soaked up astringent air, his spirit sank with his body.

"Did you and your wife have a lot of friends? Did you throw dinner parties?"

He knew they hadn't. They kept the doors shut, the curtains drawn.

"We didn't have no dinner parties. We didn't know nobody."

His distance from the town, his isolation from his peers, maybe it wasn't because they were ashamed of what they had or didn't have. What if his father had lacked the confidence to move through the real world? Had his mother loved him enough to shield him from the harsh light of broken boundaries? Inside, his father wasn't nearly as gnarled and knurled as he'd seemed. They were all just fragile people in a world of sharp edges.

"Did you have any kids?"

"Got a son. He visits sometimes. Opened a store somewhere, I think. Don't know whereabouts."

Kyle ran his thumb along the ragged edge of the paper and creased it back along its folds so it would lie flat on his lap. He'd never been one for tears. Sentiment didn't float to the top for him, but right then, it lumped in his throat like curdled regrets. His father's mind had been a foggy mystery since Alzheimer's cast its blanket. It had been at least six months since a real memory surfaced, since anything that Kyle recognized as reality had made itself known in the mist. The nurses and pamphlets said it was like that, some days would be clearer than others, but he hadn't expected that his father was listening.

Rapid blinks kept tears at bay, kept them from plunging to the paper and soaking it through.

"I bet it's a great store," his father said. "Something about kitchens. That boy is smart. He'll do good with it. Didn't learn none of it from me. Rotting away in this place, forgotten."

He wanted to reach out and touch his father's arm, to give the man the reassurance he never got as a kid. He wanted to say that it would all be okay, that there was nothing unknown lurking in the darkness, that he'd learned a ton about being strong and having a stiff upper lip and working hard even if it was at a desk instead of in a field. But nothing that came to mind made any sense. All the words were gibberish, drowning in emotions he didn't know how to express.

"Your son did get a lot from you. You seem smart."

His father swatted at the air and tiny fibers from his blanket swirled in patches of sunlight. "I ain't smart like him."

"What would you tell your son if he led a nice girl on and made all her friends angry? What if he could lose his store because everyone turned against him?"

"I'd tell you to stop being a moron and go get the girl." He ran over his lined face with a papery, wrinkled hand. "Don't make things so damn hard, son. You've always made things so damn hard."

"Dad?"

"What?"

Kyle's insides twisted and the room turned on its axis. The eyes that blinked back at him never changed. The bones got thinner, the muscles failed, the skin hung loose and the mind eroded, but his father's eyes hadn't changed a bit.

"Nothing. You want me to read the paper?"

"Yes. Apologize to the girl, be nice to her friends, and read the damn paper. The sun is going down. I got to watch *Wheel of Fortune*."

# CHAPTER TWENTY-SIX

Kyle's feet were planted to the floor of Adelle's flower shop. He couldn't move if he wanted to. It smelled like her, like fancy white flowers and earth. He couldn't shift his weight, and the tension was making his knees wobbly. He hated confrontation and hadn't been that intimidated by a conversation since he lost a client in his first year running his own accounts and had to tell the boss. But he had to make things right, not just for his business or his reputation in town, and not to win back Adelle's favor, but for himself. He had to tell her the truth, that relationships were hard for him, that desire was louder than the reasonable voice in his head that told him to shut up and walk away, that he had to preserve himself and stay focused on the future because he was terrified. For so long, his shoulders had been heavy with angels and devils screaming at him, distracting from the fact that she was a friend, and he valued that. He didn't have many.

She deserved better than him, anyway. He'd been stupid and selfish, and couldn't find the words to make it right.

He folded his arms and unfolded them again.

"What is it you want from me?" Adelle didn't look up from her flower arrangement. She snipped the end from a purple floofed stem, and the shard flew across the counter and onto the floor.

He folded his arms again. "I was wondering if I could—"

"Are you cold or something?" Another snip. Another flying shard of stem.

He tugged at the hem of his flannel shirt. "I've been busting my ass to get this store together, because you were absolutely right. If I hadn't been so horrible to you, I wouldn't have realized what I needed to do. I owe all my progress to you."

"You came over here to tell me that you've been busy?" It wasn't a question. Not the way she said it.

*No. Not like that. That's not what I meant.* Kyle opened his mouth, but the synapses in his brain wouldn't fire. *How does she do this to me?* He cleared his throat, forced all his weight to one foot, and took a reluctant step toward the counter. "I want to make it up to you."

"Mm-hmm." She spun the arrangement and glared at it as if it had offended her as much as he had.

*Apologize, you moron. Make the words. I'm sorry.*

She grabbed an offending stem and ripped it from the vase, and threw it on the counter.

*Or not. Just keep going.*

"I'm holding my first cooking class. We talked about maybe me using some of your herbs and selling them. I mean, if you're still interested I could sell little pots of them like we talked about. Maybe customers will want them for their windowsills or whatever once they cook with them. If I haven't completely destroyed things..."

Adelle threw the stem in the bucket under her counter and stormed to the back of the store, vases chattering on the shelves as she stomped.

The floor creaked as she moved around, and half of him wanted to inch to the door, sprint across the street, and retreat to the comfort of his own domain. But he came for a partnership, to rebuild the rapport that he broke, to continue on with life, and for the love of everything complicated about living in a small town, he was going to resolve this with her and then go on his merry way. Life would have to get back to normal eventually.

"Adelle?" His voice was louder than it needed to be.

"Here." She emerged from the hall and pushed a black plastic tray into his hands, full of little terra-cotta pots. The tray's edges were sharp, but he welcomed the sensation of it digging into his fingers. At least he had something to do with his hands.

Adelle tugged her apron tighter and wiggled a new stem from the bucket beneath her counter. "You were right, too. All of this is just a business transaction. Maybe I'd do more business if I weren't so damn nice." She clipped the stem, and a piece went flying. It skittered off the counter onto the floor. "Mark them up however you want, but you need to keep my tags on them."

"Of course." He hunched over the tray. "Adelle, I…"

She hadn't looked at him once, but he could still see the anger in her eyes. That and the pink tips of her ears said he wasn't going to cool the fire by hanging around. Trying to explain himself hadn't worked with anyone else. She wanted him gone as much as he wanted to be gone. He turned to the door.

"You what?"

He pivoted. "I'm stupid."

Her eyes softened one degree. "I know. How's Jacques?"

Kyle bit his lip. Was this an opening to apologize? She paid him no attention, though. All her concern was directed at a daisy.

"I, um. Jacques. He would like some company. He misses you." *Apologize, you fool. You actually like her. She's a nice person. She's a better person than you are, anyway.*

She raised an eyebrow. "Maybe."

*Say you're sorry.* Kyle opened his mouth, but she turned away, and he closed it again. His brain fumbled the apology because there were just too many to make all at once. The way he acted, the way they left things, that he hadn't come over earlier, that he'd gotten his whole life wrong so far and always made the wrong decisions, but his heart was good, he could swear to it. He never intended to hurt her or make things hard or awkward, but somehow his mouth always messed things up, and this time the apology wouldn't spill even out. Not the way the indignities had. She was hurt, and he caused it. And why couldn't he just string together a sentence to make it better?

"Thanks for these." He lifted the tray. "I'm looking forward to cooking more."

*For her, dummy. Tell her you want to cook for her again and make it up to her.*

"Uh huh." For the first time since he entered the store, she looked at him, utterly blank. All emotion and care had been drained from the woman he admired.

He crossed the street in the biting cold, the plastic tray imprinting his fingers.

He shrugged his shoulders against the wind and let them drop when he stepped into the recessed doorway, fumbling in his pocket for his key. Jacques was curled up in the window inside.

A throat cleared behind him, and he jumped. Stuart stepped into the doorway.

"You again. Come up with another way to destroy my life and the town?" Kyle jiggled his key in the lock and pushed the door open.

"I wrote a retraction and an apology."

"No one ever remembers that. They only remember the controversy. Everybody knows that." He stepped inside, but turned to block the door. Letting Stuart in the first time was one time too many. A little pot of thyme tumbled onto its side, spilling soil into the tray. It was the last straw. "Like life isn't hard enough without you following me around trying to make things worse."

Stuart held the door open with his foot. "I'm trying to fix this. I want to offer you space in the paper."

The tray landed on the floor with a thud. More pots of herbs rolled onto their sides. "I don't have time for your shit, today. We're done. Got it?"

Stuart pushed his way in and closed the door behind him. "No. We're not done. Neither one of us will survive in this town if we don't fix this. I'm trying to find a way to be supportive."

Kyle threw his hands on his hips to keep from balling them into fists. "By refusing to leave my store? In a perfect world, we wouldn't both be in it. Get what I'm saying?"

Jacques woke at the commotion and padded to his food bowl.

"It's free marketing. No editing. I promise. You write the story, and I print it. But it has to be relevant to the paper, otherwise the whole paper turns into a series of editorials where everyone airs their grievances."

Kyle forced his jaw to relax. "Like what. What are you talking about here? What's the offer?"

"A column. A weekly food column. That you write. I'll fix punctuation and spelling, but I'll print just what you give me."

A piece of Kyle's colossal anger fell away, but his trust in Stuart had already been broken. There had to be a catch. "What's in it for you?"

Stuart lifted his chin. "Less work. I'm struggling to get the paper on its feet. I never meant to suggest you were the one who didn't belong here. I'm the one who doesn't belong. I moved here and started this newspaper, and it's hard to find content to fill the whole thing."

Kyle raised an eyebrow. "So you fill it with fiction instead?"

Stuart flinched. "Ouch."

"Where did you come from, anyway?"

"Philadelphia. I was a creative writing professor."

*Figures.* Kyle kept his comment to himself.

Stuart shifted his weight, and the floor gave out an uncomfortable creak. "I'm trying to keep my head above the water here. I love writing hard-hitting news, and maybe there's just not enough of it around so I lost the truth in the local stories for all the fiction I saw in the shadows." He stuck out a hand. "I'm sorry. I am. Can we start over again?"

Stuart's hand was clean, his nails perfectly trimmed. Kyle shook away a flashback of boring business meetings with manipulative coworkers and set his jaw. Every road in that town was paved with forgiveness, but that didn't mean they were easy to navigate. It was hard not to be a little jealous of the guy. He made apologies look easy.

Stuart rolled his eyes. "Look. I'm just trying to belong here. Everyone knows everyone else, and I'm not doing a good job of fitting in. I want this place to be home, but…" Stuart trailed off, running a hand through his hair. "I apologize. I'm an outsider here, and I don't want to make enemies. Especially not with someone who can make a blueberry pie."

He couldn't make a pie, but Stuart didn't need to know that. He grabbed Stuart's hand and gave him a firm shake. "It's a deal, but I want it in writing."

Nodding, Stuart pulled a business card from the front pocket of his messenger bag. "A contributor agreement. We can do that. Email me. I'll write up an agreement and send you some ideas to help you get started. It'll be fun. I'm not a bad person. You're not either. We can make something better out of this."

The card sat hot in Kyle's hand. It weighed a ton. It was a chance to turn around public opinion, to offer something back, and build a better name for himself. Maybe it wouldn't make things right with Adelle, but it was a start.

Stuart paused at the door. "You know, I think you're going to do fine. This store looks great. It absolutely belongs in Ramsbolt. I'm not just saying that."

# CHAPTER TWENTY-SEVEN

The giant fiberglass horse outside the log cabin steakhouse was smashed to bits. Brown-painted chunks of legs, tail, and shoulders were sprayed across the concrete walk. Kyle hopscotched through them.

"You're late." Emma stood at the top of the stairs, her arms folded and eyes narrowed in the late afternoon light. Sun picked up gold in the highlights of her newly blond hair.

"I had my SATs this morning. The bus was late. What the hell happened out here?"

"Someone dragged it with a rope we think," she said.

He took the stairs two at a time. "Blonde looks good."

"Yeah? The brown faded too fast." She ran a hand down her wavy hair and flipped it over her shoulder.

"You should try sticking with one color for a week and see how it goes." Kyle wrapped a hand around the wrought-iron door handle and tugged. The door weighed a ton.

Emma followed him in. "You should get a car and try being on time."

"Funny." Kyle snorted. A car was the last thing on his priority list. He needed every penny he could get to pay for college.

Emma slipped behind the hostess podium and wrapped a fistful of silverware in a paper napkin. "Garrett is pissed as shit, by the way."

"I'd imagine so. I wouldn't want to clean up that mess." Kyle crossed the dining room, pushed through the door and into the kitchen, Emma in his wake. He grabbed an apron off a hook and spun to the prep station. The prep crew had done their job. Finally. "That horse has been there since I can remember."

The horse had captivated Kyle when he was a kid. It was much bigger than a real horse, and no one remembered where it came from or how long it had been there, but it stood outside the log cabin diner since the dawn of time. On the rare occasions he ate there as a kid, he'd patted its leg as he passed it by.

"He's not pissed about the horse. Well, he is. But he's pissed at you."

"Me?" Kyle tied the apron tight. "What did I do?"

"Beats me. Might be because you're always late." Emma shrugged and swished through the door.

Not likely. She wasn't wrong; he was always late. But it had never been a problem before.

Kyle loved his job cooking for Ramsbolt and random visitors who found the place on their way into Canada and back. He craved the adrenaline rush, the pace and the pressure of cooking meals, plating them, getting them out to the tables in the right order. It was frantic and anxious. Missing one piece would throw the whole night awry. It was a logic puzzle, a dance, a competition all rolled into one. Even on nights he wasn't cooking, just sitting in his room cramming for tests and filling out college applications, his mind would drift to cumin and brown sugar and chili powder slathered on a slab of salmon. He'd make recipes in the margins of his books. He was great at his job, and he loved improving recipes.

His heart sank. That had to be what pissed off Garrett. Fiddling with the recipes.

"Kyle!" Garrett's voice could stretch across a crowded dining room and slap you in the back of the head. "My office. Now."

Kyle knotted the apron strings and pushed through the door and into the hall. Garrett's office was no bigger than a utility closet, tucked between two bathrooms and smelling every bit like one. A plank of wood fixed to the wall with brackets supported his computer monitor. Papers were taped to the wall. They littered the shelf and the floor, where a massive computer tower in a yellowing case whirred and hummed.

"Shut the door, kid."

Garrett was a wide man, nearly as wide as the room. He motioned to an empty folding chair and Kyle sat, the metal cold on his legs. At least he didn't have to stand for his lashing. He never knew how to just stand there.

"What did I do?" He couldn't afford to lose his job. He needed every penny he could get to pay for college.

"That's what I'm trying to figure out." Garrett leaned back in his chair and folded his hands across his stomach. The chair creaked like a sinking ship.

"It's because I got creative, right? I tried to stay true to the menu, to what it says."

"That so?"

Kyle wiped his sweating palms on the apron and regretted knotting it so tight. His fumbling fingers would stall a hasty exit. Shrugging one shoulder, he said, "I guess I just wanted to change things up. There aren't a lot of places to eat around here."

"And you figured you'd just take it upon yourself to update the menu."

He couldn't look Garrett in the eye. He'd never been truly scolded before. Garret would josh him about being late, but he'd never been in any real trouble. Not since he was a kid. "No, not the whole menu. I just added some spices and freshened things up a bit."

The word *freshened* hung in the air like poison. "I didn't mean that. I mean, a dash of this, a splash of that. A little lemon and garlic can do amazing things to mashed potatoes."

He didn't want to say that the food needed improvement and that plates came back to the kitchen with side dishes piled high, instant potatoes running down the sides. Grainy, runny potatoes had been a staple as a kid, and he hated serving them to people for money. It cost the same to serve people better food.

Garrett raised an eyebrow. "What else? What did you do to the pork chops?"

Kyle bit his lower lip. He'd done a lot to the pork chops, actually. For a few days he'd used thyme. One day he'd added caramelized pearl onions. "I grilled them and served them with apple butter."

"That's not all."

"And I made an apricot glaze, once."

His boss tilted his head to the side, lowered his chin, and glared at him like a parent who knew they'd been lied to. "Is anything still the same?"

Kyle sat forward, tucking his feet beneath the chair. He laced his fingers. One wrist bore the scar from a fryer burn. "The tea."

Garrett sighed and threw a menu at his feet. "Spill it. One at a time. Hurry."

The words swam together in a blurry alphabet soup. "Nachos. I switched out the runny cheese for melted cheese instead. It costs the same and tastes better. Fresh salsa instead of jarred. I make it a day ahead. The soups are all fresh. No more canned. And I pepper crusted the steaks. I wanted to sell one with blue cheese, but it's not on the menu."

"There has to be a reason you wouldn't clear this with me."

"But I asked and you said—"

"Four nights a week you cook here. The other three, customers come in here and tell me the food doesn't taste the same. At first I was like, well, different cook. It just tastes a little different. But then Arvil tells me he had some sweet orange sauce on his pork chop, and I'm wondering why because I don't sell a pork chop like that." Garrett's eyes were wide.

Kyle fumbled for words, looking for a combination that would get him out of trouble. *Sorry, I won't do it again, Mommy* didn't seem like the right response. He shrugged. "I asked before, if I could make some changes. You said no, and I did it anyway. I made a mistake."

"With which one? Which plate?"

"What do you mean? All of them, I guess."

"You guess, or you know? Why did you do it?"

Kyle scratched behind his ear. "I want to constantly improve. I love to cook. This is my dream job. Not this, exactly. I want to make fresh meals with local ingredients and get people to fall in love with what they choose to eat."

"Why? Why in God's name would that matter to you when you're that smart and you have your whole future in front of you. Don't you hate going home smelling like a deep fryer? Don't you want to work nine to five like a normal person and get a billion weeks of vacation?"

"You don't. You're here more than I am."

"You think I want to be?" Garrett's voice shot up an octave. "You think this was some dream of mine? To look like this because I eat like crap, and I'm on my feet all night, listening to people whine? It's like hostage negotiation sometimes trying to find people I've already hired who will wait on the damn tables. And I swear to God my shoes are always sticky."

He lifted a folder from the makeshift desk and let it fall. "All these bills? Money in and money out. It's a cycle that never ends. And this is your dream?"

Kyle picked at a clean fingernail. "I want to run a store and teach cooking classes. One of those kitchen stores with cast-iron cookware and… It doesn't matter. I'm sorry I messed up the menu. I won't do it anymore."

"God dammit, kid." Garrett leaned forward in his chair, his voice booming between the bathrooms. "I would love for you to do this full time, but it's dumb of me to ask. I want you to write down what you did so we can make a new menu and replicate it. I'll have to teach those other asshats how to do what you do."

Kyle looked up from his hands and into the eyes of his boss. He hadn't expected to find pride, but there it was, mixed with an eyeroll of exasperation. He chewed his lip to quash a smile.

"If they can learn it," Garrett said.

"I hate to let you down. I love working here a lot." Kyle hated the mile walk to work in all kinds of weather when he couldn't catch a ride.

He hated the hours, and the wages were low. If he were honest, Garrett was right. He hated the smell, too. The fryer, the kitchen, and the god-awful bathroom disinfectant smell of that tiny office. "I really like cooking here, but I'm going to college."

Garrett took the folder from the desk and held it out. "Kid. College is a good thing. If you stick around here, you'll only end up doing this paperwork crap in a dusty, greasy office. I'd rather see you do something you love."

"I'd rather cook and open a store, but I need college first." College had never been a question for Kyle. College first, then a job where he could build a safety net and save enough money to start his business. Then he'd find a place in some bustling town and open a store full of dreamy kitchenwares. "I need to learn business, build a foundation, that's the next step."

Garrett leaned back in his seat, the folder still clutched in his hand. "Then what?"

"One step at a time. Until I make it."

# CHAPTER TWENTY-EIGHT

Slivers of onion and drops of tuscan white bean soup seared to the stovetop. This batch roiled his stomach, tied forever to Adelle, to his horrible timing, to his inability to get his life together enough to be with someone who might actually care about him. He flicked an onion heel into the trash while soup boiled furiously in his stock pot, filling the store with savory smells that gave him a headache.

His recipe for his first newspaper column was becoming more of a story about how food gets tied to memories when you're not expecting it. One of his favorite hearty meals was now inextricably chained to his affection for Adelle, how he'd led her on, let her down, then slammed her plan to fix the town. Soup, for all its fluidity, had become a wall.

He grabbed a notepad and wrote down the ingredients. Onion, carrot, celery. White beans soaked overnight with herbs and garlic. Diced ham and soup herbs, two boxes of chicken stock. Mixing unchecked emotion and unbridled pride. Trap the present in a sachet of the past and tie it tight so you never lose it. Throw it all at your dinner companion and expect them to handle it well.

He threw the notebook down on the prep table.

Jacques lifted his head from his spot in the corner, stretched his legs and went back to sleep.

"Sorry, little guy. I got carried away."

Anger boiled within him. Tracey kept creeping into his mind, the way she slurped her soup and scraped her bowl, her fake nails clawing at her spoon. She'd sat across from him at dinner and said he wasn't making forward momentum in his life. Every day he'd gone to work in that soulless office and busted his ass for a promotion, even when the deck was stacked against him. Just living through that was the epitome of momentum.

He'd nursed his wounds that night with four ounces of rye, telling himself that she was just out for more from a man. More money, more stature, more of something he didn't have, and she probably couldn't put her finger on what. She was out there somewhere, probably being as demanding and unsatisfied with someone else.

She'd never even cared about his job. She only asked about it when she wanted to know how close he was to being a partner or a vice president. Then she had the nerve to say he didn't live a decisive life and never made a definitive move on anything, which she would have known was totally wrong if she'd ever bothered to ask.

The timer on the stove went off, and he silenced it. He lowered the temperature and stabbed a wooden spoon into the pot and gave it a twirl. Bits of carrot and bean caught up in the whirlpool, slowing until they settled.

If Tracey had hated his cooking that much, she could have said so two years before that terrible dinner, and she could have left some food on her plate when he cooked for her sometimes.

"Whatever."

He tossed the spoon on a spoon rest shaped like a pig and rubbed his face against his shoulder, brushing his hair from his eyes.

Indecisive. If she thought he couldn't make a decision, she should have seen him the next day. That asshole boss, Carter, calling him into his office and doing exactly what Becker said he would, throwing all the work in his lap.

With a high-pitched tone, he mocked the man who was years and miles away.

"Oh, Kyle. Go ahead and finalize the details of that plan you proposed and put your head together with Huntington. You'll find him down in the corner office with his name on it, playing *Super Mario Brothers* on his Gameboy. He gets the big paycheck, but we're gonna need you to do the work for him. M'kay?"

He stirred the soup again and spun, waving it at Jacques, whose forehead wrinkled when he raised his ears. "I worked damn hard for that spot." Droplets of soup landed on the floor.

He was never one to burn a bridge. Growing up in a small town had taught him that you'll always cross paths with your own regrets. But it had snowballed that day into an avalanche, and he'd ridden it all the way to the bottom.

"Know what I did?"

Jacques took in a deep breath and let it out in a winnowing sigh that heaved in his chest, his eyes closed tight.

"I stormed the records room. Walked right in there and took a box of files, dumped them on an empty desk, and I packed all my crap in that box."

He turned to stir the simmering soup.

"It wasn't much. A coffee cup, that old business card holder, and my planner. I could have carried it all in one arm, I guess. It kinda sucked that was all that was left of a life I dedicated to that job."

He smashed a simmering carrot against the side of the pot.

"I pried my name plate off the door and walked straight past Carter's office carrying that box like I was the hero in some bad '80s movie. I was going to make my own happy ending. No more waiting on other people to tell me when I could be happy. It took five damn years, but there I was doing it."

He threw the lid on the pot and left the soup to simmer.

"See? Now I'm doing what I want. I'm happy. Dammit."

And then there was Adelle. How could he have been so stupid to let his guard down? He'd flirted with her, and then when she picked up on it and flirted back, he let her down. At least she'd understood and didn't take it too much to heart. But every time he made this soup for the rest of his life he'd remember this feeling of never being good enough, of working so hard and always falling short of what he wanted for himself.

He set the timer for forty minutes, grabbed his notepad, and moved the cluttered backroom that he intended to transform into an office.

An old door without hinges or a knob leaned against the wall. Kyle wiped it down with a rag and set it on two old sawhorses to form a desk. He plopped his laptop on it and turned it on. An update started, a spinning wheel counting down a timeless bout of waiting, so he grabbed a bundle of mail instead, held together with orange rubber bands and untouched since Riley dropped them off. He'd been getting really good at avoiding stressful things lately.

He scraped a paint-splattered metal chair across the room, and it echoed in the small space. He fell into it and tore rubber bands from the mail while Jacques padded across the dusty floor and curled up by his feet. He'd hoped for a better ratio of junk mail to bad news, but at least it was sorted. He made piles of what remained. Things to file. Things to trash. Bills to pay.

Between an annual fund plea from his college and an offer of cheaper car insurance was a simple envelope with a stiff insert. He sliced open the flap with a boxcutter and mail from his credit card company fluttered to the counter.

The people who gave him the fancy silver card had replaced it with one of orange instead. A sticker on the card urged him to call and activate it.

*After regular review, your credit score no longer meets eligibility requirements and according to our findings, your income has dropped below the qualified amount. The enclosed card features a new account number. Your balance has been transferred, and you will see a rate increase as well, detailed in another mailing. Please call to activate this card upon receipt and dispose of your old card securely. When your credit score and income meet qualifications again, please feel free to call and reapply. For more information on how interest rates are calculated, please visit our website.*

"I know how interest rates are calculated, you horrible, greedy people."

He pulled his wallet from his back pocket and tossed it open on his door desk. The little silver card was in the back, where he'd kept it safe. It had been great for getting the best concert tickets. Maybe it was a bit shallow, but he'd enjoyed the look he got from waiters when he handed it over to pay for meals, and he'd loved the look he got from his parents when he took them to dinner. It was the last remaining piece of that life that still fit him. Though he hadn't used it until he needed the stoves, it had been a small comfort to know it was there.

At least his mother didn't have to see it all stripped away, and his father thought he was just a guy who read the paper.

They never wanted him to live like they did, fighting at the dinner table every night over money and never making amends because the money never showed up to fix the problem, but they'd stayed together, which was more than Kyle could say. They fought bitterly about how to dig out of every hole, but they did it together. He couldn't get past a first date, and apparently he'd never learned to apologize.

He tossed the card on the desk and leaned back in his chair as the wheel on his laptop spun and spun.

"I'm really sick of coasting through disasters and catastrophes."

Jacques padded over and plopped his squeaky duck on Kyle's shoe.

"Mom got sick, then her funeral. Dad got sick, and I fought with the government. It's like one day just keeps rolling into the next. I always thought things would go back to the way they used to be. They never did."

Jacques grinned, tongue dripping on the floor. Kyle put the orange card in his wallet.

"I never really wanted concert tickets anyway."

Sure, the card was his last tie to a successful life, the last tangible thing he could hold in his hand to show that he'd made it. But it was just a card. The status that came with that stupid silver card status didn't count for much in Ramsbolt. It didn't put food on the table, and he hadn't used it for years.

Kyle grabbed an end of the toy, wrestled it free from Jacques's grip, and gave it a toss. Jacques barked and chased after it, nails scraping the floor.

"It's just stupid credit card. Who cares? I don't have to impress anybody, and I'm not going back to that life, anyway."

He grabbed a pair of old tin snips left behind by a former occupant, and he cut the card into strips.

Jacques returned with the toy in time to sniff the trash can as Kyle scattered the remains of his old credit card.

Laughter found its way in from outside. Kyle pulled back the stained and rotting curtain that shielded the office from the back parking lot. His neighbors—all three of them—were sitting in lawn chairs around a fire pit, drinks in hand. A sad twinge came over him, like the adolescent ping of being left out, but Adelle was having a good time. She deserved it.

Someday, when he didn't have so much work to do, he could relax like that.

Jacques dropped the squeaky duck on Kyle's foot and nudged him with a bark.

"I can't little guy. Not right now."

His laptop woke, and the icons on his desktop showed up like fireworks. He brushed the mail aside and opened a file to start his first column, but Adelle made for a haunting shadow.

There wasn't time to figure out where he'd gone wrong with her, why it was so damn hard to make things right, why he couldn't be the kind of guy to give a woman the time and attention she deserved. He couldn't solve it with a list or a plan, and God knows his heart and his gut hadn't been any help. And there wasn't time to play.

* * *

"This was a great idea, Helen. So much fun. I had no idea pumpkin chili was a thing." Logan joined Helen at the register, clutching the handles of her take-out bag. Her shoulder-length brown hair was held back with a rubber band, and her T-shirt was stained red with chili. "I'll take this little tray of herbs, too. They'll look cute on the windowsill, as long as I don't kill them."

Helen leaned on her cane and patted Logan's arm. "Just keep them watered. They'll be fine. You know, I bet you could use pumpkin puree in the chili, too, if you don't have time to roast diced pumpkin."

"Or you could brown the ground beef ahead of time." Kyle added small containers of chives and sour cream to their bags. "Dump it all in a crockpot on low, and it's ready when you get home from work."

He handed over their receipts and packed the tray of herbs in a small box, wrapping paper around the plants. His hands could barely hold the box as he dropped it in a bag with tissue paper. Exhaustion set in, but adrenaline still sparked beneath his skin, keeping his brain wired. He would sleep like a rock for the first night in weeks, if he could turn off the inner trembling of shame and stop glancing at Adelle's shop, hoping it would look reachable across the divide.

Jacques tugged on the leg of his jeans. "Thanks for coming. If you think of it, I'd love a review. Maybe tell your friends."

Logan exchanged glances with Helen. "Will do. I don't get away from the tavern very often. This was a treat. Thanks for the great night. I would definitely do this again."

"I thought it would make a fun outing." Helen smiled. "I haven't cooked much since I turned the diner into the tavern. It's been years since I made a good meal when it wasn't a holiday."

"And you have a really cute dog." Logan smiled down at the puppy, who whimpered his disapproval at being ignored.

Kyle's first cooking class was a small group, half occupancy. But it was a cozy start, and more fulfilling than sitting on a stool all day waiting for shoppers.

"I'm sorry to say that I never knew the diner. I don't get out much myself," he said. "I'll have to stop by the tavern for a drink sometime."

Helen leaned closer and whispered. "It's been a rough start. You deserve one."

It was no secret, then. Kyle offered her a lopsided grin. "I was a bit surprised anyone signed up for classes at all."

"This town is weird sometimes." Logan slid the bag up her arm. "I had a hard time when I first moved here. But it's a pretty forgiving place."

"You just have to hit the right note." Helen turned to the door, Logan at her side.

Jacques growled and tugged at his pant leg in a game of tug-of-war that Kyle couldn't play. "Okay, little guy. Give me a minute. I just need to close up. Then we can play."

Kyle was alone in his store, alone in the silence. He adjusted his cooking apron and wiggled onto the stool. His closing procedures played out in his mind like a theater performance, choreography from someone else's dance routine. Instead of counting down his drawer, his eyes locked on the counter, his brain turned off, and his puppy curled up in the corner with a deep sigh. Jacques had given up.

"Kyle?"

He blinked to wash the sleep away. Adelle stood just inside the door. He couldn't bring himself to look at her. The shame of the way he rejected her was nothing compared to the inferno it became when he couldn't apologize like a normal person. As tired as he was, he would definitely make it worse if he opened his stupid mouth.

He fumbled with the apron's strings and pulled it off over his head, letting it fall on the counter like his deflated ego.

"I wanted to see how it went tonight."

Jacques lifted his head and blinked at Adelle. He sprang to his feet and lunged for her.

She bent to rustle his ears. "I'm here to pet you, too. Yes I am, you little cutie. I miss seeing you. What a sweetie you are."

A wave of anxiety welled up from his toes, flooding his chest and making it hard to breath. His hands shook. He tried to crack his neck, but the tension was too thick. He unfurled a paper towel from a roll and wiped down his counter. "I sold a set of your pots. I'll write you a check in the morning."

"I'm not in a rush if you want to wait." Adelle stood and shifted her weight, hands in her pockets. "I didn't come here for that."

He wadded the paper towel and tossed it in the trash. The business guy in him, the one who never showed his cards, put on his poker face. "I was a total dick. Is that what you came to hear?" Arms folded, he leaned against the brick wall.

Her face flushed red. "That's not what I came for at all. I came over to make things better, not worse. I can't afford to fight with a neighbor. Marissa told me what she said to you. I'm the town manager; I can't be involved in divisiveness here. It's too small. Life would be a lot easier if I could go on hating you forever, but it's just not that easy."

"Fair enough." He threw his hands up in surrender, squeezed his arms tighter around his middle and stared at his shoes. They were the wrong thing for being on his feet all day. His heels ached. "I'm never going to be able to say the right thing around you, am I?"

Adelle sighed, and the store filled with both of their tensions, tugging at the air.

She took one step, but stayed on the black rubber mat. "I understand the attraction wasn't mutual, and you're not required to feel anything for me at all. I crossed a boundary I shouldn't have, and I came to put things right between us. I just want to be an adult about this."

He curled his toes and leaned his head back, the bricks like sandpaper against his scalp. "Adelle, I keep getting this all wrong. I wanted to apologize to you. I never meant that the attraction wasn't mutual. It was. And Jacques has been very sad and scolding me..." He kicked his feet out, slumping against the wall, hands in his pockets. Damn poker face. "This is so stupid, this thing I do where I try to act like I don't have feelings."

He pushed away from the wall, but his feet were frozen, stuck to the floor. He pulled at the hem of his shirt. Adelle made no movement, no sounds. She stood on the rubber mat, held back by some invisible wall, but that was as close as he wanted her to get, anyway. His ears burned, and he rubbed at the tip of one.

"This is stupid," he said. "I don't know why I do this. I need to take some responsibility for the shit I create, and pretending like Jacques is the one who's hurt is just a childish deflection. I don't know how to apologize. That's what it comes down to. My parents fought like cats and dogs, and I never saw them apologize for a damn thing. They just went on like it never even happened, so maybe that's my whole problem. You have your whole life together. You have the balls to come over here and try to create something better between us, and when I went over there to apologize to you all I could do was stare at my hands. I'm a numbers guy, and I like to cook. I'm just not good at relationships."

Adelle's arms hung at her sides, a surrender he knew well. "I do *not* have my life together. It might look like it because I have some town manager role, but I'm so bad at relationships the only real friendships I have are Marissa and Penny. I'm trying, though."

The hard shell cracked. A yolk of empathy bled from him. It was too fragile to collect, and there was too much of it to hide. Of course she understood. It was a universal truth, wasn't it, the search for belonging? That's what business was all about, putting on suits and standing up tall. Shopping in the right places and not being seen in the wrong ones. It was a code, a standard of operations that brought people just close enough to profit from each other and just far enough apart to justify the process. That's why he'd been so good at it. It was a great place to hide.

Of course Adelle understood. She wasn't all that different. The perfect small town florist. The brave town manager. Inside, she was just as raw as he was.

He pressed the heels of his hands against his eyes and fireworks erupted in the dark. "I'm sorry. I didn't mean to hurt your feelings, or break your heart. I didn't mean to lead you on. It's just that when it looked like something might come of it, I clammed up. After all these years, I'm finally realizing that—" He searched the ceiling for the right words. "I've watched a lot of relationships fall apart because of bad timing. I have a lot of things to sort out before I can get involved with someone. Money. This place."

Adelle's nod was nearly imperceptible. "It's not true, you know, but I understand it. I guess I always thought I couldn't have a relationship until I found someone who would be satisfied with the status quo. It always felt like people were rushing off to find something better, and I wasn't going to waste my time unless I found someone who wasn't going to leave me for something better."

"They'd be crazy to leave you."

"You'd be crazy to wait." Adelle shifted her weight, hands in her back pockets. "Life doesn't happen in stages like that, you know."

"It does if you want to be happy in the end."

"What about being happy now? I'm not trying to change your mind. I'm just…"

"No. I know. You want to understand. I always believed there were dues you had to pay. You can't have the corner office until you put in the work. I don't know if I believe that anymore."

"Real life isn't corner offices. You don't earn one thing at a time."

"You do if you don't want to sacrifice everything at once." Kyle shook his head. "How could I invest in a relationship if my head and my heart are somewhere else?"

Jacques pawed at Adelle's shoe and blinked up at her. She gave the puppy a weak smile that almost looked sad. "All I know is that we're neighbors, and neither of us can afford for this to be awkward. I don't know how to pretend it didn't happen, and I don't want to be embarrassed every time I see you. Is there any chance we can get over the awkward part?"

Kyle chewed his lower lip. He didn't want the awkward either. "Yeah. I was horrible to you. I hurt your feelings and my own. You're way too nice for me to use you for some short-term comfort. I'm very sorry."

Adelle took a hesitant step from the mat, and Kyle shifted his weight, inching further down the wall for the cold, hard comfort.

"You're sorry you felt it or sorry about the dinner?"

"Both? Can it be both?"

"Of course." Adelle smiled and turned a little, her shoulder pointed to the door. "There's something comforting in your line of thinking. I mean, if your hypothesis is correct, the universe owes me a lot of happiness for all the work I put in. I haven't seen the financial payoff, but if you're right, it should be here any day."

The lighting changed when she smiled at him. Her sad, weak smile said her heart didn't mean it, but the room seemed warmer somehow. The tension snapped like a rubber band, and it sent his heart racing all over again. He was too tired to fight with his own emotions. All he wanted to do was climb the stairs, climb into bed, and hide.

"You deserve all of it," he said. "The whole five-leaf clover. Faith, hope, love, luck. Someone who can give you everything."

"Thanks." Adelle's eyes curled at the corners and her nose wrinkled when she grinned. She pushed the door open and cold air fluttered in. "Maybe someday you'll believe you deserve it, too."

Jacques hopped in the window and pressed his nose to the glass, his tail wagging his body as he watched her go.

# CHAPTER TWENTY-NINE

Kyle synced a picture from his phone to his laptop. He tapped his foot on the stool while it uploaded to his new website. The internet had always been a wild unreachable planet, full of pictures without substance and pages without form. But after a few hours of work and the cost of a lunch, he had a basic site where people could sign up for classes and get directions. As achievements went, this one ranked up there with his college diploma and the first time he changed the oil in a tractor without using a manual.

He snapped a picture of the homepage with his phone, something to remember the day by, and hit the publish button.

*Loading.*

A pen slithered across the counter as he tapped his foot. He caught it before it hit the floor. Across the room a woman pressed buttons on an Instant Pot that wasn't plugged in.

"Let me know if you're looking for something specific." The ball spun around and around.

The woman waved. "Will do."

*Published!*

Kyle clicked the link to view the site. It wasn't elaborate. No one would mistake him for a big fancy store with a marketing team, but it was a really good start. And someday, if he worked hard enough, that Visit Us page would have several locations to choose from.

Outside, an early autumn snow squall pushed up the street. The light from Adelle's shop was barely visible through the wall of clumpy flakes flying sideways. It was nice to look over at her store and not feel the stabbing shiv of guilt in his chest that had plagued him the day before. Things might still be a little awkward, but at least they weren't mad at each other, and he didn't have to hide from her.

The door creaked ajar, and Helen entered, brushing snow from her hair. Kyle waved, and she returned it with a shake of her cane.

The Instant Pot woman set a pumpkin spice candle on the counter and dug her wallet from her purse, her eyes fixed on the door. "Is it supposed to snow like this all day?"

*Tourist.* Kyle pushed his laptop to the side. "Flurries in the morning with a few squalls coming through. It's just about over, I guess."

"Thank God," she said. "It looks festive, though."

He ran her card and tied the bag handle with ribbon. "It does. I'd rather get through Halloween first, but I don't mind a little snow. Makes travel dangerous so stay safe out there."

"Will do. Not much further to go." She accepted the bag and walked to the door. "Thanks. You have a cute store here."

Kyle nodded with a smile. He'd never tire of hearing it. "Thanks. Come again."

Helen plodded around the old candy table. She held up a turkey shaped cookie cutter sideways and tilted her head. "George Washington?"

"Turkey."

"Hmm." She carried it to the counter. "I need a new griddle. The nonstick coating is flaking off my old one, and apparently you can get tragic diseases if you cook on it. I've got one new knee, one very old knee, and an aversion to lesions. Do you have cast iron?"

Kyle slipped from the stool. "Single burner or double?"

"Goodness, me. Single. I'm not that popular." She tossed her purse, the size of a beach bag, on the counter with a wallop. She pulled from it an umbrella, a hairbrush, and a full-size box of tissues. "My wallet is in here somewhere."

Kyle grabbed a griddle still in the box and placed it on the counter. Helen plopped the cookie cutter on top.

"I love having Logan and Grey over for holidays. Which reminds me..." She shook her wallet at the ceiling. "Darn this thing. Always goes right to the bottom. Anyway. When is your next cooking class? Please tell me it's on a Monday."

Kyle skimmed his calendar. "Monday the fifth."

She slapped her debit card down on the calendar. "Sign us up, please. Me and Logan."

"Do you want to know what we're cooking?" He opened his calendar on his laptop and entered their names into his schedule.

Helen waved her hand. "No, no. She's like a daughter to me. Kids these days are so used to convenience foods. It's my personal mission to teach the girl to cook." She leaned across the counter to convey her secret. "It's very hush-hush you know, but Logan was very rich once. No one ever taught the girl to cook. She thought food fell from the sky when I met her. But it's something fun we can do together."

"I can't imagine not knowing how to cook." Kyle shoved tissue paper into a bag. "Is this everything?"

"Indeed."

"Baking. Bread I can make, but I can't bake a pie to save my life."

Kyle ran her card while Helen shoved tissues and umbrellas and a pair of socks back into her giant bag.

"I knew your grandmother well, you know. Too bad she didn't pass on those pie skills."

He snapped to attention. The few people who remembered her referred to her as the pie lady. His father rarely told stories about her. "Knew her well?"

She took her card back and slid it into her wallet. "Oh, yes. Talked to her all the time. I knew your dad, too, when he was a kid. Precocious child. The kids used to play traffic cop in the streets. Hopscotch. He'd hide in my hydrangea and play cops and robbers."

"What was my gran like?" *Never mind my father.* "Can you tell me about her blueberry pie?"

She put a hand to her heart. "That pie was the best I ever had. And consistent, too. I'll never forget the last one; it was just as good as the first. Of course, I didn't know it was the last one at the time. The best things in life are that way, aren't they? You never get a chance to say a proper goodbye. But if I did have a chance, I would have sent a piece off to science to figure out what made it so good."

"You and me both. I never knew her and never had the pie, but I have her recipe. It just comes out with lumps of flour and a soggy bottom."

"You gotta blind bake your crusts, son. Everybody knows that." Helen's eyes narrowed. "And why are you putting clumps of flour in a pie?"

"The recipe said to toss the berries in it. It thickens them up."

Helen's jaw dropped. Her eyes widened, incredulous. "She didn't use flour. I don't know how old that recipe was, but she used corn starch. I know 'cause I lent her some once when she ran out." She tapped her temple. "Squirreled that away up here."

"Corn starch. And blind baking. That makes sense. I tried to follow the recipe, to make it just like she did. Never occurred to me that it might have been written down wrong."

Helen clutched her purse. "You get that right, you're sitting on a gold mine."

He laughed and wrapped the cookie cutter in paper. "I doubt that."

She grasped his hand, her knuckles white. "Share it with me. I would pay a fortune for another slice of that pie. Of course my idea of a fortune isn't anything like Logan's, but I would pay a lot for it. Can I make a copy of it? Pretty please."

"Oh, no." He dropped the cookie cutter in the bag. "There's a stern warning written on that recipe."

She accepted the bag with mock disdain. "Then you must learn to make it and save me a slice. I'll make tea and tell you stories about your grandmother. Anyway, I'm glad I can support her grandson. If anyone is worthy of her recipe, it's you."

"Worthy." It's what his gran had written on the recipe. Only a truly worthy Nolan could figure out the secret. "Do you know if she had a secret ingredient?"

Helen paused in the doorway and shrugged. "Beats me. But if anyone can figure it out, I'm sure it's you. Always liked your cooking."

The door closed behind Helen, and Kyle leaned over the counter, looking for Jacques.

"You want to go for a walk now that the store's empty?" He listened for the jingle of the puppy's tags, but the store was silent. "Jacques?"

He slipped from the stool and around the table, poking his head into the window nook, but Jacques's bed in the window was empty.

"Jacques?" Flinging open the door to the narrow back office, he expected to find Jacques curled up under the desk, but Jacques wasn't there. The door to the basement was locked, but he threw it open anyway. The stairs were dark.

Kyle's voice echoed off the stone walls. "Jacques? Are you down here?"

Of course he wasn't. Jacques never went in the basement. Locking the door, he rushed back into the store, his heart thundering in his chest. He took the stairs to his apartment two at a time. *Don't panic. He can fall asleep where he stands. He's probably under the table or on the bed.*

But he wasn't.

"Jacques! Where are you?"

Kyle tossed the covers off the bed and threw himself to the floor, pushing aside boxes.

"Jacques?"

He wasn't under the bed with the sweaters or on the bathmat or curled up under the tiny dining table. He wasn't curled up in any cabinets or under the chairs.

Kyle rushed back down the stairs, spinning in place in the middle of the store. He rubbed an eyebrow as his racing heart steadied.

*Think. When did I see him last?*

He peered out the door wiping his sweaty hand on his pant leg, eyes darting up and down the street. He clutched his shirt, his chest, where heartburn flared.

He must have slipped out when Helen came in. Or that lady from out of town. He rubbed his eyes and tried to think. There was a couple this morning. They bought a french press. It was snowing when they left. Then the woman with the candle.

Kyle shoved the door open and stepped outside.

"Jacques?" He called out as loud as his voice would go, his word bouncing back off the stone storefronts.

Wind whipped through his thin dress shirt, carrying his breath away. He folded his arms and clutched his elbows trying to keep in the warmth, but his breath froze, and he lost feeling in his nose. The sky was darkened by the snow, and everything was covered by three inches of white. There were no paw prints in any direction. Just Helen's footprints fading in the drifts.

*He's been gone a while.*

"Jacques!"

A gust of wind blew him backward. Tears welled in his eyes, and his breath hitched in his throat. He winced and covered his face with his hands, shaking from his core.

He flung the door open and stumbled back inside. His hoodie hung on a hook at the bottom of the stairs. He jammed his arms into it and flung himself back into the snow. It came down thick and heavy, blowing into his face and making him blink. He squinted against the icy cold and peered in every doorway.

"Jacques?" His throat was frozen, and the words seemed to hang in the air.

The street emptied onto the turning circle and the park. The yellow glow from the streetlights couldn't reach the ground, clumps of snow streamed through. Kyle studied the ground for prints, but there was no puppy huddled under the benches or cowering behind the sailor statue. If he slipped out the door before the couple came, he could be anywhere. His footprints would be covered no matter where Kyle looked. He sprinted, screaming Jacques's name, slipping on slick patches, down Main Street, but there was no sign of the puppy.

His heart thundering in his chest, he turned back, racing up Main Street to his store.

The lights were still on at Adelle's. He brushed snow from his hair and stomped his boots on the curb before peering into her window. She was there, cutting chunks off some plant. She must have heard him, because she looked up and waved him in.

Inside, her store was warm. There was no time to let it soak in. His hands were numb, and he rubbed them together hoping the feeling would come back.

Concern spread across her face, and she let her scissors fall to the counter. "Is everything okay? You don't look so good."

"Jacques is gone."

She grasped his hands. A day ago, her touch would have burned him. A week ago it would have set him on fire. But it was comfort, as cold as it was. He let her lead him to a stool.

"Sit. When did you see him last?"

He shook his head. "I don't know. Earlier. Before the snow. I was making a website, and people were shopping."

"Have you been outside long? You look frozen solid. Where's your coat? You can't run around in this cold in a sweatshirt. Do you need tea?"

"Tea?" How could she think about tea at a time like this? "I don't need tea. I need Jacques."

"Where did you look?"

"The park and Main Street. It's so hard to see. I called for him, but—"

Adelle rushed to a room in the back. She was only gone a second, but when she returned she was wearing a thick coat and a woolen hat. "I'll be back. I'll check the cemetery."

"The cabin. That old hunting lodge in the cemetery. He always pulls on the leash like he wants to go there."

"Stuart's house. I'll check there. You go back to the store in case he returns. Get your phone and post in the town Facebook group. Let everybody know he's missing, to keep an eye out."

"Good idea." He slid from the stool. "Thank you. I'm lost without him."

She reached out and touched his arm. "I know. We'll find him."

Snow peaked in wind-blown banks as he crossed the street. It blew sideways, pushing his hair into his eyes. He didn't deserve the warmth of the store, not for being negligent, and oblivious to the thing that mattered most in his life. He was so stupid to think that Jacques would stay put in the store, that he wouldn't get distracted by something shiny and wander off. And it was so cold out. Jacques was growing, but he was still so small. He held his phone in shaky hands and posted online to let the town know, to beg for their help, and he paced the floor, tugging at his hair and leaving dirty clumps of snow that melted to muddy footprints.

The door flung open and Adelle rushed in, her arms wrapped tight around her middle. She joined him by the table. "He wasn't in the cemetery. I went everywhere."

"Did you check the cabin?"

Adelle nodded. "I checked. Stuart hasn't seen him. I'm going back to my store to make some flyers. Stuart said he'd print them. You need to get something to eat."

"I can't eat. I'm not hungry."

"You look pale. You should eat."

"I can't sit still. I need to go out there and look for him."

Adelle grabbed him by the shoulders and lowered him into a chair. "You need to stay right here, in case Jacques comes back. He probably will. Did you post online?"

"I did." He ran his finger around the silver edge of a dish. All these things meant nothing if Jacques wasn't okay. He pushed up from the chair and retraced his paces, but the room spun and his vision was blurry. Adelle had a point; he didn't feel well. He fell back into the chair.

She was gone for just a moment that seemed like a year. The snow had slowed when she entered again, planting her feet on the rubber mat and waving some flyers.

"I called Penny while I printed these. Nate is going to call around and make sure all the stores downtown know. He said he'd come and sit in your store to keep an eye out for Jacques so you can help look. Penny and I are going to hang these on every surface in town. Wanna come?"

"Thank you. Yes. I'm coming." He leapt to his feet and grabbed his coat and Jacques's leash.

Adelle held the door open, and he stepped onto the sidewalk. "You're welcome. This is what neighbors do. I love Jacques. I'm just sorry I couldn't find him."

"If I hadn't been so focused on this stupid store, I wouldn't have lost him. He's the only important thing I have. I have to get him back."

# CHAPTER THIRTY

The sky hinted at dawn. Kyle could just make out rooflines and tree tops from his shop window. Most of the snow had melted, leaving only tiny clumps where late-day shadows had lurked. Jacques was somewhere out there, alone and cold.

Kyle paced the floor where yesterday's dirty footprints had dried into soot-colored smudges, leash wrapped tight around his hand. The shop was haunted by the lack of sound. The spaces where puppy snorts and jingling tags ought to fill were vacant, as hollow as his insides, a silence so deep it seemed the walls were closing in. He trembled with hunger, yet he couldn't eat, and he hadn't slept.

The streets were empty. Adelle's windows were dark. It was barely five thirty. Resting his forehead against the cool glass of the door, he made foggy splotches with his breath and rubbed the back of his neck. He squinted into the puddles of streetlight, hoping to see his best friend, flappy paws and floppy ears, bumbling his way home.

Kyle dug a pen from under the register and scrawled a note. *Jacques is still missing.* He stuck a piece of tape to the back and grabbed his sweatshirt from the banister. With the leash still tight around his hand, he rushed across the street and slapped the message to Adelle's door, facing in, so she'd see it first thing. Then he turned toward the park, walking down the center of the road that ran from the town to the farm, calling out for Jacques as he went, looking under every shrub and car along the way.

The mile walk took less than half an hour, but his hands were too cold to check his phone as he crested the hill. He had no idea what time it was. The farm came into view. The lights were still out in the old farmhouse, but Dan's truck idled on the gravel path, clouds of exhaust heaving into the air and hanging low. Golden light spilling from open barn doors. Whoever replaced him liked an early start.

Kyle picked up his pace. If Jacques had stumbled back to the farm, he could be anywhere. Maybe someone took him into the house for the night. He felt horrible for not thinking of it sooner. His legs cramped from the cold and lack of rest, his body shivered as he bolted down the gravel path.

"Dan? You here?" He panted outside the open barn door.

Dan crunched past him and dropped an oily cardboard box in the truck. "What are you doing out this way? At this hour even."

"Jacques is missing."

"What's a Jacques?"

"My dog. The puppy."

Dan wiped his hands on his pants and winced at the blast of icy air sweeping up the drive. "I ain't seen no dogs here."

Kyle twisted the leash tighter around his hand. "You'll keep an eye out? Let everybody know?"

Dan nodded. "People'll be showing up here. We'll keep an eye out.

You wanna stick around? Get a cup of somethin' warm and take a look around?"

Part of him did want something warm, just enough fuel to tear every inch of soil from the earth until he found his friend, that little furry face and his sweet little ears. But it was daylight now. No time for warmth. He needed to keep searching, and the more ground he could cover the better.

"No, thanks. You'll look around?"

Dan nodded. "Course. Nobody wants to see harm come to a little dog. I'll get everybody on it first thing. We'll bring him down to your store if we nab him."

"Thanks." Kyle waited until he was on the road to run. No use twisting an ankle in the gravel now. He tore down the street, and hopped the curb, slipping down the muddy bank toward the creek, his eyes fixed on the ground for puppy prints. Clumps of ice still laid in the crux where tree trunks rose from the earth. Water bubbled over rocks in the creek. No sign of Jacques.

He climbed the hill and crossed the narrow bridge, pausing to catch his breath in the park.

The town was waking. Posters hung the night before fluttered in the morning breeze on every pole, and the cloudless blue sky seemed cruel. Light-headed and thirsty, he took the rest of the walk one step at a time.

If he'd stopped to play and gave him more treats and wasn't so focused on things that didn't matter like a stupid website, Jacques would still be here. The leash was wrapped so tightly around Kyle's hand his fingers were white, but he couldn't loosen or let it go. It was the last tether that held his life together. Jacques was gone.

Kyle's body wore down; the hunger caught up to him. It took all his effort and energy to make it from the town park to Marissa's. It was the only place open at that hour, light streaming from her window, stretching into the street. Light-headed and winded, opening his eyes wide against the head rush, he froze outside Marissa's bakery.

His mouth went dry. Marissa hated his guts.

A bell rang out when he opened the door. Marissa tore into a sleeve of paper coffee cups and dumped them on a stack. She turned, rooted to the spot, one eyebrow raised.

"My dog ran away." It wasn't at all what he wanted to say. "It's been a long morning, and I'm famished. Can I buy breakfast? You're the only place open at this hour."

Marissa slipped behind the counter. She balled the sleeve from the cups and threw it into the trash. "Of course you can." She flipped a switch and lights came on above the counter. "You look like crap."

"Thanks. I deserve that."

Marissa folded her arms. "What'll it be?"

He ran a hand over his face, and it came away wet and clammy. He hadn't showered or shaved. Nothing looked good. Everything looked revolting, and the smell of something from the kitchen turned his mouth sour.

"Plain bagel? Toasted? Some carbs would be good."

She threw a bagel in the slicer. "You need more than that. I'll make you a sandwich."

"You don't have to do that."

Lifting a shoulder in a half shrug, she said, "I know I don't. But I want to. I can't send you back out there without a proper meal. Adelle would kill me."

"No, she wouldn't." Kyle fell into an empty chair by the coffee station.

"Yes, she would. She told me not to be so hard on you. Girl doesn't know what's good for her."

He picked at the sharp stray edge of the metal band around the table's edge. "I talked to her. We're good. I was selfish, pretending the only feelings around here were my own."

"You don't have to explain anything to me." She turned her back and inched toward the door.

"Clearly I do." His heart couldn't handle any more. The shop and the money, messing up with Adelle. Losing Jacques. It was all too much. He ran a hand over his forehead. "I apologized to Adelle, and we're good now. Sometimes I think that I don't owe anybody anything. Maybe I don't owe you an explanation about what happened between Adelle and me, but we both know what kind of town this is, and I don't want you to think I'm that kind of person. I didn't mean to lead her on or hurt her feelings. If you don't think I'm good enough for her, you're not wrong. But she and I patched things up anyway. If you're still holding a grudge, that's fine. But if you want to resolve it, I'm right here. Sure, I should be out there looking for my lost dog, but if you want to hash this out, let's do it."

Marissa wrapped a sandwich in paper and tucked it into a bag. She hovered by the toaster, waiting for the bagel. "I don't hold grudges around here, because I can't afford it any more than you can. I don't need enemies in a town that runs on forgiveness."

The bagel slid from the conveyor onto the tray. Marissa grabbed a toasted half and tossed it on a plate. "Shmear?"

"No, thanks." Kyle pulled his wallet from his pocket and hauled his weary bones to the counter. "What do I owe you?"

"Nothing. I'm sorry about your dog. I'll keep an eye out." She handed him a paper cup. "Grab some coffee before you go."

"Thanks. I could use it." Kyle took the bag and the cup. He filled it from a carafe. "I mean it. I'm serious about fixing this. I don't have time right now, and my brain's not firing on all cylinders, but soon. I don't want fake niceties; I want to make this right. I'll bring food or something, and we can talk about it."

Marissa nodded and said with a smile, "We're good. I'm sorry I got defensive. But I won't turn down food. Especially if it's your grandmother's blueberry pie. It's legendary. Rumor has it you have her recipe."

His breath hitched in his throat. "You know about my grandmother's pie?"

"Doesn't everybody? I gave up trying to make pies. Nothing out of my kitchen was half as good."

# CHAPTER THIRTY-ONE

*If I'd stopped to play and given him more treats, he wouldn't have taken off. He's lonely. He needed me, and I spent a day making a stupid website.*

Kyle's body eroded. The store seemed to get further with each step. Never had a bagel and a sandwich weighed so much. Marissa's coffee burned his throat and seared his insides on the way to his stomach, where it churned, threatening.

The crowd in the flower shop could be heard two doors down. It took all Kyle's strength to open her door. Inside, Adelle was on the phone, finger to her ear to block out the commotion. Nate hunched over a notebook on the counter, Penny inspecting her phone at his side. Stuart pounded keys on his laptop.

"Hey, guys." The door closed behind him.

"No luck, huh?" Penny looked up from her phone. She gestured to Adelle. "Adelle is calling everyone. Diane will be here soon. Carol's closing up the hardware store now, and she'll meet us in the park. Riley said he'll keep an eye out on his rounds today. And Nate's making a map of town so we can organize a search party."

Stuart's eyes were fixed on his laptop. He typed while he talked. "I'm emailing the flyer out to the newspaper's local distribution list."

Kyle's empty insides coiled. "You guys are going through a lot of effort. This is so nice of you. I don't know what I'll do if—"

Adelle pressed a button on her phone and tossed it on the counter. "I left a message for Grey. You look terrible. Did you eat?"

Kyle shook his head and held up the bag. "I checked the farm, and stopped at Marissa's."

"Where's your coat?" She kicked a stool in his direction and pushed him onto it. "You never wear a coat."

"I didn't take one." He dug the bagel from the bag and took a bite.

"I keep telling you, you're going to freeze to death running around town in a sweatshirt." Hands on her hips, she scrutinized him, lip curled.

"I'm too hot. I feel hot." He spoke with his mouth full.

"You look like crap," she said.

"There. Six zones." Nate clicked the pen closed and dropped it on the counter. He turned to Kyle. "I get it. Too restless to sit still. We'll look everywhere."

Kyle brushed bagel crumbs from his jeans. He tried to force a smile, but his mouth was too stubborn to conform. His nose was frozen, and his eyes felt hot and wet. He wanted to be excited, to be hopeful and at least look like he was happy and grateful for the help but every ounce of him wanted to slide off the stool and onto the floor.

Penny locked her phone and put it in her pocket. "I did some research. Somebody says you should put something that smells like you outside so he can find you. Like your pillow case or a blanket you use or something."

His stomach clenched. He shoved the bagel back in the bag. "I can do that. I'll do it right now. Thanks for your help, guys." He reached out and touched Adelle's arm. The move would have been unthinkable even hours before. Now her comfort was all he wanted, aside from getting Jacques back. "We'll definitely find him with all this help."

He hoped they believed his words, because he didn't. The night had been so cold, Kyle feared the worst.

Adelle grasped his hand and squeezed. "Where did you look?"

His breath caught in his throat, and he swallowed hard. "The farm. Down by the creek and under the bridge."

"Okay. Let's get to the park and meet Carol." Adelle grabbed her coat and flung her clover scarf around her neck. "Kyle, you stay here. You need to rest. We'll cover the town."

Penny spread her fingers in her gloves. "I'm sure we'll find him. He's just out having a good romp, and he'll be back in no time with a million stories to tell."

The three of them left, and Kyle was alone in Adelle's shop, surrounded by flowers and a soft crackly radio station. It was twenty-six and sunny just this side of Canada and coming up next was a four song block to get the day started.

He slinked across the street to his store, flinging off his sweatshirt and throwing it as far as he could. The zipper scraped against the floor. The crash wasn't satisfying enough. He wanted to grasp the dishes and hurl them at the walls, shatter the pottery and flip over the tables, but he was too weak for the rage to budge. He snagged his sweatshirt, opened the door, and threw it outside instead. Just in case Jacques could smell it.

He yelled at the ceiling. "How could I be so damn stupid? If I'd spent a fraction of my energy telling him how much I care, if I listened when he pulled on my pant leg or played with him when he asked or gave him just one damn minute of my time instead of spending all my energy on this stupid store, we'd still be safe and warm at the farm. How could I be so naïve as to think that anything mattered more than him?"

An alarm went off in Kyle's stomach. He needed more than two bites of a bagel. He needed protein, fuel for his brain, or the day would spiral into the darkest of nights.

Falling into a chair as the room spun, he dug the sandwich from the bag and thanked Marissa for knowing better than he did what he needed.

*All I have to do is eat and be here in case Jacques shows up. How hard could it be?*

Dog tags jingled from the back office, and he sprang to his feet, knocking his sandwich to the floor.

"Jacques?" He sprinted to the back, running into the corner of a prep table on the way. He rubbed his thigh where a bruise was sure to form, limping through the office. No Jacques.

Out of the corner of his eye, a small form moved in the shadows. He searched beneath the desk, but no puppy.

Rubbing his eyes with the heels of his hands, he returned to his sandwich.

*Five second rule.*

He took a bite, holding it between his teeth, commanding his stomach to hold it down. His sweatshirt lay in a crumpled ball on the sidewalk outside. Dragging his chair so he had a clear view, he settled and chewed, one foot tapping the floor, jiggling glasses on a shelf nearby.

A bird landed on the curb, pecking at gravel. It hopped to the sweatshirt and tugged on the drawstrings and flew away frustrated. No

Jacques, though.

Creaking floors and sun-warmed windows popped in their frames. It was all in his imagination, puppy footsteps all over the store. If he closed his eyes tight, he could take for granted it was Jacques, playing and prancing, begging for treats. Taking Jacques for granted was exactly what he'd done. He never made the puppy feel secure, at peace, and at home. No wonder he'd run away.

A wall of cold air blasted into him, and Helen stumbled in, her giant bag slung over her arm. Her cane made a glassy puddle where she rested it.

"So glad you're open." She ran a hand over her wet hair and dried it on her elastic-waist khakis. Kyle blinked up at her, unsure if she were the apparition of a delirious mind. "It's such an ordeal, getting into the car these days. Of course I was halfway here when I thought I should have called. The weather being what it was. But what are a few flurries among Mainers?"

He opened his mouth to validate the reality of her, but she pulled a giant freezer bag from her purse, holding it high like a holy grail.

"I've got a few of these," she said. "You can have 'em."

Whatever was in that bag, its form was indistinct. Dark and frozen. "Blueberries?"

She tossed the frozen bag of lumps on Penny's table, on a platter, and slung her purse at their side. Bag after bag of frozen berries, slicked with condensation landed on his dishes.

"Your grandmother wasn't just a pie lady. She was the blueberry lady. She never wanted anybody to know that."

Kyle shook his head. "What does that mean? Blueberry lady? And why not?"

Helen gestured widely to the street. "All those bushes. They don't come from nowhere. Your grandmother done that. I used to help her, back when I had a back. She needed berries. The best berries. But she didn't have any land to grow 'em. A woman raising a boy on her own had to take some short cuts. If you know what I mean. I'd go over there for tea and help her pot the stems out to make more bushes. I never told nobody that. She swore me to secrecy."

Kyle stood and paced between the berries and his shelves. "Hold on. I didn't get a lot of sleep. I may not be putting these things together right. Are you saying she planted the blueberry bushes?"

Helen nodded. "All over this town. Along driveways. Between houses. Down by the creek. Adelle ain't the only one who knows how to make a plant. Your grandmother found the best berries and propagated new shrubs from 'em. She'd dig up the bad ones and plant better. Did it all over this town. Then she'd go out early in the morning before the town was up and pick what she needed. She didn't want anybody yelling at her for planting things or stealing her berries, I guess. So she kept it on the down low."

He jumped to his feet and grasped Helen by the shoulders, pulling her into a hug that knocked her off her feet.

"I got a bad knee!" She steadied herself with a chair.

"I'm sorry. I'm sorry. I am. I get it now. Only a true Nolan from Ramsbolt can work out the mystery." He said it to himself, but Helen's face twisted with questions. He brushed them aside. "Something my gran wrote on the recipe."

He grasped a bag. "I can have these? Really?"

"Of course. That's what I brought 'em for. Been in my freezer. More where that came from all over town. When the time is right, though.

Nobody deserves them more than you."

He gathered the berries in his arms, holding them to his chest. "Thank you. This is so kind. I don't know what to say. This is some kind of miracle."

"Not a miracle." Helen hiked her purse onto her shoulder. "Just kindness."

He dropped the freezer bags onto a stack of pie dishes and carried them to the back of the store. "Come back this afternoon. Around two," he called over his shoulder, "You can have some legendary blueberry pie. It may not repay all the kindness, but it's a start."

He turned to thank her, but she was gone.

# CHAPTER THIRTY-TWO

Kyle dumped bags of tiny blue berries on baking sheets that lined Penny's old farm table. While they thawed, he plucked out stems. His grandmother's crust was flour, sugar, and salt, blended and mixed with butter. One teaspoon at a time he added cold water and mixed with a fork until the dough came together, a trick he learned from YouTube. Then he divided the dough into two even parts, wrapped them in plastic wrap, and popped one in his fridge upstairs. He did this six times, for six matching pies. If he was lucky.

But luck had nothing to do with it. Not this time.

He rolled out clumps of dough until they fit in the glass pie pans. While they prebaked in the ovens, he sprinkled the berries with a teaspoon of lemon juice, tossed them with sugar, cinnamon, and cornstarch, then poured them into the baked pie shells and dotted them with butter. Making lattice from the rest of the dough, he topped the first pie, brushed it with egg wash, and made foil bands to protect the crusts.

Just like his grandmother used to.

He pushed up his sleeves, the same shirt he wore the day before, and rubbed at the stubble on his chin. There was nothing satisfying about baking while everyone searched frantically for Jacques. With every minute that passed, the puppy was ten times less likely to be found. Keeping his hands busy was the only way to keep his mind from wandering to dismal places or his feet from rushing out the door to look on his own, leaving the store—Jacques's home—unattended. Adelle was right. He needed to be here in case Jacques returned. One eye on the door, the other on his pie lattices.

He popped the first pie in the oven and checked his phone. It was nearly eleven. No texts, no calls. A hundred notifications on social media that offered condolences, a report of a stray cat, but no sign of Jacques. A hot lump in his throat threatened to choke him, and his eyes grew warm and wet. His pies felt less like magic with each minute that passed. And every time he glanced out the door and his eyes fell on his hoodie in a damp, snow-frosted crumpled pile, he felt less confident Jacques would be found, and more worried about the fate that had met his little friend.

The whole town was out there looking. If his puppy were out there to be found, he'd have been found already.

He laced strips of dough over the rest of the pies with blue-stained fingers, mind kicking up tragic scenes, flashes of terror involving wildlife and car tires. At best, some passing car snatched him up and took him home to some distant town where a kid snuggled him.

*You should have had him microchipped. It would have been a better use of that credit card than inventory no one will ever buy.*

Kyle stood and stretched his lower back, tugging at the hem of his shirt while he paced. Jacques's leash puddled on the counter, bowls of food and water untouched.

He went to the display window and peered out to the street. The whole corner smelled like Jacques. The little plaid dog bed still wore the depression Jacques had left behind after his last nap. Kyle couldn't bear to move it. There was a hollow place in his chest where his heart used to fit. He clutched at it, balling his shirt in his fist.

Outside, a car passed slowly, cutting through the cold air and swishing down the street.

Even with the radio on, the place was so empty without the yips and yawns and jingle of tags that the very air seemed constructed of sadness and loss.

Whatever would be, as one day might pass to the next, as the leash and bowls found their way to a closet, as Jacques's little bed was fluffed and shuffled into a box with other memories and tucked in a corner under the bed, as moments of joy and boredom crept in to make gaps in the grief and relegate his dog to just another broken tile in a mosaic of a life lived, he owed his friends and neighbors a fitting thanks. When they did return, he'd have to paint on a smile, thank them for all their efforts.

And he owed to himself a proper goodbye, but not now. In its own time.

*You can't just stand here and stare out the window for the rest of your life, wondering if he got trampled by a moose or picked off by a bear. You can't just watch the door and wait for something to happen. No more waiting. Do something.*

He had to keep busy. If he stopped moving he would shatter.

A timer dinged. He raced to the ovens and shoved his hand into his fish-shaped mitt. He leaned into the blast of hot air when he opened the stove and pulled out a perfectly baked pie.

He pulled the foil wrap from the edges and admired the pie his grandmother made. Generations apart and just a few dozen steps from where it began, his grandmother's Blueberry Window Pie rested on his stove. The universe might have taken his dog as punishment for not being a worthy dog daddy, but it had deemed him worthy of his grandmother's legacy. At least as far as he could tell until it cooled.

A car silenced its engine at the curb. Helen scrambled out of it and shuffled in the door. Behind her, the door heaved open again, and Adelle rushed in with the cold air, expressionless, her face white, cheeks red from the wind. She tugged off her gloves as Penny and Nate tumbled in behind her. Marissa, Diane and Carol crowded the doorway. Logan, the bartender from the tavern, wiggled through with her boyfriend, Grey, Stuart at their side. All of them, frozen.

An icy chill spread from his stomach through every cell in his body. They were giving up.

Adelle shoved her gloves in her pocket. "Kyle—"

He put up a hand, still clad in a fish mitt. "Don't say it. Please. I can't bear to hear it. I'm grateful you all tried. I've always had my nose to the grindstone, and I never thought I'd have friends who'd—"

Riley's towering figure pushed through the crowd, his six-foot-six frame soaring over Helen. "Hey, Helen. I got your mail in my bag somewhere."

She tapped her cane on the floor and shuffled to the side. "I came by for pie. What are you all…"

Riley let his mailbag fall gently to the floor. "It's under this dog."

A yellow bundle of quivering fur bolted from the bag and across the floor. Kyle's heart leapt into his throat. He had so many questions— where was he found and was he injured. Kyle fell to his knees, arms outstretched, and scooped up the puppy who squirmed and wriggled in his arms, licking his face. The puppy wiggled free, bounded past the waiting crowd, jumped in his window, and sat on his pillow as if nothing had happened at all.

The room spun. Lost for words, Kyle leaned against the wall, his heart racing.

Logan stepped forward. "I found him playing by the tavern dumpster. He was chasing a leaf."

"That's it? That's where he was?" Kyle rubbed his temples. "I walked past the tavern this morning, when I went to the farm. I didn't even look there."

Logan shrugged. "He wasn't there when I closed last night. Someone at the tavern saw your Facebook post, and I looked out for him. It was a slow night at the bar with the snow and all. I had plenty of time to look. Anyway, I didn't have a leash or anything, so I carried him back toward town."

"We were looking down by the creek." Penny had a tight hold on Nate's hand.

Nate nodded. "I wrapped him up my coat, and the three of us headed this way. What is that smell?"

"I was crossing the park." Riley hoisted his bag back onto his shoulder. "This bag holds a lot of weight and keeps me pretty warm. I figured he'd be cozy in here. That's when we ran into Adelle. Is that pie?"

"I was at Sparky's." Adelle slipped out of her muddy shoes and crossed the room. She stood close to him, thaw coming off her skin, sending chills up his arms. "I was looking around all those broken lawnmowers. I figured that place would be like an amusement park to a small dog."

Kyle fumbled for words. "You guys looked so hard. I don't know what to say."

"I was so afraid we wouldn't find him." Adelle shrugged. "How could I ever come back here and say that we gave up? I'd never be able to forgive myself."

"It wasn't your fault he went missing; it was mine. I was careless and selfish. All he wanted to do was play, but I never had time. I was always working so hard, putting all of that effort before anyone else."

"Don't blame yourself." Penny shook her head. "He's fine. Just a little cold and tired, that's all. Look at him, getting cozy already. If he could talk, he'd have a hell of a story to tell."

Jacques was already back in the window, circling his bed and preparing for a well-deserved nap.

Kyle motioned to the back of the store, to the counter between stoves where the pies rested. "I made some pies to say thanks. I hope they're okay. The last few times I tried, the bottoms were soggy, and the berries were runny. I think I got it right this time, though. With a little help."

Helen broke from the crowd and scuffled to the back, hovering over a pie. She closed her eyes and serenity took over her countenance as she breathed in deep.

Adelle rubbed her hands together, warming them. "Is it your grandmother's recipe?"

"It is. At least I hope it is."

"It's famous around here. My dad talked about Blueberry Window Pie all the time."

Helen turned to Kyle. "It smells just like I remember. Can I?"

Kyle flung open a prep table drawer and pulled out forks and paper plates. The forks clattered on the stainless steel counter. He handed her a knife. "I hope I did it justice. It's the least I can do to say thanks. For everything."

Helen sliced pies into wedges while Penny held plates and passed them out among friends. They ate and chatted, told him it was wonderful, but it was Helen's opinion he wanted the most.

He slipped beside her. "What do you think? Is it close?"

"It's perfect." It might have been the crust she swallowed back hard, but if Kyle had to guess, based on the look in her eyes, it was a lump in her throat. "Your grandmother didn't have much, but she never wanted for friendship. She was years older and lifetimes wiser, and she was the best thing in this town. The best friend a woman could ask for."

"Does it taste like hers?"

She balanced her fork on her plate and patted his arm. "My God, son. Yes."

Adelle pulled on his shirt sleeve, tugging him aside. She swatted him with a glove. "See, you made pie. You had faith."

"I wish that was true. With everything you guys did for me, I just thought it was a good day for pie." He clasped one of her hands. "The truth is, I haven't had faith in anything. But that changes right now."

# CHAPTER THIRTY-THREE

Kyle filled an old margarine tub with his favorite cheesy garlic mashed potatoes. He snapped the lid on and added it to the bag with the rest of dinner. After tying a strand of green ribbon to the handle, more habit than function, he gave the bag a test lift. He didn't have to travel far, just across the street, but spilling mashed potatoes in the middle of the road was the wrong way to impress a woman with his cooking.

He turned to Jacques. "Your turn."

The puppy wagged at his side. Kyle grabbed an old collar with a black bow tie. He fought off kisses to put it on, but the collar didn't fit. Jacques had grown since they moved into town. His snoot had grown longer, and his head had grown into his ears.

"What are we going to do with you? You're going to outgrow everything."

The dog stood expectant, with his trademark yellow lab grin.

"You still want a bow tie, huh?" Kyle fashioned a new one from leftover green ribbon and tied it to his collar. "How's that?"

Jacques barked his approval. Kyle faced him, hands on his hips.

"Now look, this is a really big deal. I have to be on my best behavior. Not you, you're always perfect. So I need you to be the best wingman you can be tonight. If we get over there and Adelle has other plans or you pick up on a vibe that she doesn't want us there, you need to do a little pee-pee dance and save me. Got it?"

He put his hand out, and Jacques gave him a shake.

"Use all your magic. We need to use those puppy dog eyes to our advantage."

Kyle shrugged into his new black pea coat and wrapped his neck with a gray scarf. He leashed Jacques, grabbed the bag with Adelle's surprise dinner, and descended the stairs.

Outside, wind howled up the street. It was colder than usual for the middle of October. Light pooled on the sidewalks outside store windows, and the gaps between told the story of how far Ramsbolt had fallen since its heyday and how far it had to go. Things were already looking up for Kyle. He'd turned a profit early that month. It was enough to afford to cook better and treat himself to a new coat.

A few doors up, a truck was parked at the curb. Faint hammering sounds could be heard from the building within. Another store coming soon. Another resident chasing a dream. He'd ask Adelle about it, if she let him in.

Behind him, someone tapped on a window. He turned to find Penny grinning out from her store, holding a black paper bat with green eyes. Her window was half decorated with tombstones and black cats and flying bats. She gave him a broad smile and a thumbs up. He gave her an uncertain shrug and mouthed, "We'll see."

He tucked his chin in his scarf and let Jacques lead him across the street.

Adelle cleaned up inside her store. She wore her green apron, and her hair was up in a tie, half pulled through in some kind of ponytail loop. She swiped an arm across her counter and chunks of stems and petals and leaves brushed into a trash can. Kyle stood in the street and watched her work, mesmerized by the way she moved. It wasn't just the art she made; her flowers were gorgeous. He was captivated by her in her world, in a place he didn't deserve to be but wanted to be so badly. Everything around her felt warm and soft and safe. He'd been so stupid to throw it away.

At the end of the leash, Jacques pranced.

He stepped closer to the curb. He should be shivering. The food was getting cold. Adelle wiped off a pair of clippers and dropped them in a drawer.

*Stop staring at her like some creepy stalker.*

A car passed, and light from its headlamps caught on her necklace and its five-leaf clover pendant. He stepped onto the curb and reached for the doorknob, and her head snapped up.

She rounded the counter and pushed the door open.

"What are you doing here? Hey, Jacques." She bent to ruffle the dog's ears. "I love your new bow tie. Very dapper."

Kyle hoisted the bag onto her counter. "I brought dinner to share. If you'd like."

"After the day I've had, that sounds great!" Adelle folded her arms and leaned her hip against the counter. She raised an eyebrow and gave him a sly smile. "What's the special occasion?"

"I need a do-over."

"Kyle. That's not necessary. I told you; we're good. But I won't turn down dinner." She peered into the bag.

"Excuse the containers. I used what I had. It's what's inside that matters, right?"

"Of course." She poked at a ball of aluminum foil. "Did you bake fresh bread?"

"And cupcakes. Chicken, veggies, cheesy garlic mashed potatoes."

"Comfort food."

"I even brought the silverware."

"What about Jacques?"

Kyle reached into the bag and pulled out a tub of dog food. "He brought his own crunchies."

Adelle motioned to the stairs. "Do you want to come up? It won't be comfy to eat down here, and I've been sitting at this counter all day."

He unfurled his scarf, wiggled out of his coat and dropped them on a hook by the door. He wasn't running away this time. "I would be honored."

She locked the door and unbuckled Jacques's leash. "You don't need that in here, little guy."

Jacques sniffed his way down the narrow hall and bounded up the stairs, and Adelle turned to follow.

"I guess that's our cue," she said.

His stomach twisted into its familiar knot, and he unthreaded it with a deep breath of floral strain. Grabbing the bag by the handles, he followed. *Not this time. No more cowering in the corner. No more burying your feelings with work.*

She flipped a switch, and a light went on in the hall above. Her inner sanctum. Where she lived her graceful life. Her home, full of her things.

Adelle rushed up the stairs and into a room ahead, straightening something he couldn't see.

She closed a door, and he paused on the steps. "Is it safe?"

"It is now. I'm a little messy sometimes."

"Me, too. That's the luxury of living alone, I guess."

She pointed to the kitchen. Like his but more narrow, her window looked down on the street. A small table rested against one wall, covered in mail and a laptop. She scooped it all onto the counter, grabbed napkins, glasses, and a mostly full bottle of wine.

"Hey, what's going up in the street? The new store?" Kyle pushed food onto plates, and in a heartbeat, the table was set. Jacques curled up beneath it as they settled, leaving little room for their feet.

"Stuart is opening up a real office. I guess The Ramsbolt Reader is taking off." Adelle leaned over and rubbed the dog's golden ears. "Jacques, here, has made himself comfortable. You should, too."

Kyle nudged a chicken leg to the edge of his plate. "I'm a little on edge."

"Yeah. It feels like you have something to say. This isn't just a casual dinner, is it?" She sipped her wine.

"No." *As if she doesn't know.* "I owe you a lot. An apology, for starters. A real one. And a dinner that doesn't end in regret."

She swirled wine in the glass. "You don't owe me anything. Dinner is delicious, and the company is great, but you don't owe me."

He folded his hands in his lap, like he always did, and for the first time saw it as the posturing maneuver it was, intended to mask his words and inner turmoil with an outward sense of calm. He used it when giving bad news to good clients, but this time it wasn't just okay to be vulnerable. He needed to be.

"No. I do owe you. You deserve a better apology." Leaning forward, he locked eyes with her. "I should have told you that I'm sorry I didn't say yes. I am sorry. I should have said yes."

She swallowed hard. "Yes to what?"

"You said we should do dinner again. Your treat. And I said no. I should have said yes. Hell yes. I should have said that I love to cook, and we should cook together next time."

He reached across the table and touched her hand, laying his fingers across hers. The move was bold, and her eyes widened, but she didn't flinch. "I totally knew that you liked me. I picked up on every signal and instead of being honest and saying yes, instead of looking you in the eye and telling you the truth, that you're the most amazing woman I've ever met, and I can't wait to have dinner again, I was too damn scared of losing myself in this, and I ran instead."

"There wasn't anything to be afraid of."

"I'm not excusing my behavior. I was rude to you because it was easier to make you hate me in that moment than it was for me to face the truth about myself."

Adelle nodded. "I understand. I do. I've run away from plenty of things in my life."

Her hand flexed beneath his, and he pulled away to set her free. She twisted her fingers and laced hers in his.

"Don't," she said. "This is nice."

It was more than desire that coursed through his veins. Fear and longing and the pain of spilling truth on the table threaded through him. Kyle forced his shallow breaths to deepen and prayed he didn't look as anguished as he felt.

"Everything in my life is new, Adelle. Having a pet, running my own store, making a profit, being my own boss. I am absolutely terrified, and I have this stupid belief that I have to make it on my own before I let anyone in on my chaos. That, and work has always been a great defense against facing my own feelings."

"It doesn't look like chaos from here. It looks like courage. You look like one of the bravest men I've ever met. And you make that store look like a lot of fun."

"It's a great illusion. A lot of effort goes into not looking half as scared as I feel."

His hand was warm. He knew it was clammy, but she didn't pull away. He could see it in her eyes, the search for words, her need to break the silence with some kindness and consolation. But he didn't need it from her. He let his guard down.

"Adelle?" He scooted in his chair and leaned closer. Jacques snored between their feet. "All of this, the store and living in town…my entire life would be a hell of a lot more fun if you were in it more. I don't know if the store will make it, if I'll ever get to have a chain of them. I can't control the future any more than I can control the present, but I'd love it if you'd be a part of this with me."

He held his breath, waiting for the answer he hoped would come.

Adelle squeezed his hand. "I thought you'd never ask."

## CHAPTER THIRTY-FOUR

"I can't believe he thinks he can still fit under this table." Kyle's legs didn't fit in his own kitchen anymore, not with Jacques under foot. "I'd buy a bigger one, but then I'd need a bigger room to put it in."

"If things keep going the way they have been, you'll be able to afford a house soon. Then you can rent this place out." Adelle's work scattered the table, happy piles of florist bills and town business. She bent to scratch the yellow lab's ears and caught a file folder before it hit the floor.

"I think about that every once in a while. I love living downtown, though. I have great neighbors."

"I agree." Adelle smiled at him. Jacques sat up, bumped his head on the table, and put his chin in her lap, vying for attention. Full grown but still filling out, Jacques barely fit anywhere, but he insisted on trying. "Better under there than getting under your feet while your baking."

Jacques's tail thumped the floor, and his wide smile morphed into a yawn.

"We have to be at Zeb's at ten." Adelle checked the time on her phone. "It's 9:45."

A timer went off. Kyle pulled his second steaming hot blueberry pie of the day from his oven. "I'm ready once I turn off the stove."

"How long does it take to get to your dad's? Half hour?"

He waved his fish mitt over the pie. "Yeah. Just on this side of Colby."

With one warning chirp, the smoke alarm blared, a screaming siren that sent Jacques reeling, bumping into a table leg and sending Adelle's papers fluttering to the floor.

"I need to replace that thing." Kyle ripped the smoke alarm from the ceiling and yanked the battery out. After a few seconds' pause, he put them back in and snapped the alarm back in place.

Adelle pulled her papers into a pile and slipped into her shoes. She grabbed a cooled pie from the fridge. They left Jacques to his nap, locked the store, and climbed into his old Saturn.

She held the pie on her lap while she put on her seatbelt. "Have you heard anything new from the doctors?"

Kyle pulled out of the lot and onto the road to Zeb's. "Nothing's changed. Gradual decline."

"No chance he'll recognize Zeb today, then?"

As winter had thawed and the land loosened, Kyle had come to terms with it. As summer set in, the end felt near. "No. Definitely not. I warned him."

Adelle shifted the pie as they turned into Zeb's driveway, discomfort coming off her like the heat from the tarmac.

"It'll be okay."

"I've never met your dad." She picked lint from her jeans.

"I don't mean it to sound harsh, but you still won't have met him. I told him all about you, though. When he could listen."

Kyle shut the engine off, climbed out, and slammed the door. Adelle left the pie on the back seat and trudged behind him up the gravel drive. He took uneven steps to navigate to the broken mosaic of the walkway. He hadn't been to the farm since Jacques went missing months before. Zeb had done some work since then. The front door had been painted and the porch stained and sealed. A can of paint sat by a pile of lumber in the yard. It wound something within him, spooling absence and memory. He'd missed the place.

Bern flew out the door and down the steps. He tipped his hat as he shuffled past. Inside, Dan sat at the kitchen table, hat on his knee and a cup of iced tea dripping sweat on a coaster someone took from the tavern.

"What you in for?" Dan wiped his forehead with his arm. "Hot as hell out there."

Kyle nodded. "Hottest June I can remember. Taking Zeb to see my dad for Father's Day."

It was two birds with one stone. His father hadn't remembered him in weeks. The nurses said he was struggling with movement and sometimes choked when he swallowed. He hadn't been able to feed himself for months. Zeb wanted to see him before goodbye became elusive, and Kyle brought the pie to take the edge off. It was hard to outrun the feeling that it would be his last Father's Day with his real father, the least he could do was brighten it a bit for the man he'd come to think of as a second dad.

"That blueberry pie you make is damn good." Dan swallowed a sip of tea. "Bern gave me one of them for my birthday. Shoved a candle in it."

Adelle skimmed sepia photos on the wall, her hands in her back pockets. Kyle caught her smile.

"Thanks," Kyle said. "I remember when he stopped by. Glad you liked it. Happy belated."

Zeb came down the hall, running a thin black comb through what was left of his hair. "Dan, I'll be back before dinner. Don't let that damn cat in here."

"Stray." Dan finished his glass of tea. "Cheers. Have fun."

Zeb shoved the door with all his might, and it inched open. He clung to the railing and crept down the stairs.

"Looking forward to seeing your dad," he said. "I know he won't remember me, but I'll be glad to say what I got to."

Kyle gave him an arm. "I've been doing that a lot the last few visits." Aiming for lighter conversation, he nodded to the paint can and lumber. "You've been doing a lot of work here. Porch looks great."

Zeb straightened his back when he reached the walkway and aimed for the car. He looked like a child in dress up clothes, his thin plaid shirt three decades aged and two sizes old. "I took your advice."

"Which advice was that?"

A cat scampered across the drive. Corn was getting high in the fields, swishing in a distant breeze that didn't reach the driveway. Sun glared off the Saturn's windshield, blinding Kyle as he steered Zeb to the car door.

Zeb lowered himself into the seat and spun to grip the dashboard like a child preparing for a roller coaster. "I sold land."

"You're kidding." Kyle pointed to the seat belt. Zeb struggled it into the clasp. "I thought that was the last thing in the world you'd ever do."

Adelle climbed into the back, pie on her lap. "How much land?"

Zeb put his hands on his knees, eyes skimming the dash. "Is this thing safe? What'd you say?"

"Yes, it's safe." Kyle closed his door and started the engine. "She asked how much land. How much did you sell?"

With any luck it was enough to keep the place afloat and not just a paint can and a stack of lumber's worth.

"You remember that plot down by the creek with that old factory on it?"

Kyle steered onto the road to Colby. "The old mill. It was a machine shop, right?"

"Ages ago."

"I bet nobody's stepped foot in there in fifty years."

Zeb's voice picked up over the engine. "Something like that. Some guy from town bought it. Gonna put a flea market in there."

"A flea market?" Adelle leaned forward, yelling into Zeb's good ear. "Who? Who bought it?"

Zeb turned in his seat. "Some guy named Arvil."

"Figures." Adelle touched his shoulder. "We have a question for you. Maybe you should ask, Kyle."

Kyle glanced at his old boss, his dad's old friend, the man who helped keep his family afloat as long as pride and fear allowed. He owed the man a lot, and he needed one last favor.

"Adelle's dad's long gone, you know. Both our parents are gone." Kyle winced. "Almost."

He cleared his throat. "We were wondering if you would walk Adelle down the aisle at the church in the fall. And maybe let us borrow your barn for the reception."

Zeb stared long enough and hard enough for Kyle to sense a no on the horizon. The man stroked his beard and turned his kind eyes to Adelle.

"More like you walking me, but ayup. I'll do it. You gotta clean up that barn when you're done. Can't leave food in there. I'll get rats."

"Thank you, Zeb." Adelle smiled at Kyle and gave him a thumbs up.

Corn rippled beneath the clouds. It quivered and swayed in his Saturn's slipstream.

# ABOUT THE AUTHOR

A Maryland native and Pennsylvanian at heart, Jennifer M. Lane holds a bachelor's degree in philosophy from Barton College and a master's in liberal arts with a focus on museum studies from the University of Delaware, where she wrote her thesis on the material culture of roadside memorials. She resides with her partner Matt and a tuxedo cat named Penny.

**Receive free prequel stories, news about upcoming releases and more by signing up for the author newsletter at** jennifermlanewrites.com

OTHER WORKS BY THE AUTHOR INCLUDE

*Of Metal and Earth*
*Stick Figures from Rockport*
*and the*
*The Collected Stories of Ramsbolt Books:*
*Blood and Sand*
*Penny's Loft*
*Hope for Us Yet*
*A Good Day for Pie*